Freya Wolfe's debut novel, *Between the Lines*, was shortlisted for the Little, Brown UEA Crime Fiction Award 2018. She lives in Derbyshire with her husband and daughters and two miniature dachshunds.

Between The Lines

Freya Wolfe

www.freyawolfe.com

ISBN: 9798723664494

Cover by Jennifer Greeff.

For my girls

"Jase, is the camera on? Jason! Right. Give it here....no, I'll do the filming. I haven't exactly got the equipment for your role... no, don't worry, we'll dub over the voice-recording.... got some kicking beats to record over the top... you ready, Ash? Tooled up and equipment out? Jesus, look at the stupid bitch. She's still breathing, right? How much of the stuff did you give her? Nah, it doesn't matter. It's not an audience participation sport, this. As long as she can lie there and receive the goods we don't need anything else. Might make it that little bit more interesting. We know what's happened, and the good and great folk of the subscriber list will know what's happened, but she'll never be quite sure. Stupid cow. Serves her right. Thinks she's so bloody brilliant. I'll teach her. I'll teach her a lesson she won't ever forget. Who's going first?"

Dear you

I know what you did and I will make you pay, you faithless whore.

Chapter 1

Dr Vida Henrikson looked out across her audience at the Central Sheffield University and tried a smile. "As police officers, you're aware of the importance of the words you use." Her throat felt dry and she couldn't hide the flush in her cheeks. No matter how many times she lectured, talking to an audience of professionals always terrified her. She'd read enough self-help guides to recognise herself as a victim of permanent, self-imposed imposter syndrome: just not enough to know how to overcome it.

"Making sure the PACE warning is given correctly. Using the right words in an interview situation to retrieve the information you need without being accused of coercion. Selecting the best way to communicate with a witness, a suspect, or a grieving family member. You're aware of the importance of the words you use." At least this group looked more interested than her undergraduates. Before she'd started lecturing, she'd assumed that the modern student was eagle-eyed and beaver-keen due to the hefty tuition fees they forked over. Instead, she regularly encountered the same bleary-eyed and less-than-polite yawning that had been rife when she was a student. Still, to give them their dues, when she'd yawned it had usually been the result of late-night shots in the uni bar; for the modern student, it was more likely to be from the three jobs they were working outside of their degree to make ends meet.

"But think about how much can be gained by examining the words that aren't deliberately chosen, the words that unconsciously reveal so much about you. Every place you've lived, everyone you've communicated with, even what you've watched on television, can have an impact on the shape of your speech. Just by listening to a voice we can find out about where that person has been, what experiences have shaped their lives. I want you to think about your own language right now. Where does your language come from and what would we be able to deduce about you, do you think?"

She took advantage of the rhetorical question to have a break, gulping a glass of water, very aware of the fact that she was racing through her presentation. She was booked for the hour; she needed to make sure she wasn't left with empty airtime for the last fifteen minutes of it. Speaking to around thirty police officers today, her lecture formed part of the South Yorkshire Police Professional Education Scheme that was aiming to equip its officers with the tools and skills needed for modern policing. The force seemed to be desperately trying to improve their reputation after the last few years of surfacing shameful historical debacles with the Hillsborough and Orgreave Enquiries. These were the newest recruits to start working in CID, an eclectic mix of gender, age and race that represented the face of a much more accessible and forward-thinking police force. As professionally junior as they were, this didn't help with her nerves. She tucked strands of a blonde bob behind her ear once more and then took another deep breath.

The slideshow behind her flicked on to the picture of a young woman, pretty in an average kind of way, made stunning by the big smile across her face. The audience shuffled upwards, their backs all a bit straighter. Everyone found the real, practical case studies more interesting than the theoretical. Human nature she supposed to want to gape at the reality, no matter how horrible it was if you stopped to think about it. "I'm going to tell you a story now. The story of a young woman, her beautiful girlfriend and how it all went wrong. The story of how our young woman disappeared and how forensic linguistics helped to solve the case. Her story." She indicated the projected image. Finally, in the hands of the victim, her nerves settled. This was a story she'd told hundreds of times before. Despite its familiarity though, she never failed to get a thrill from her involvement in the case. It had been her first real opportunity to work directly with the police, when her eyes had been opened to the possibilities of what she'd always thought of as a near-obsessive interest in words. She'd studied Linguistics and Applied Linguistics at university, completed her PhD with no real idea of where she was going. Then suddenly what she was doing had been made real and relevant.

"This is Jenny. Nothing unusual about her. In 2014, she and her partner, Verity, sold their house and belongings and embarked on a round the world trip. A once in a life-time experience for them and Jenny, certainly, was incredibly excited." She clicked the audience through a series of pictures of Jenny and Verity, looking blissfully happy and ridiculously young. The ominous coincidence of the name Verity struck her as always; perhaps she should look into a study of names and how they might predict future behaviours. What would her own name suggest? She left the screen on a snapshot of some Facebook messages, all capturing the unadulterated joy Jenny obviously felt at the start of her adventure.

"Read her words, hear her voice," Vida said. "This is all we needed to help the police find resolution in this case." The audience leaned forward as a collective, all seemingly equally excited by the prospect of seeing the clues she had promised them. In seminars she liked to ask the students what kind of a person Jenny was. It was always interesting hearing their prejudices and discussing where they might have come from. She had no time for that here though.

"Jenny and Verity set off around the world. Europe first, moving across to Asia, Australia, the Americas and then finally returning home in a year's time. Jenny was a real homebody, very close to her parents and younger brothers and at first, they worried that she would be homesick, but their fears were soon put to rest by the emails Jenny would send them whenever she could and the regular Facebook updates. She was having an amazing time. Loving life in every way. The emails continued for the whole year." She showed them a selection on the screen, wondering whether they would be able to see what she had seen. "Sometimes they were sent daily, sometimes more sporadically, just once every three weeks or so." She still found it amazingly moving, reading about what a great time Jenny was having. It was like watching a film about the Titanic; knowing that tragedy was just around the corner heightened the emotion she felt every time.

"Then about eight months into the trip, just four weeks before they were due to come home, Jenny sent an email that shocked her whole family. She'd met someone new. After six years with Verity, she'd become bored and had decided to leave her and make a life with Izabel, an exotic South American beauty. She said she'd try and come back home soon, but not to worry. That was the last they ever heard from Jenny." The audience members exchanged glances with each other. The message was brief, almost curt. It didn't match at all with the bright and vivacious tone of the earlier messages. "Her family was distraught. They sent messages back but got no reply. They tried ringing the mobile that Jenny had taken with her, but it was always switched off. They tried to email Verity, but apart from a short message saying that she was broken-hearted by Jenny's actions and couldn't face talking to them, they heard nothing more."

"So, in desperation, Jenny's parents went to the airport to meet the flight that their daughter should have come home on. They met Verity at the gate. She said she'd not seen Jenny for over three weeks, and she walked away from them." She couldn't imagine the despair that Jenny's family must have felt. It should have been such a joyful home-coming but instead they were tormented by the fact that they hadn't heard from their daughter for a month and only had Verity's account of events.

"You're all police officers. What would you do if two worried parents came to you and said they were afraid for their daughter, who had willingly set off around the world and who had seemingly willingly agreed to stay in Brazil.

In a practical sense, there was nothing to investigate. Thankfully, they found an officer who was receptive to a gut feeling. They knew in their heart of hearts that something was not right. And what's more they thought they knew who was responsible." She clicked onto a picture of Verity. She was beautiful, but Vida had always been sure that she could see a hardness around her eyes and in the lines of her mouth. Perhaps that was just wishful thinking though, a knowledge and prediction of human behaviour she hoped she would have been able to apply if it had been her.

"The relationship had been happy, but not perfect. Jenny was perhaps sometimes a bit flighty and Verity was sometimes a bit controlling. But overall, they had worked. Although the decision to go round the world surprised her parents, Jenny seemed enthusiastic about it and so, with misgivings, they gave it their blessing. And it's hard now to know whether the trip was a positive thing, or whether it was always part of Verity's plan." It was the first time she'd referenced Verity directly in the role of machinator and she saw a few of them noticing her direction.

"Brazilian police were contacted, and they could find no trace of either Jenny, or the mysterious Izabel she had apparently set up home with. In fact, they could find no trace of Jenny ever even entering the country. And so started a manhunt that took in countries across the world, tracking Jenny's movements. Throughout this whole experience, Verity stuck to the Izabel story. She couldn't account for the fact Jenny had not entered Brazil; perhaps it was an administrative blip. In the end, the last entry point they could find for Jenny was Argentina. With Verity firm on her version of events and no physical trail to follow, the case seemed destined to be unsolved." What must that be like? To have a feeling that something terrible had happened, but never being able to know for sure.

"It was a chance encounter that brought Forensic Linguistics into it. The policeman who had originally spoken to Jenny's parents met Dr James Harrington at a Masonic dinner." It wasn't often you could be grateful for the old boys' network, but it had definitely had a positive outcome here. "He'd been working on various research projects involving Forensic Linguistics and suggested that this might be a science that could help. Perhaps, if we reviewed the messages that had been sent from Jenny, we could find something that might give us answers."

"The science at this time was experimental and when we started the project, we were not certain what we would find. But then, we found this." She filled the screen with two messages, one dated the end of March, the next the start of April. It still gave her a thrill now, seeing the breakthrough. Casting her eyes across the audience, most of them seemed to be confused but there were a couple who were nodding as if understanding.

"A team of researchers analysed all the messages that Jenny had sent." This time, she made air speech marks around 'Jenny'. "We looked at her word choice, phraseology, the way she signed off, the average length of her utterances, the punctuation she used. We built a pattern of her style. Of course, there are anomalies. A message sent in an Internet cafe when there's only a few seconds left on the clock, or a message sent after a long silence. But overall, we can see a picture of her language. This message is typical of her. You might notice her tone, or the words she uses or maybe the way she uses this smiley face emoji at the end of the sentence. This message, however," she said, indicating a new email on the right of the screen, "is not Jenny Whittaker."

There was a collective gasp and Vida couldn't help the reflexive smile that sprung to her lips. "But more than that," she continued. "It was possible to show that not only is it not Jenny Whittaker, it is Verity Callahan."

The gasp this time was even more resounding.

"At some point between March 26th and April 3rd, Jenny disappeared and Verity took over sending the messages. Armed with this new information, the Sheffield police were able to close down the time span for Jenny's disappearance and could liaise with local police to try and find her. They could also use the information to reinterview Verity. Finally, she confessed. She and Jenny had fallen out badly. The whole trip had been one big argument, despite Jenny's apparently happy emails, and Jenny had told her that as soon as they returned to England, she would be moving out. Verity flew into an enormous rage and attacked Jenny. She remains adamant that it was an accident, that she didn't mean to hit Jenny so hard, but she didn't seek any help and obviously the way she dealt with the matter afterwards didn't indicate remorse. She also refused to tell the police where she'd left Jenny's body. Ultimately, through the fact we could narrow the date of the event to just a few short days, local police found a shallow grave off the side of a road just outside a tourist town together with a gentleman who had been paid $50 to bury Jenny. She had been stabbed. This was murder." She left the story there, not wanting to bore them with the months of legal wrangling over whether or not the linguistic analysis would be accepted in evidence. Thankfully it was.

"This was just the start of the possibilities of the science," she said. The audience seemed a lot more engaged now; an actual case made the science relevant to them. "Our language takes us far. And it's not just our spoken language. The same variances that can distinguish a Geordie's oral utterances from that of a Londoner can be used to examine the written word. If you just stop for a minute and think about all the utterances we make during the day, whether oral or written, then you can begin to see the potential for this science in helping you to identify criminals and achieve convictions. Suicide notes, ransom demands, hate mail, abusive tweets and written confessions can all be linguistically analysed to help determine authorship. And they're just the obvious forensic texts. Think about the possibilities that are open to us if we consider all the routine communication that occurs and how we can use that in pursuit of justice. The possibilities really are endless."

She opened the floor to questions, dealing quickly with the usual fervent detractor who argued that Forensic Linguistics would be as much use to them in finding criminals as asking a Fairy Godmother for help. She didn't think it was sexist to note that 90% of the time said detractor was male and the vocal commentator here had been no different. Young, cocky, thought he knew it all, he'd peppered her with questions about the validity of the data and the realistic potential of an actual crime-solving solution, while treating her responses to teenager-worthy eye rolls. Thankfully, everyone else seemed pretty open to what she had talked about and she had the practical cases to back the research up.

"Thank you." She drew the questions to a close, nodded her head and walked off the stage quickly to a smattering of applause. The shuffling in seats and stretching started before she'd even left the room.

"Good job, Vida," her supervisor, Myfanwy, hailed her with a taut voice, stilettos drumming an imminent attack along the corridor. She was a diminutive woman, but what she lacked in height, she made up in steel backbone and ferocity. "Just caught the tail end and it seemed to be as powerful as ever." Vida didn't know how the woman had the brass to be so superficially nice while stabbing her in the back as soon as the battle tide turned. "I'm telling the Vice-Chancellor great things about you and the work you're doing with the police at the minute. Covering yourself, and the university with glory. Exactly what the powers that be want to see." Myfanwy paused, as though waiting for Vida to acknowledge the praise.

Vida tried to turn her natural grimace into a polite smile. Myfanwy's compliments were always bathed in underlying tones of financial woe and student number panic. Vida had joined the university after the Whittaker case had helped raise the profile of the science and had been lured by the promise that Forensic Linguistics would be front and central of the university's new Linguistic strand. She wasn't surprised that the promise had slipped, and she considered herself lucky to be able to deliver an undergrad module and these professional lectures. Myfanwy seemed to be permanently disappointed that introducing the subject hadn't led to an immediate jump in student applications. Vida had tried to point out that it took time to establish new courses and to attract new students to new fields, but Myfanwy's eyes had swum with the instant gratification required in modern university management. There were even murmurings now that Forensic Linguistics might be dropped from the offering altogether. Vida wasn't sure what she would do if that happened.

"So, actually Vida, I'm glad I caught you," Myfanwy continued. Caught? More like ambushed. Vida wondered how long she'd been waiting for her to emerge from the lecture hall. "Got a little proposal for you. Some friends of the Vice-Chancellor have a problem and we were wondering whether you'd be able to help them out."

Inwardly, Vida groaned, but tried to maintain neutrality on her face. "I am quite busy at the minute, Myfanwy," she said, "you know, it's dissertation time of year."

"Oh, I know Vida. I know. And I wouldn't ask if I didn't think it was important. The Donaldsons are big university donors though. He owns Spintech," Myfanwy said, naming one of Sheffield's biggest technology companies, "and they've always given very generously."

"Right," said Vida. She recognised the magic words, pursed her lips and squashed a sigh.

"It's not just the money though. In fact, it's not the money at all here. I'd really like it if you could just hear them out and decide whether you could help or not. If not, it's fine, no pressure. Peter, Mr Donaldson that is, was really adamant that he wanted it made clear that this is not a task he's forcing you to do."

Human interaction was funny Vida thought. If you just took the semantics of the words, you might be inclined to believe Myfanwy. But pragmatics told her that while Peter Donaldson might not be forcing her involvement, Myfanwy definitely was. Vida knew that a decline on this request would be marked straight in the 'Reasons Forensic Linguistics is a waste of money' column. "OK," she agreed. "When do I meet them?"

Myfanwy smiled, an uncomfortably feline curl. "Excellent. Now. They're in my office. I checked your diary and you've nothing until a 3pm tutorial. Plenty of time."

Vida needed to start blocking off time in her diary if it was going to be tracked like this. "Thank you for your efficiency," she said, evenly. "I just need to get something to take notes with and then I'll be with you." Myfanwy nodded and marched away as Vida headed towards the stairs to make the climb to the Linguistics floor, avoiding the lift her daily concession to keeping fit.

Chapter 2

It was the worst of February weather as DI Gabriel Slater strode hard up the hill towards the furtive activity ahead of him. Just past ten in the morning, he could tell that this was a day that was never going to see sunlight, the rain too spiteful to hustle up and snow properly, with the kind of invasive dampness that got inside his bones and made it feel like he'd never dry out. Even the streetlights were uncertain about whether it was day or night, half of them flickering on and off. There'd seemed little point bothering with an umbrella in the face of such meteorological malevolence.

He frowned as he saw the crowds of people hustled around the barriers. He'd hoped that the weather would have put off the gawkers, but they were out in force with their camera phones held aloft. Pushing past, he flashed his credentials to a young officer stood manning the crime scene tape and then ducked under. He ignored the clamour of shouts asking for information. Some were possibly genuine journalists, the rest just wannabes ready to share salacious pictures on Twitter. It was getting increasingly hard for him to tell the difference. Not that it mattered. He didn't really have time for any of them. The officer manning the inner cordon handed him a package of an unopened protective body suit and carefully entered his details on the scene log.

"Stick this somewhere," Slater said, shrugging off his raincoat and handing it to a nearby PC. He'd dressed in preparation for the cold and wore a thick, cable-knit navy sweater under his coat. Hauling on the white coverall and yanking plastic booties over his shoes, he cast his eye over the scene around him. He knew that the photographer would already have taken shots in the round of the whole area, but the flat light of a picture didn't tell him nearly as much about the scene as just being here did. Strangely, the sounds of the city seemed muted here, the traffic itself skirting the edges of the horror that awaited him. The cordon marked off the end of an alleyway, cornered on one side by a bar, the other by a vintage clothes shop. He was grateful that this had kept the victim out of eyesight of the crowds at the cordon. Opposite stood the great and good of Sheffield's nightlife: the Wetherspoon's in the old Waterworks building, sitting uncomfortably next to the grand City Hall. It was fairly well patrolled by uniformed officers and PCSOs because of the proliferation of bars, pubs and clubs and he wondered how a crime could have happened in such a visible area without anyone noticing, even if it were later at night.

"Handy location," offered his sergeant, Mark Dawson as Slater approached.

"Nice to have a bit of fresh air on a morning," grumbled Slater. The scene was just a ten-minute walk away from their base on Snig Hill; in truth, he'd have preferred something a bit further out so that he could have justified his car and its heating. "What've we got?"

"Body found by the bar staff coming to open up this morning at 8am." Dawson nodded to the bar on the corner.

"Bar opening at eight?"

"Diversification, boss. Can't just be a bar anymore. Got to offer brunches and afternoon teas."

Slater contemplated the front of the bar, which looked more upmarket than most, freshly painted with relatively clean windows. He turned his gaze back towards the alley. It was tight, too small to even fit a car down, and black plastic bags were heaped up on either side, narrowing it even more. Further crime scene tape marked the far end, a burly officer preventing anyone from entering. Slater pulled the hood of the suit up around his head, stopping the rain from dripping down his neck and stepped gingerly around an accumulation of muddy puddles. Activity was on the right, scene of crime officers already busy swabbing and taking relevant samples.

He surveyed carefully, trying to be scientific in his gaze, avoiding the emotions that always swirled when he was met with the remnants of life. The body of a young woman arched backwards over a pile of rubbish, her positioning almost graceful despite the hideous surroundings. She looked like a black and white movie star in the shades of the February day, her skin grey, hair pale. A scene of crime tent had been erected quickly above her, but the rain had already slicked her skin, moisture catching the light as he moved towards her and creating the illusion of life. The acrid aroma of urine hung in the air and Slater didn't like to contemplate the number of late-night drinkers who might have been taken a slash in the alley.

"Any idea who she is?" Slater asked, turning to Dawson.

Dawson shook his head. "Not yet. No sign of any ID or purse or anything."

"Sexual assault?" Slater hoped not but was fearful.

"Impossible to say right now. She's not wearing knickers. Again, could be a lifestyle choice rather than they've been removed. Bit of date night fruitiness."

Slater was well-practised at sifting through the relevant comments from Dawson's more off-colour statements. He stepped carefully closer to the body. Activity around them stopped momentarily as he studied the poor girl whose life had ended in such a horrible way. He thought she'd probably been beautiful, but it was impossible to tell now. Beauty was about spirit and life, and this lass had neither of those anymore. Blonde hair, stained rusty red in places, haloed around her head. Her face was turned towards the wall, the angle pulling open the garish wound on her neck. She was wearing a short, silver-sequinned dress that was ruched up around her waist, revealing long legs and a pubic area too bare for Slater's taste. A large dark pool spread out from beneath the plastic bags, saturating the ground below. It was impossible to tell if it was blood or something more innocuous. From what he could see, in addition to the gaping neck, the body was covered with what looked like shallow slashes, punctuated by deeper stab wounds. He'd seen some horrible scenes in the past, particularly when he was in uniform and attended a massive pileup on the M1, but there was something especially unnerving about such deliberate death.

"Divisional surgeon been?" He directed the question towards Dawson without wanting to look away from the scene. It was important to him that he faced it head-on, noticed everything he could, from the way she was positioned, to what she was lying on through to the smells around them. Whoever she was, nobody deserved to find themselves here and if he could show a little respect by not shying away from the brutality she'd suffered, then that was what he'd do.

"Yep. Confirmed death."

"Give us a rough idea of cause?"

Dawson consulted his notebook. "Wouldn't give much away. Did say that the slash to the neck was ante-mortem, before she carked it, and was possible cause of death. Reckoned the rest of the wounds could be window dressing. He wouldn't commit on the possibility of sexual assault either."

"Time of death?"

"Again, we've got to wait for the post-mortem, but he reckoned sometime after midnight and before two this morning based on temperature. Said they can do some more tests later to close it down a bit more."

"Any weapon?" Slater knew he was firing questions at Dawson but wanted to make sure he didn't miss anything in this first swoop. The quicker he got the information, the quicker he could assign tasks and work out their approach.

"Not found yet. Still got a whole lot more to sift through."

Slater studied the body a little more, eyes desperately searching for anything else that might help the victim, a clue to her identification or what had brought her here.

"Watch it, Bitch-in-Charge," Dawson hissed. Slater stood up and turned to face the alley entrance, frowning at his sergeant. The name was apt, but he disliked its use. For some reason, he had the urge to salute every time his DCI came near. There was something about Zahra Hussain that inspired fear. Perhaps it was the ruthless ambition that obviously accompanied someone who'd made DCI before 35, despite being female and Muslim. Even with the force taking positive action, Slater knew it was a challenging climb and rumours said it was only to be a brief stop as well, before she moved up to Super and beyond. He found her an inspiring woman.

"What have we got?" she barked, before she even made it within five feet of him. Her face was stern, framed neatly by the white coverall she'd donned.

Slater filled her in quickly.

"Hmm," she said, sounding suspicious that they were failing her already. She stepped forward and surveyed the scene. "I want details. Update in my office as soon as you get back." She spun round to face him, nodded and then stalked away the way she came, back ramrod straight. She was a tall woman, but the officer on the tape went up on tiptoe to lift it over her head so she barely broke stride as she moved under.

"Thanks for the royal visit," muttered Dawson. Slater simply shook his head, staring after her. He was never entirely sure that she didn't have extra-terrestrial hearing and was particularly careful not to say anything that could be misconstrued. She was unusual in even attending the scene. Most bosses in his experience preferred to stay well behind the desk, but she still liked to keep her nose in. It made reporting to her much easier; he admired the way she contributed her own ideas, probing his mind to tease out solutions.

Slater caught the eye of the Crime Scene Manager, Tony Fairbright and stopped quickly for an update. "Blood spatter analysis could give us some interesting data. This is the kill site and spatter over there," Tony pointed to the wall opposite the body and then gestured further down, "And there might tell us something about the weapon and the assailant or assailants. There's going to be loads of contributory DNA here so we're just swabbing everything we think might be pertinent. Lots of loose items to take and sift through. It's a volume job really. We've set the cordon fairly tight but even then, masses of potential evidence. We're going to need to keep it tight on the budget though." He seemed quite upbeat about the task ahead, despite its obvious mammoth nature.

"Tony!" The CSM and Slater turned their heads towards the shout. A SOCO in anonymous white came towards them, waving a silver bag. "Tony, sir," she said, addressing the pair in turn as she approached. "Just found this underneath those rubbish bags over there." She gestured with her hand.

"Open it," Tony instructed. Gingerly, she unzipped it.

"Some money, looks like about hundred quid in twenties. Lipstick. Mac, nice. Some paracetamol. Some sort of letter. And this." She pulled out a driver's licence and presented it with a flourish. Slater scanned it without touching.

A low exclamation behind him alerted him to Dawson's presence.

"Do you know her?" Slater asked over his shoulder to his sergeant.

"You mean, you don't?" Dawson replied, rolling his eyes.

"Kitty Morton," contributed Tony, reading the licence.

"Mean something?" Slater said, annoyed.

"If it's her, then she's known as Kitty Wakelin," Dawson said.

Still meant nothing to Slater.

"Singer? Just nominated for a Brit Award for Best Newcomer? Sheffield's best apparently." Dawson barely hid the disbelief at Slater's lack of knowledge.

Slater shrugged. He wasn't keen on music. Any music. All those passions and emotions just left him feeling slightly disorientated.

"If she's so famous, why didn't you recognise her?"

"Well, you know... I didn't really look. She was all bloody and facing the wall and stuff. Couldn't really see her," replied Dawson sheepishly.

"Right, well, we'll be having a slightly more definite ID before notifying the media I think," he said, dryly.

"It's her." Dawson was confident and bizarrely jovial. "And you know what that means? Career make or break."

"Thanks. We'll leave you to it and coordinate when you know a bit more about what there might be," he said to Tony, who nodded to the SOCO. She strode off to bag and tag the evidence. "Right then," Slater said, turning towards Dawson, "let's have a quick chat with our barman."

Chapter 3

Myfanwy had bagged herself a beautiful corner office, but even her status couldn't improve the hectic view of the city beneath them. Vida often wished that her faculty could have been based in one of the university's other buildings overlooking parkland, instead of the metropolis that sprawled beneath them. She loved the view in the twilight though, when the orange streetlights twinkled on and brought the city a sort of magic. At this time of day, a watery February daylight barely penetrated the gloom, and even floor to ceiling windows didn't preclude the need for lights.

Vida knocked and entered without waiting for an answer. The office was a lot tidier than her own, tall bookshelves lining one wall, a neat and virtually empty desk positioned in front of the window. She'd never managed the paper-free thing herself, and although she liked to tell herself that a busy desk showed a busy mind, she suspected it was more a messy desk showed someone who needed to get a grip on organisation. Her friend and colleague, Caroline, had told her about some research that suggested the more intelligent you were, the messier your desk. She was fairly sure Caroline was just being kind.

A couple were sat huddled together along one side of a small meeting table. They seemed nothing like the wealthy donors that she'd met in the past, perfectly polished and well groomed. These two were worn down by what Vida quickly identified as grief. Both had red-rimmed eyes that spoke to tears and sleepless nights, and while Mrs. Donaldson's hair was obviously expensively coloured, it barely looked brushed. Mr. Donaldson looked slightly more together, but there was a slight disarray about his suit, the tie not quite aligned, a smudge of dirt on his shirt collar. Myfanwy was bustling around in the corner, a capsule coffee machine whirring and clunking as it distributed an array of coffee styles. She introduced Vida to the Donaldsons, smoothing over the faux pas as Jane Donaldson firmly corrected her title to Doctor. Coffees were distributed to the Donaldsons, all accoutrements present as though it was the finest coffee shop in Sheffield: a saucer, a teaspoon and that all important coffee biscuit. Vida got a matching set, only strangely without the biscuit. How would Myfanwy respond if she pointed it out?

"Now, where were we?" Myfanwy asked, looking around at them. "Peter, do you want to explain a little more to Dr Henrikson about your problem."

"Yes, please," Peter said, smoothly mannered despite his and his wife's obvious distress. "It's about our daughter, Maggie. She died in May of last year. They've just held the inquest and they recorded a verdict of suicide."

"But it wasn't!" burst in Jane, suddenly, her voice harsh. "It wasn't. She couldn't. She just wouldn't have killed herself."

Peter lay a comforting hand on his wife's knee and she subsided, retreating physically. "Jane and I both feel that the verdict was a mistake. We can't believe that Maggie killed herself. She had absolutely everything she ever wanted. Her whole life was in front of her. She was bright and beautiful and..." He took a shuddering breath. "I'm sorry. We just still find it so hard. And we thought the police investigation and inquest would give us answers but instead we have more questions than ever before. We just can't accept it."

"I'm so terribly sorry for your loss," Vida said, "but I'm not quite sure where I come into this?"

"It's the note," he said. "Maggie supposedly left a letter. But it was typed and only her name was signed. Is that normal? We don't understand why she typed the letter. Don't people take the time to handwrite their suicide notes?" He seemed bewildered and it was Jane's turn to rest a soothing hand on his knee.

"Not always" Vida said. "Not now, when more and more of our communication has been moved online and onto computers. I bet that virtually all your communication is online these days?"

"Well, yes. But surely a suicide note is different? Anyway, it's not just that it was typed. We just don't think it sounds like Maggie. She was always a beautiful creative writer, and so expressive but this letter is just dull, and we were having dinner with Philip, Dr Lacewing," he said, naming the university's Vice-Chancellor, "and he mentioned that he'd got this Forensic Linguistic whizz who was working with the police and specialised in authorship matters. He said that you'd worked on suicide notes before and could tell whether or not the person who is supposed to have written them did write them."

Vida sipped her flat white and wondered whether it would be social suicide to use her finger to get the froth out. Shrugging, she opted for partial humiliation and used the teaspoon to scoop it up. "I think Dr Lacewing may have been a little kind with that introduction," she said gently, swallowing her mouthful of foam. "I have worked as part of a team in the US for a few weeks looking at suicide letters, but I would by no means call myself an expert. And the science itself is inexact. We can draw some conclusions by comparing different writing styles, but they cannot be definitive ones. The science is at its best with volume texts, where we can really build up a body of style markers. It's difficult with a single letter."

The Donaldsons' faces dropped even further and Vida felt like she'd just stamped on their puppy.

"Is there nothing you can do?" Peter asked, desperation lacing his voice.

Vida sighed. She sent pleading eyes towards Myfanwy, hoping that she could extract her from this situation, but she was scrupulously avoiding her gaze. This wasn't going to go well. "I can take a look for you," she finally conceded, "and presuming you've got other texts that Maggie wrote, I can compare them to see if there are any recognisable markers of Maggie's style in the suicide letter. But I can't promise I will find anything, and I also can't promise that I will find something that suggests Maggie's suicide note wasn't written by her. All I can do is look at what the evidence tells me."

Peter leaned forward eagerly. "That's all we want Dr Henrikson. That's all we want. Just take a look please."

Chapter 4

Slater was relieved to be out of the mizzle. The station was not exactly roasting, but it was dry and there was the occasional radiator attempting to heat the space. During the short walk back to the station, the cold had slapped his cheeks and frozen his nose. He felt the fizz of his features thawing as soon as he entered and blew his nose delicately before shrugging off his coat and hanging it on a nearby coat stand. DC Louise Watson met him with sheaves of paper in her hand. A fairly new addition to his team, he'd been cautious around her to begin with. Being an older recruit at 42, he'd questioned her motives for joining but she soon proved she had all the enthusiasm of someone just out of sixth form. She was particularly superb as Office Manager and despite her relative inexperience, Slater knew she had the eye for detail and precision needed for the role.

"Kamal's sent me over the list of bar staff working last night. I've already run them through the database. Got one hit for possession from a Sasha Turner but everyone else is clean," she said.

"That was quick. Thank you, Louise," Slater replied. "Once we've got a firm ID or a clean shot of the face, we'll go and talk to them all. The bloke who found the body didn't have anything particularly meaningful to offer us. See if anyone else saw her in the bar last night or knows her from anywhere. Any CCTV looking over that road?" he asked.

"Cameras at the junction at the end of the road, where Carver Street crosses Division Street, private car park just down the road has one and then there's one further up at the other end of the road, just down Devonshire Street. We've got coverage all around the pedestrianised areas of course. Nothing directly pointing at the alley. I've requested all the recordings."

"Great. If we can find her on the cameras, we might get lucky and find her with someone suspicious. You know, someone wearing black, face covered with a balaclava, a knife by their side, that kind of thing." She smiled weakly at him, obviously uncertain when he was joking or not. He nodded approvingly. It was good to have someone so efficient, made his job substantially easier. "I'll be in with the DCI for a few minutes. Can you get the team round?"

Hussain looked up appraisingly as Slater knocked. She was sitting behind a large glass desk, busy on a laptop and nodded him in. Her office had a nice view over the river, looking down across some of the old mills that had helped make the city profitable in the 19th century. The room felt clinically bare though, apart from the usual policing awards, pictures of her meeting Very Important People and a single picture of an Asian family Slater took to be Hussain's. He'd never asked her. She was scrupulous about keeping her private life private and he had no idea what her living situation was. Not a million miles away from the way he preferred to live his life. He didn't suppose Hussain's family offered the same risk to her professional life as his did though; he was fairly certain the sister she seemed to have in the picture didn't dabble in drugs and violence in the same way Slater's brother did.

Striding in, he met her forthright gaze with his own, waiting for her signal to sit down. Finally given, he sat sharply in the chair, back upright.

She pushed her laptop away from her. "So, what have you got?" she asked, directly. He knew it was a loaded question.

"Not much more yet, ma'am," Slater kept it brief. He liked to keep some things in reserve so he could use them at a later, less productive time. Not that he had anything to keep in reserve on this one so far.

"ID?"

"Nothing certain yet but..." he hesitated. He knew she liked direct information; she didn't like guesswork and sloppy police investigation. But this was potentially too important to keep to himself even at this early stage.

"Spit it out," she nodded, a frown settling on her face.

"Bag at the scene gave us a driver's licence, name of Kitty Morton," Slater admitted.

"The singer?"

He wasn't surprised that she knew the name where it had slipped him by. He was fairly sure she was omniscient. "The very same," he acknowledged. "Dawson thought it was a match."

"Slater," she said, her tone low, "if it is her, this is going to be a massive pain." She rubbed her temples as though to emphasise her point. "We will have to get this solved quickly. Media outlets will be all over it. I'll need a statement for the media asap." She broke off talking to him, dialled an internal number. "Julia? Potential problem. Give me ten minutes and then come down." Her attention once more on Slater, her eyes bored into him. "We have got to stay on top of this thing. It'll be a bloody nightmare."

"The team is out of the blocks, ma'am. We've not been slow on this." Slater tried to keep the edge out of his voice. Sometimes it felt like even if they solved it and secured a conviction on sight of the crime it still wouldn't be enough for her. He was always stuck between immense pride that he worked for her and immense annoyance that he never quite felt good enough.

"I know," she said, slightly conciliatory. "But we need to be quicker. Let's go." She rose and disappeared into the open office, leaving him to bring up the rear.

The team was already assembled, seated around the central board. Currently, quite small, Slater knew numbers would swell to deal with all the additional lines of enquiry that would no doubt follow, especially if the victim did turn out to be a celebrity. It was disgusting really that more press pressure bought more police officers. It shouldn't be that way, but it was a fact of life he was used to living with. He watched as Hussain delivered the briefing speech. She inspired confidence, even though she lacked people skills. It wasn't that she didn't know how to deal with people, it was more that she just didn't care enough to do it. He knew that she'd had a tough ride to get where she was and even now he would still hear people calling her The Token. He bristled when he heard that and struggled not to respond. Not that she needed him to leap to her defence. Men and women alike withered before her gaze and more than one police officer had had a shortened career thanks to a mistimed comment.

Still, he supposed he should be grateful that the face of modern policing had moved on from the time when he would have been the token. His dark skin fitted in generally now, but his father had had to fight discrimination every single step of his career from Police Constable to Detective Sergeant. Not that being black was entirely plain sailing, even now. There was still enough of the old guard around to make it uncomfortable from time to time, and racism was alive and kicking on the streets of Sheffield. The people who lived around him suffered from the kind of racism that used the media's representations of a race to judge people by, rather than the individuals they knew and liked. The media narrative seemed to have largely moved away from the Caribbean immigrants though, firmly targeting all those supposed Muslim terrorists that haunted the dreams of the Daily Mail-reading British. Another thing for Hussain to have to fight against.

As she finished, he stood up to additionally brief the team, but Hussain didn't bother to wait to hear what he had to say. She'd done her bit and now moved swiftly on to dealing with the PR machine. He waited until she'd left the room, looking around at the collection of faces, feeling the slight tremor of nerves and excitement he always felt at the start of an investigation. Those same feelings were reflected in the faces of everyone in front of him. "Right then folks. DCI's given you the info. Body's with the pathologist at the minute and we should know more after the postmortem's been carried out. Me and Dawson will attend that when it's listed." Everyone was scribbling things in their assorted notebooks, jotting down key points and questions that they had.

"This next bit, hush hush, confidential, softly, softly," he said, his tone indicating deadly seriousness. "This could be sensitive in that we found ID at the scene that suggests this might be Kitty Morton, who is apparently better known under the name Kitty Wakelin. Mark's informed me that she is a Famous Person, and we all know what that means." A groan went round the room. Policing by the press was everyone's least favourite way of managing a case.

"Remember, at this stage, any ID is speculative. Family will be informed and will be coming to give a firm ID, plus we will confirm with fingerprints. We do not want any errors here. We've got video coming in from a variety of sources, footage from the bar, CCTV, Davies, I'd like you to get onto reviewing that. We're looking for any sightings of our victim, anyone that could possibly be her, anyone looking suspicious. You know the drill. I need two teams on door to door. Canvas the other properties on the street and those that back onto the alley. Someone might have seen or heard something. Jog some memories. We'll get a good picture of her face to show round. Priority is tracking her movements; just where was she before she ended up in that alley?" He looked around, his face calm. These men and women made up an excellent team of police officers; he knew though that a team was only as good as its leader. This was on him alone. "Last job is finding the bastard that did this. Let's go."

Chapter 5

"That wanker!" spat Simon. "Complete and utter tosser!"

Vida forked what was an extremely good carbonara into her mouth while musing on the prevalence of male-oriented insults being obsessed with masturbation. Female insults were more concerned with promiscuity; she always found it striking that so-called gender behavioural rules still made their way unseen into everyday life, despite them living in a supposedly equal world. Her pondering kept her linguist's mind distracted while her husband stalked up and down their small, galley kitchen. She'd long learned to just let Simon get his expletives out of the way. Beyond making small back-channelling noises, there was very little she could offer to the conversation. He didn't want practical solutions and she'd had her head bitten off more than once for trying to get him to approach things from a different side. She was beginning to think that he liked having something to rant about. There was always something, always somebody who'd committed some small slight that he could take offence at. And boy did he offend easily.

Squall suddenly calmed, he sat himself down opposite her. She smiled at him, handsome despite his frown, and carried on munching. There was something in the sauce that she couldn't work out, an unfamiliar tang she'd not tasted before.

"Great carbonara," she offered. It was a treat for a working woman to have dinner on the table when she got home. An early one tonight as Simon had something or other that he needed to do in town later.

"White truffle from Piedmont. Can you taste it?" he replied, mollified. "I had to go up to Leeds to get it. Cost a small fortune."

She nodded, knowing better than to point out that perhaps if he spent less time on sourcing specialist ingredients and more time on his PhD, he'd have finished it by now. They'd had that argument before too, and she knew there was little to be gained from restarting it. Now he'd had his initial outburst, he'd be tolerable company for the rest of the time.

"Yes, it really brings out the flavour of the... pancetta?" she offered, hopefully.

"Completely. This Italian woman on a blog I'm following suggested it and just wow!" He kissed his fingers pretentiously and "mwah!"

"Lovely."

"It's got this really weird consistency," he carried on. Vida nodded, listening but not really, as he talked to her about truffles and microplane graters and soft, grey shavings. They'd been together for nearly twelve years now, having met as undergraduates at Warwick and while she felt her face was beginning to show signs of the last decade, he seemed almost physically unchanged, a handsome man still. His best feature was a generous mouth, capable of the most winning smiles, when he wasn't bitterly spewing abuse.

"So, when did you see John?" she asked, cautiously, trying to keep any note of accusation out of her voice but adding quickly, "excellent wine too, Si," to defuse, taking a sip of a particularly nice Soave Classico.

"I drove over this morning." He pursed his mouth, annoyed again. "I mean can you believe it? I mean, seriously. Who does he think he is?"

She bit back the response that said Your PhD supervisor and opted for "I don't know," instead.

"He talks to me like I don't have a clue. Suggesting that my research was based on a faulty premise. I've been working on this for the past three years. No way is this a faulty premise."

"Did he suggest any alternatives?"

"He wants me to change the whole bloody focus to the Dalmatians. They're barely even relevant to the work I've done so far." He stabbed at his plate, showing no mercy to the targeted pasta.

"Mmm," contributed Vida, non-committally. She felt sure he'd changed his focus so many times already, once more could scarcely make a difference. She was also fairly sure that John had probably not told him to throw out the baby with the bathwater. Simon had a particularly unhelpful habit of hearing what he thought was being said instead of what was actually being communicated.

"It means of course that I'm going to have to cancel plans this weekend. I'll have to be in school." They'd planned to go walking in the Peak District, a nice meander followed by a pub lunch.

"Of course," she murmured, resigned to another weekend alone. She missed the times they'd spend visiting different cities around the UK and he'd impress her with his virtually encyclopaedic knowledge of every church and public building in the country. Still, that was what happened when you'd been with someone for a decade. People grew apart. Marriages changed. It didn't have to mean anything sinister. "I got a new case today," she changed the subject hopefully.

"Oh?" asked Simon, barely looking up from the iPad. She hoped he was at least reading the paper, but she suspected he was more likely playing Sudoku.

"Yes, a teenage girl committed suicide. Her parents don't think it was suicide though and it sounds rather mysterious. Could be really exciting to get involved in such a live case."

"Surely, a dead case."

"Well, fine. A live dead case if you like. It would be really good for our reputation at the university. Maybe give me some more ammunition to try and get them to deliver on what they trapped me with."

"Sounds promising," Simon offered. He looked up and flashed her a quick smile. "Why don't you go and sit in the lounge? Put your feet up, I'll bring you another glass of wine and I may have bought you a little treat."

"Oh, that sounds lovely. I might take the laptop and do some reading too," she said. It was no wonder her waistline was ever-increasing with such delicious treats. "Thank you." She dropped a quick kiss onto his waiting cheek. A cosy fire, research to do, and something delicious, and she hoped sticky, to munch on sounded like the perfect way to pass the evening.

Flopping on the sofa, she opened up her laptop, and googled 'Maggie Donaldson suicide'. The search term returned hundreds of results ranging from newspaper reports, through the coroner's 'Preventing Future Deaths' paper and then a tribute page set up to Maggie by her friends. Clicking on the Sheffield Star link, she was taken through to 'Maggie's Tragic Last Night', the newspaper's re-enactment of her last steps. A photo of Maggie smiled out from the top of the page. She had been a beautiful girl, luminescent skin, shining dark hair and soft brown eyes. The very picture of radiance. "What a waste," Vida murmured.

"Tragic Maggie Donaldson made her final journey across Sheffield at around 1am on Tuesday 10th May. Here we reveal those last moments," she read. "Maggie had spent the day at Sheffield High School for Girls, as she did every other school day. She laughed and joked with her friends. Nobody thought she seemed sad or worried. "She was the life and soul of every day," her best friend, Tamsin Jennison told us. Tuesday afternoon was netball practice so after school finished at 3.30pm, she stopped on to captain the netball. Her mother, Dr Jane Donaldson, a prominent local GP, collected her from school at around 5pm. They went home and watched Pretty Little Liars until Maggie's father, Peter Donaldson, tech-millionaire owner of Spintech, arrived home at around 7pm. The family ate dinner together. Laughed together. Discussed their day together."

Vida looked up and rubbed her forehead. The matter-of-fact reporting was painting a particularly vivid scene that she was finding it all too easy to imagine. She was an only child herself, and while her parents hadn't been wealthy, their evenings had been similarly full of laughter and discussion. She'd inherited her love of language from her Swedish father, although he was eternally disappointed that she'd chosen to focus on English rather than becoming a polyglot like him.

"Maggie said goodnight to her parents at around 10pm, telling them that she was tired and needed a good night's sleep. Then she climbed the stairs, sent a few goodnight texts to her friends and got into bed.

"What happened next has been pieced together through CCTV footage and witness statements. At exactly 12.52am, the alarm on the front door was disabled, presumably as Maggie left. Her parents were asleep and didn't hear the front door or any movement around the house." Vida wondered if it was just her being over-sensitive but there seemed to be some sort of implied criticism in that statement that it must have been the Donaldsons' fault for not taking better care of their daughter. Never mind the fact that nothing in nature could control a wilful sixteen-year-old girl.

"She walked into the city centre, down Fullwood Road and out along the River Don to the east of the city. She seems to have been alone and there was no sign of anyone else on the footage. The walk took a little under two hours. As she reaches the pedestrianised track next to the river, the CCTV of the city cuts out and so we have no further recorded sightings of Maggie. At 3.30am, a houseboat owner was awoken by a loud splash. There was no scream, no wail, no human sounds at all. He presumed that somebody had dumped some white goods into the river and looked out of a window but saw no sign of any human life.

"At 6am the following morning, Blake Huntley, a council worker walking to his job at the Council Houses, came across a neatly folded coat on a pedestrian bridge crossing the river. On top of the coat was a typed note, carefully preserved in a punched-pocket and weighted down with a large rock. He phoned the police and within two hours, police divers had found the body of Maggie Donaldson. Her ankles were weighted down with weights taken from her father's home gym. Cause of death was found to be drowning." Vida sat back in her armchair and took a contemplative bite of the rum cake that Simon had magicked to her side. She wondered whether the police had been able to tell that Maggie was carrying something heavy from watching the CCTV. Certainly, the walk seemed to have taken her longer than expected. Maybe she'd had to steel herself for what she was about to do. Or maybe the Donaldsons were right and there was something more to this than just a suicide. She returned to the article.

"Police believe that Maggie committed suicide. According to released statement, there is no evidence that anybody else was with Maggie on that night. The Donaldsons however feel very strongly that their daughter could not have killed herself. 'She had everything to live for. She was just about to take her GCSEs and all her teachers were expecting 9s. She wanted to go into medicine, like her mother, but specialise as a Paediatric Surgeon. Her whole life was waiting for her and we just cannot accept that she was feeling suicidal and we knew nothing about it.'" Vida suspected that that was the rub. How could you live with yourself if your teenage daughter had killed herself and you'd suspected nothing? What must that make any parent feel like?

She quickly scanned a couple of the other articles, jotting down anything that she thought might be relevant, including the name of DI Gabriel Slater, who was given as the Investigating Officer. Maybe the work she'd been doing with the police recruits would give her some credibility to ask him what he thought and if there was anything at all to support the Donaldsons' opinions. Finally, she turned to the tribute page and as Maggie's kind eyes glimmered at her from her laptop screen she read epigraph after epigraph, all saying how loved Maggie was and how missed she was going to be. A sea of teenage grief scrolled in front of her. She knew teenagers were infamously two-faced, especially girls, but if just a handful of these comments were accurate then it seemed to support Maggie's parents' view that she had everything to live for. So how on earth did she end up drowned at the bottom of the River Don?

Chapter 6

Assigning the final tasks of the day, Slater's phone buzzed with the news that Adam Marriott, Kitty's boyfriend, and her parents had been taken to Adam's house following their formal identification of Kitty as the victim. It was late and the Family Liaison Officer was already there, but Slater set off immediately to meet them there. This was for both pragmatic and emotional reasons: pragmatically, nobody would know Kitty the way her parents and boyfriend did; and emotionally, he knew from personal experience how important it was to see the person that would be seeking justice for their lost family member. He'd never forgotten the man who'd worked his father's case, a gruff DCI who was remarkably colour-blind despite the prevalent racism of the time. He had treated Slater's mother as any other grieving widow, with sensitivity and care. Of course, at that time, the police force hadn't been quite so publicly supportive, and the FLO role hadn't even been conceived of yet, but the DCI had done his best to keep his mother informed throughout. Slater knew that she'd appreciated that, and he'd always done the same thing; be kind and informative. He hoped the FLO here had managed to keep the family away from their phones and the breaking news that was scrolling across all the news feeds and trending under the hashtag #kittykattragedy. Too many of those voyeurs this morning had snapped the body bag being escorted from the scene. Where was their shame and sense of decency?

Whatever he'd been expecting from the home of an on-the-verge-of-a-breakthrough singer, it wasn't this tiny working-man's terrace. The red brick rows characterised so many Northern towns, functional little boxes that had been built by mill owners for generally selfish reasons, but which had housed hundreds of families over the years. Slater's own childhood had been endured in one of these houses and his mum was still determined to see her days out there. Gentrification of the area had taken the terraces one of two ways: either they were tarted up, extended at the back and top and sold with all mod-cons at top price; or they were left to be eyesores, neglected and barely maintained and rented out to the city's student infestation. This one looked like the latter as he pulled up outside a front door badly in need of a coat of paint. The windows were still the wooden-framed affairs, splitting and peeling. The street was quiet but heavily populated with 'To Let' signs proclaiming student shares and rooms at a dirt-cheap rate. He knocked firmly on the door and was ushered promptly in by the FLO.

She briefed him quickly; Adam was virtually mute, Kitty's mother reduced to an occasional sob and her dad on the edge of angry belligerence. He took in what he could quickly as he moved inside. The interior of the house was no more prepossessing than the outside. There was very little sign of what Slater would consider a feminine touch. Stepping straight into the front room, he was immediately struck by how dark the house was. A heavy, working-man's club green covered the walls, with heavy dark green velvet curtains hanging at the window. If the fire had been lit and the curtains closed then perhaps it would have been cosy, but with nothing more than a dim stream of streetlight peering in through the windows it was cold, unloved and uncomfortable. The furniture looked like it had been sourced from the back of a house clearance van, evidently picked for its cheapness rather than its comfort. Bookshelves lined the alcoves, piled high with textbooks and battered paperbacks. The only evidence at all of Kitty ever even being here was a single photograph propped on the mantlepiece. In it, she and a man he took to be Adam stood, her smiling at the camera with her arms wrapped tightly around his waist, him unsmiling with his arm carelessly draped around her shoulders. Slater picked it up, studying closely the expression on Kitty's face. She looked happy, but the closer he looked, the more he realised that it wasn't a joy that spread to her eyes.

The FLO coughed and he replaced the photograph and went swiftly through into the back room. A small extension had expanded the space back here, providing a tiny but functional kitchen off from a space he'd loosely describe as a dining room. It did host a Formica dining table with four chairs scattered around it, three of them occupied by Kitty's loved ones, but the room was dominated by a large old-fashioned desk in the corner and more overladen bookshelves. These had spilled onto the table and it looked like they had been hastily shoved to one side, along with the detritus of a disturbed morning, a hastily folded paper and a half-drunk mug of coffee. A quick glance in the kitchen revealed more surfaces crammed with papers and books, and a sink piled high with dirty dishes. Out of the back window was the bare cement of a functional backyard, no greenery or flowers or trees. There was nothing glamorous about this house;

nothing at all that he could match with his perception of the rising pop star Kitty was supposed to be.

His attention turned to the three people sat around the table. All nursed drinks, two cups of coffee and then what looked like whisky for the father. They were silent, the weight of grief heavy in the air as they stared without seeing at the tabletop, not even looking up as he entered the room. Kitty's parents were both bottle-blonde but while Slater knew that sorrow had a habit of ageing people in different ways, he suspected that Mr Morton had at least fifteen years on his wife. She looked to be around her late fifties, immaculate in that uniform way that so many middle-aged women seemed to conform to. Her hair was neatly styled, with the immoveable look of a close encounter with a can of hairspray, but the precision of her hairdo didn't take away from the intense redness of grief-stricken eyes. Mr Morton was bulbous and fleshy, his hand clasping the whisky so tightly, it was surprising that the glass didn't shatter under the pressure. He had impressive wispy eyebrows that looked as though they might have a life of their own, even set now in a deep frown. Finally, Adam Marriott, a sallow and washed-out looking man of around forty. Still nothing here that could explain what a bright light like Kitty Wakelin was doing in a dirty, little terrace in Studentsville.

He introduced himself to them and then pulled himself the last seat out to sit on. The FLO busied around, making him a cup of tea, checking on the others. A shake of the head from the trio; they were as fine as they probably ever would be over the next few weeks and months.

"I wonder whether Kitty had mentioned anything that she was worried about, the last time you spoke?" Slater asked. He disliked poking at people when their grief was rawest, but a murder investigation couldn't wait, and statistics said that 44% of women were killed by their partners or other family members.

Marriott stared at the table, his finger intently moving around a loose crumb he'd found. The Mortons looked at each other, pondered before they started. "No, no she didn't," began Mr Morton, eyebrows working expressively, dipping and knitting.

"We didn't really talk very often," admitted her mother, her hands clasped in front of her. "She was so busy that it was hard to squeeze in that much time with her."

"Mr Marriott?" Slater asked, turning to Kitty's partner. In the flesh, he looked even more of a mismatch to the vibrant woman of the press photographs. Short dark hair and a bushy dark beard framed solemn brown eyes, wrinkled at the corners. Unlike the other two who were hunched over the table, he was slouched back, long legs stretched out in front of him in dark green corduroys and an Arran sweater.

He shook his head. "No. I mean, I did talk to her obviously, but she didn't say anything about anyone bothering her in person. There are those sickos that parade around social media being abusive for no reason at all and there were plenty of those with something against her.

God knows what. Someone always found fault with something. Didn't like her hair, her dress was too short, she said something that someone in deepest darkest Peru might find offensive. Pretty fucking sad if you ask me. Why don't they have better things to do with their pathetic little lives?" His eyes met Slater's as though expecting him to answer the question. When no solution was forthcoming, he shrugged and returned his gaze to the frigid coffee in front of him. "She'd been getting some hate mail too recently," he said, more quietly. "I know that had shaken her up a bit."

"In the post? Do you have these letters?" Slater asked.

"No. She didn't keep them here. I think they're at her flat."

"Her flat?"

"Yes, she kept a flat in the town centre. A crash pad I suppose you'd say. Somewhere she could sleep if she was back late and didn't want to disturb me. I don't sleep well," he said, slightly defensively. "Anyway, that's where her Vile Pile is. That's what she called it, her Vile Pile."

"Do you have keys to the flat?"

"No, I never went there."

Slater made a note to get Louise to contact the landlord. "So, some abuse online and in the mail but there were no more immediate threats that she was worried about?"

"She seemed pretty happy to me. Not like anything was worrying her. Always happy." Adam's face dropped still further, and he steeled his jaw, pushing his teeth together.

"She was a happy child," her mother interjected. "Always laughing, always singing. Do you remember?" she said to her husband, touching him gently on the knee.

"She was doing really well," Adam interrupted.

"And Mr Marriott, you didn't report her missing; is there any reason for that?"

He scowled as though about to object but then again, tightened his jaw and shrugged. "I just presumed she'd stopped in town."

"Did she tell you that was what she was doing?"

"No, no, she didn't. Which was unusual, I suppose, because she was normally pretty good at letting me know where she was. I just thought she'd got caught up. I tried her mobile; it seems to be dead. That wasn't like her. Her phone is always on. She's always got to be tweeting this, that or the other. Keeping everyone up to date with how the amazing Kitty Wakelin is doing."

Slater kept his face expressionless but didn't miss the increasing bitterness in the man's statement or the fact that he was shifting the attention from Kitty to how her life impacted on him. Nor it seemed had Kitty's parents, who exchanged another look. "Are you not a fan of social media yourself, Mr Marriott?" asked Slater, mildly.

Adam checked himself and then shook his head, curtly. "No, I'm not. I'm a private man. I like my privacy. I know that it was just part of Kitty's job though," he acknowledged, begrudgingly. "And thankfully, Laila reckoned we should be as under-the-rug as we could be, for not wanting to put off the fans who might fancy her, so she was pretty good at keeping me out of the limelight."

"Sorry, Laila?" Slater asked.

"Yes, Laila Khan. She and her brother, Rashid are Kitty's management team."

Slater nodded and made a note. "And did you have plans for last night?"

"No, I didn't. If Kitty's out doing something else, I just tend to catch up on my boxsets. Working my way through House of Cards."

"Anyone ring or visit?"

Adam's eyes flashed. "No, I don't have an alibi. If I did, it would have been Kitty as she's pretty much the only person I see out of work."

Slater wondered whether that was his choice or hers. He couldn't get a sense of what made this couple work. Louise had mentioned they'd been together for years, but there seemed to be no glue of common interests that he could see. Two very opposite people. "And was your relationship happy, would you say?" he asked, holding a hand up to forestall the outrage Adam was preparing. "I know, sir, and I do apologise. This is a horrible time for you all. Can't think of anything worse than having a policeman asking a load of questions at a time like this. But it is necessary. I will not intrude any longer than's needed and I will only be asking questions to find out who has done this to your loved one." It sounded glib to him, but Adam seemed appeased.

"Yes," Adam slumped back into the corner and folded his arms in front of him. "Yes, okay. Yes. Our relationship was very happy. We were talking about getting married, making it permanent."

"She seemed so settled since she'd met Adam," her mother said. "So happy and he is just so good for her. Was, I mean," she tailed off and her hand hovered towards her husband's knee. He caught it, squeezed it and then lay it gently on her lap.

"Kitty, well we called her Cat," her husband said, gruffly, "wasn't always so happy or settled. I'm afraid she had rather a mixed-up time as a teen. No, no, Nessa," he soothed his wife, "they'll already know from their files. She got into rather a bad crowd and before we knew it she was caught shoplifting. A few times. I think that was probably the very least that she was up to, to be frank, Inspector. She was a late child for us. One of those miracles I suppose that you hope for for so long and then when they arrive they just seem so precious that you're afraid they'll be taken away from you again. I think we were probably too lenient when we should have been hard and then too hard when we should have been easier. Cat and I... well, we butted heads. Too much like each other I think." He gave a short humourless bark. "Don't know how you put up with the both of us," he stroked his wife's arm affectionately. "After the conviction for shoplifting, and the fine and community service, we didn't know what to do. We staged a bit of an intervention, I supposed they'd call it now. We called it tough love. Which isn't easy with a teenage girl who's supposed to be working towards her A-Levels. We pretty much sat on her all the time, grounded her, you'd probably say."

"And it worked?"

"Yes." He smiled to himself, wistful. "Yes, I think it did. Not straight away of course. My God, those first few weeks, months, you'd've thought she was imprisoned in Guantanamo Bay the amount of abuse she threw at us about breaching her human rights. But suddenly, something seemed to click. Finally wore her down and she started putting that energy into her music instead."

"And how did the relationship with yourself start, Mr Marriott?"

"We ran into each other outside the library. Literally," he smiled. He cast a fond look at Kitty's parents as though encouraging them to remember happier times. "Love at first sight you might say. If you're the sort of uncynical person who believes in that kind of thing."

"And do you?" asked Slater.

"Not really. I believe in the right time and the right place and the right person, and that's what Kitty and I were. Oh, I know we look like the odd couple, Inspector, but we weren't really. We both liked quiet nights in and walks in the countryside. It's just that Kitty's leisure time was interrupted with gigs and the public whereas mine is taken over by the Council and business efficiencies."

"She was so happy with you," said her mother, smiling at him through tear-laden eyes. "Adam didn't do this to my daughter." She turned to Slater, fierce now in her statement. "Please, just find who did."

"We will do our best," replied Slater. The temptation to promise was always there, but he knew nothing could be gained by making vows he might not be able to keep. And this was already shaping up to be a case where he found more questions than answers.

Dear you

I know what you did and I will make you pay, you faithless whore. I am your dark storm and I will have our vengeance.

Chapter 7

An uninterested landlord met Slater and Dawson early Tuesday morning at the door of Kitty's apartment at City Point Velocity, one of the starkly modern blocks that seemed to grow almost organically from the dust of industrial past within a matter of days, despite local opposition and bigwig grumbling. The landlord gave their warrant cards a cursory glance before unlocking the door and ambling away.

"It's not glamorous being famous in Sheffield, is it?" Dawson commented. "I thought there'd be like doormen and what-you-call-ems, concierge thingies. She'd not taken off proper yet though, I guess."

"So, she was on her way up?"

"That's what they say."

Slater pushed open the door and the pair stepped inside. This place was a massive contrast with the dismal front-room he'd been in yesterday. Despite the looming clouds outside, ceiling-high windows along one wall dragged in every little bit of light the struggling February morning had to offer, the white of the walls bouncing it around and amplifying it. His next thought was how cold and uninhabited the place seemed. It was modern and stark, and there were no signs of life anywhere that he could see. No pictures, no clutter, nothing at all to tell them anything about the woman who lived here.

"I'd've thought there'd be more stuff," Dawson voiced his thoughts. "Women normally have more .. you know…

things. This place looks like yours," he grinned at Slater, who narrowed his eyes in return. He didn't make it a habit of socialising with his work-colleagues but had taken Dawson to his apartment to sleep it off one night after he'd drunk too much and had a fight with his wife. Slater'd not heard the end of comments on his home-furnishing choices since. They moved further in, footsteps deadened as they moved from stripped wooden floors to deep-piled rugs in shades of innocuous strewn across the floor. "Where are the shoes? The coats? The missus has got them layered about ten deep all over ours."

"Maybe she was just really tidy," Slater offered. The flat was open-plan, white leather sofas that showed no signs of ever having been sat on, glass topped dining table that looked box fresh and kitchen appliances whose stainless-steel surfaces were still mirror-new. "Take-aways all the time? Or maybe just didn't eat here?"

Pulling on nitrile gloves, he walked into the bedroom, as spacious as the main living area but with a few more signs of life. Opening the wardrobe, there were a couple of dresses hanging up. Drawers revealed a few sets of lacy underwear and the bathroom yielded toothbrush, toothpaste and an expansively stocked makeup bag. "There didn't seem to be much at Adam's house that belonged to her, no more than we've got here. She clearly wasn't into material possessions. A bit of a monk's life."

"With Chanel makeup," replied Dawson. "Sophie'd kill for this lot. Looks like that shopping list she emails me every birthday."

"Hello?" a strange voice queried. Slater frowned and quickly returned to the living area to find a man, short and dark leaning languidly against the door frame. He was dressed in an outrageously loud turquoise suit, the sort of thing that wouldn't have looked out of place on Prince but was completely over-the-top for Sheffield. His hair was dark, cut sharply around his ears, stylised stubble across his chin. Slater knew that level of facial art took serious dedication. As the man pushed himself to upright, he twisted his neck, revealing a dark tattoo snaking its way under his collar. Years of police work had taught him the dangers of judging a book by its cover, but he also knew that covers were often completely appropriate for what they contained. Cocky bastard.

"Sir, can I ask you your business here?" he asked, holding his hand up to forestall the man's further entrance.

"I'm Rashid Khan." He looked at Slater, clearly expecting recognition. Slater remained carefully neutral. Let the man spell it out. Maybe take him down a peg or two. "Kitty's manager," he added finally. "The landlord rang me. Said you were poking around." He raised an eyebrow, demanding.

So not as uninterested a landlord as he'd seemed then. "Hardly poking around Mr Khan. Conducting an investigation."

A glimpse of sudden pain flashed behind his eyes. He'd blustered but couldn't keep the memory out.

"Yes. Kitty," he said simply.

"I'm glad you're here now," Slater said, genially, "saves us the bother of having to track you down later."

The spider to the fly. "You got here pretty quick. Did you have far to come?"

"I'm in the building," he shrugged. "Just a floor down. Kitty liked it that way, having someone she trusted close by."

"Is there something specific that she was worried about?"

"Have you found her box file yet?"

Slater shook his head. "We've only just got here, as you know."

"May I?" he gestured with his hand. "I mean, can I come in? Can I show you?" Slater moved aside and Khan entered, making for a glass-fronted cabinet in the corner. He pulled out a large grey box file from the drawer underneath and brought it back. Sitting down at one side of a coffee table, he placed it reverently in front of him. "This is what worried her," he said, opening the file with a flourish. Slater and Dawson both moved closer, peering to see what was inside. "Letters," offered Khan.

"Her so-called Vile Pile?" asked Slater.

"That's it." He scooped out leaves and leaves of paper, all shapes and sizes, colours and textures. Slater caught sight of handwriting, scrawled messages and neatly typed lines. "Kitty Wakelin, you are pathetic, and you sing like a drowned cat," Khan began to read. "That's quite a mild one actually. Here, this is more like it. You bitch, who do you think you are? I know what you did and I will make you pay." He sheafed through them, reading a few lines at a time. Slater reached across and picked up a few; those immaculately typed words hid real malice.

"Is this normal?" Slater asked, brow furrowed. "Do singers like Kitty routinely get this kind of abuse?"

"Snail mail makes up the tiniest amount of hate mail these days. Most of the abuse comes online. I don't know which is worse. People say such shit stuff on Twitter, things they'd never dream of saying to you face to face. It's a throwaway comment and they don't think about the person on the receiving end at all. Some people must spend hours of their lives abusing these people who they've never even met, just because they're jealous. But these ones," Khan nodded to the large heap of letters, "I think these ones might be worse. There's effort gone into these. I mean look at them..." He rummaged through and found one where the letters had been painstakingly cut out of a magazine. "How fucking old school is that? Someone's sat down, time and effort put into writing a letter to cause misery and pain. Twats," he said, vehemently, his previously amiable face angry.

"Seems to be a lot of people with time on their hands here," Slater commented. "Did anyone ever do more than just write to her?"

"Not as far as we know. She's got the super-fans turning up from time to time, but she likes those, treats those ones nicely. Always willing to give 'em a smile and a signature. She's really good at that side of the business. The adoration. But these bastards," he indicated to the pile again. "These ones she didn't like."

"And she kept them here?"

"Yes, didn't want them in her home."

"Why keep them at all?" asked Dawson.

Khan looked surprised. "It was one of your lot told us to keep them. Reckoned we needed to keep hold of them just in case. He didn't say in case of what," he said. They all fell silent; was this the in case they'd worried about?

"You've reported this to the police?"

"Nah, not like that. Kitty didn't want to make a fuss. I just asked a mate of mine."

Slater frowned. "Why would you not want to make a fuss?"

"Dunno, really. I asked her. She just said she couldn't be bothered. Too much to do."

Then why keep them? Slater couldn't work out the motives of someone who didn't want their time taken up by the venom, but who still kept hold of the letters.

Khan had made himself comfortable, slouched into the sofa; he'd taken his peacock jacket off, but the shiny trousers and natty waistcoat remained. What was the point of a waistcoat apart from to boast to the world that you had enough money to afford an extra useless bit of suit? Khan's hands were resting on his knees, slightly darker patches betraying a nervousness his confident manner belied. Slater and Dawson exchanged a look with each other and then sat down on the sofa opposite the manager.

"Mr Khan, Rashid, can you tell us a little more about your relationship with Kitty?" Dawson asked.

"Well, like I said, I'm her manager," Khan said. He shifted a little in his seat. He didn't look entirely comfortable with his statement. Interesting.

"Which means what exactly?"

"I take care of bookings, contracts and that sort of thing, organise schedules, manage the promotional. It's basically my job to make sure Kitty is taken care of and gets everything she wants."

"Sounds like hard work," Dawson commented, injecting a note of admiration into his voice. Slater nodded approvingly. "Pretty full on?"

"Lots to do, for sure." He paused. They waited. "Kitty's just on the verge of something amazing. Lining up London for her. It's looking like she'll be moving down there by the end of the summer. Would have been I mean," he said, catching the tense. He sighed expressively, the back of his hand pressed to his forehead. "Sorry, I keep forgetting. You get so used to someone being there and then you know, what? They're just gone? And just like that you're supposed to change how you talk about them and what you think about them? Messes with your mind." He fell silent.

Again, they waited, but this time Khan didn't continue. "Tell us more about Kitty," prompted Dawson.

"She's amazing. Was," he said again, this time with a grimace. "She was so committed and dedicated to her work. I've been a manager now for fifteen odd years, and she was just the easiest person to work with. We've worked with some real twats over the years. Oh, they're all nice and well-mannered at the start, just so chuffed that you're willing to work with them, but it doesn't take long before those pound signs take over and they're after everything they can get. And they're fucking mercenary about it. Lose sight of what got them into the business in the first place and it's all about financial worth. It's sad really. In some ways, I reckon the money's ruined the music industry. It used to be about talent but now it's about marketability." Slater nodded, surprised to find himself agreeing with him. He didn't like music himself, but at least the music he'd grown up with, the likes of Delroy Wilson and Bunny Lee had made music that infected the soul with its musicality. The so-called hits today just left him feeling cold and faintly nauseous.

"Kitty was a change from the norm?"

"Yep. I mean, thankfully she was talented and marketable, so she made my job easy in that way. But there were a million small things she'd do that would just make managing her a breeze. She'd happily play any venue I sent her too. She liked the small ones; all those other tosspots would be like 'Yo Rash, when you getting me the O2?'" he cruelly mimicked his other clients, "like it was something you'd achieve overnight! I'm not sure she'd ever have wanted to play that big a venue."

"Would that have been a problem?"

"Not really. Plenty of artists keep it small and still make a decent living. And that's all Kitty wanted. Well, maybe not even that. It was about the music for her. She kept that close. Maybe that's what made the difference in her performances, someone who actually feels like lyrics rather than just stringing a bunch of faux-emoticons together in a line." He snorted disparagingly. "I'm not really selling the industry here, am I? Maybe I've been doing it too long. But Kitty, she was so different, she made it worse, if you know what I mean. Here's this lass, and she's only been making music for a few years, and she's from this safe middle-class background. They're the worst, the ones who have got the money but they're always really grabby about it. Kitty was lucky that she had financial support from her parents, but she'd've made it anyway. Somehow she gets it. And the gap between her and all those others is just immense." He stopped suddenly, choking on his words. Dawson and Slater looked away as he wiped his hand across his eyes. "She was bloody perfect. I don't know what I'm going to do now." He clasped his hand dramatically to his chest.

"Did you know of any threats beyond those?" Slater asked, nodding his head towards the pile of letters on the table.

"No, not that she'd told me. She did sometimes look a bit... well, worried. But she'd just say that nothing was wrong if I asked her."

"And when did you see her last?"

"I spent the day with her Friday last week. We were up on the industrial estate working with a producer in a studio up there. We all get little less distracted if there's no pubs or shops around us. The burger van doesn't hold quite the same allure. We were working on her new album. The one that's she's going to move to London to launch. Fuck it, was. Anyway, we spent the day together. I was going to get some food in at about six, but she said she'd got somewhere to be and so she was out of there by about five. I was supposed to meet her by the canal yesterday morning for a photoshoot, but she was a no show. That wasn't like her. I should have known, should have guessed that something was wrong. Maybe if I'd called you guys?" He looked up, eyes brimming full.

"It wouldn't have made a difference," Dawson stated. "We wouldn't have actioned a missing persons report on an adult so soon and unfortunately, she was probably already dead."

Khan winced.

"And what did you do after Kitty left you at five?" Slater asked.

He paused before answering, letting a fat tear escape his eye. It was getting annoying trying to distinguish between the fake and real emotions here. Slater reckoned he was a right one to criticise the musicians for their false feelings when he was clearly such a master himself. "I stayed at the studio until about six thirty, listening through what we'd got and making some notes. Then I came home, got changed and went out to a party at around 9.30pm. I was there until about 3am and then I came back home. My sister, Laila was with me, and look, let me write down the names of some of the other guests. They'll confirm that I was there." Dawson tore out a page from his notebook and let Khan scribble a series of six names onto it. "I texted Kitty a couple of times. Just you know, I miss you, wish you were here, a couple of bitchy comments on some people we both know, but she didn't reply."

Slater was struck by the poignancy of those messages, half a conversation that was destined never to be completed. And thanks to the wonders of technology, they'd stay there forever, just hanging in the ether like those equally tragic telegrams in the World Wars. Testimonies of a life cut short. Dawson saw Khan to the door, admonishing him to stay close in case they needed to talk to him again.

"What a poofter," he scoffed, slumping down next to Slater.

Slater turned his gaze on his sergeant. "What do you mean?"

"Well, that bloody suit for a start. And then all that 'woe is me'," he replied, dramatically sweeping his arm across his brow.

Slater frowned. "He's not gay. He's in love with Kitty. Funny he never mentioned his sister until the end. Laila, is it? Marriott put her name first in the pairing yesterday. I wonder if she knows he was here today." They fell to silence, contemplating the pile of letters on the coffee table. "Right, bag those Mark. Get them to forensics and see if we can get fingerprints off them. We might just be able to close this case nice and quick after all."

Chapter 8

By 10am, Vida was approaching the gates of an impressive, detached house in one of Sheffield's most desirable areas, Totley. She'd awoken early and had slid out of bed gently, careful not to wake Simon beside her. He considered himself a night-owl and so was rarely up and around the right side of midday. Another reason why his PhD seemed to be shaping up to be a mythical beast, she thought ruefully as she indicated left and pulled onto a gravelled drive. The gates opened seamlessly as she approached and Jane Donaldson was standing outside the porch, a long, thick cardigan wrapped tightly around her. Gravel crunched under Vida's tyres, spitting up as she applied the brakes a little too hard. Jane didn't flinch.

Vida felt the anxiety burn her throat. She'd never been out in the field before, so to speak, always preferring the safety of examining her documents in her office, but Peter Donaldson had been adamant that she should come out to their home and see Maggie's room itself, her natural habitat. She didn't have the heart to tell him that it made absolutely no difference to her analysis. It worried her that they seemed to be pinning a great deal on her possible success. Desperate parents who wanted answers she maybe couldn't give were not going to be the easiest of clients and Vida wondered if perhaps she should give Myfanwy a heads-up in case she wanted her to decline the investigation. Hell hath no fury like a donor scorned and Vida felt that this had the potential to go badly wrong for all involved. Still, Myfanwy was no fool and she seemed willing enough to let her take it on. She'd let her deal with any potential fallout when the investigation was concluded. Remembering that it was her specialism on the line, potentially her job if this went wrong though, made Vida's stomach churn. She hated this political tightrope. Balance had never been her strong point.

Vida got out of the car and approached Jane, offering a bright smile. "You have a lovely house." Vida was no expert, but it looked to be Georgian, with thick ivy climbing the walls, intruding into the corners of sash-windows. On closer look though, the house bore the same slightly neglected air as its owners on the outside, the winter gardens looking just a little more bedraggled than she expected from a house like this.

Jane turned as if to gaze on her home for the first time. "Yes, it is. Just a bit big," she shrugged. She stepped indoors and Vida followed her in. The entrance hall was surprisingly light. Vida had somehow expected it to be as dark and brooding as the outside. A sort of pathetic fallacy for houses. This looked like a normal family home. The stair wall was covered in family photographs and Vida immediately recognised Maggie's eyes smiling out at her from numerous shots. She tried not to stare but Jane nodded. "Sometimes it makes it better. Seeing her face every day. Remembering how beautiful she was. Sometimes it doesn't. Please, come through to the kitchen." She led Vida through the hall into a large and spacious kitchen-diner, the kind of home-hub that Vida would have killed for. Sadly, her academic salary together with Simon's inability to bring home anything beyond his expensive Italian food meant they were stuck with the tiny Victorian terrace. The walls were cream, the units a soft grey, centering around a large island. Along the other side of the room was a large oak table. It was impossibly huge, and Vida found herself wondering just how comfortable this family home had ever been given that there were only the three of them. She couldn't deny the magnificent view out of bi-fold doors however, stark in the February grey but stunning nevertheless. A large lawn was terraced down to a line of leylandii but beyond that the whole city was lying at their feet.

"Wow, what a view," Vida said.

"Yes, it is," replied Jane. "Can I offer you a tea or coffee?"

"Coffee would be lovely please. Milk, two sugars."

"Please, take a seat," she gestured towards one of the chairs around the massive table.

"How long have you lived here?" asked Vida, awkwardly. Small talk wasn't her forte at the best of times, let alone when talking to a grieving mother. She preferred studying the conventions of phatic talk, rather than participating, but it felt too callous though to just get straight down to business.

"Around fifteen years now? We bought it as a bit of a wreck, just after Maggie was born, before Peter's business took off. We were going to fill it with a large family. It's only in the last few years that we've had the money to make it how we wanted it. And now... it just seems very empty," she said, sadly. She bought a cafetiere over and set it in front of them, then looked up expectantly.

"Thank you," Vida said.

"No, thank you. I'm really pleased that you've agreed to have a look at this again. I know the verdict is wrong. I just know it. I'm her mother, for heaven's sake. I mean, I'm not naive. I know teenagers have secret lives. We all did, didn't we?" Jane smiled tentatively, sliding into a seat opposite Vida.

Vida thought back. Her teenage years had been anything but secret. When you grew up with parents who embraced all new age thinking and living, there was little point having a secret life. Your parents were already openly doing everything you could think of plus more. Vida's teenage years had been spent studying. "Of course."

"I tried to be an approachable mum. I know it's always awkward talking to your mum, especially as you get older, but we were quite open about sex and drugs and drinking. We encouraged her to be a teenager, to experiment. Safely, of course. But then, is it ever entirely safe?" she asked wistfully.

Vida didn't know what to say. This conversation was far beyond her remit. She could do little but nod and encourage Jane to continue.

"I'm sure she had secrets. But not this. Not such a big secret. And how could she even contemplate doing what she did? She had everything she could ever have wanted. She was popular at school, with girls and boys."

"It was a girls' school though, that she attended?"

"Yes, but it's got an associated boys' school and so the two had quite close relationships. They shared games facilities and that kind of thing. Is that important?" she asked, suddenly a little panicked. Her hand went to a small gold crucifix at her neck and she rubbed it quickly.

"Oh, I probably don't think so," reassured Vida. "I'm just trying to get a sense of Maggie's life." Like it had any relevance whatsoever to what Vida could do. But it seemed to be important to Jane for her to talk about her daughter. People often seemed to think avoiding a topic was the best way to deal with it; it was a selfish move though that left the grievers with no-one to talk to. They couldn't avoid the subject by just not talking about it.

"Well, she was. Popular I mean. And the teachers loved her too. She was doing so well. Excellent grades. She wanted to be a doctor, you know?" Vida nodded. "But she wanted to work with children. She had such a good way with children."

"There was nothing at all you were aware of that might have suggested she might be having... well, dark thoughts?" Vida felt so out of her depth. Her science was black and white, words lining up on a piece of paper. Picking it apart at word level took her away from the emotion. Here it was brutal and raw and hard. She cursed Myfanwy again; if this backfired, Vida and her science were going to pay a very public cost.

"No," Jane said. "Nothing." They fell silent as she plunged the coffee and then poured it steaming into small, delicate coffee mugs. She slid one across to Vida who dropped two sugar cubes in and stirred gently. Neither woman spoke, Vida looking out at the city while Jane seemed entranced by the whirlpool motion of her coffee.

"Dr Donaldson," Vida eventually started, "Jane. I'm really not sure I will be able to help that much. Forensic Linguistics isn't a magic pill. I won't ever be able to tell you definitively that Maggie did or did not write that letter. I might not even be able to tell you with any level of certainty." Jane continued her in-depth study of the coffee. Vida tried again. "I can look at what you've got, and I can offer you an opinion, but that's all it will ever be. I'm so sorry but I'm not sure what I can offer will bring any closure."

"Just take a look," Jane replied, so quietly that Vida almost couldn't hear her. She looked up and her face was wet with tears and exhaustion. "Please. I understand what you're telling me. I'm not an idiot and neither is Peter. We're intelligent people. We understand the science and we understand its limitations. But please. Please, just look."

"Okay." Vida blew on her coffee and took a sip. Her eyes travelled back to the view of the city, wondering if Maggie had embraced having the city on her doorstep. So much easy access to so much potential trouble. She loved living centrally, being able to walk everywhere she wanted. But she'd never been much interested in life's darker pleasures. A gin and tonic in a nice bar and occasionally, okay more than occasionally, a chocolate too many. For a teen, the possibilities could have been enticing indeed.

"Do you want to look in her room?" Jane asked, suddenly.

"Okay," agreed Vida, not entirely certain still about what she was expected to find.

"Do you mind just going by yourself? I'm afraid I still can't bring myself to go in there. Peter goes in sometimes," she confided. "It's up the stairs and the last door on the corridor to the right."

Vida held her breath as she walked up the stairs, keeping her footfalls light as though she were at risk of disturbing someone or something. It felt immeasurably intrusive; this was the family's most private area, and she was little more than a stranger. Thankfully, Maggie's room was easy to find, signalled by a vibrant 'Maggie' in fuchsia and surrounded by manically flashing fairy lights. Who switched those on every day? Or were they never turned off? Would the batteries be replaced when they finally died? She turned the doorknob gingerly and pushed open the door.

An almost supernatural stillness occupied the room. Only a year since it had been inhabited and yet it felt like it was a museum exhibit from the last century. Someone clearly cleaned in here as there were no cobwebs and no sign of dust on any of the surfaces, but even that interaction wasn't sufficient to create a feeling of inhabitancy. An involuntary shiver ran down her spine as she stepped inside and broke the seal. It wasn't just the room's occupant that was dead; the whole room had died the night that Maggie Donaldson had jumped off the bridge.

At the back of the house, the room shared the same view as the kitchen, Sheffield sprawling but strangely beautiful at her feet. If Vida lived here, she would have slept with the curtains open, watching the city breathe, humanity and nature in tandem as daylight fell and nightlights rose. The wilderness clashed awkwardly with the tasteful decoration inside the room though. From one angle, it felt more like a guest room. Polite Laura Ashley oriental wallpaper, a tidy bed with accent pillows. But as Vida turned she saw Maggie and the teen room came to life. The door wall was covered, floor-to-ceiling with pictures, polaroids and printouts of a thousand teenage faces. Vibrant, beautiful children beamed out at her, their whole futures waiting to be unrolled and explored. This was life. Along from the door stood a dressing table, littered with designer makeup and expensive looking brushes. Vida moved quietly into the room, pulled out the dressing table stool and sat in front of a mirror. Her own pale blonde face stared back at her, but it wasn't hard for her to see Maggie's face there instead, carefully applying the teenage flicks of eyeliner and edging lips in cherry red. A single photo was clipped to the side of the mirror, showing Maggie tightly encircled by her parents. Together like this, Vida could see Maggie's eyes were in fact Jane's and her upturned nose and full lips came directly from her father. An idyllic looking family indeed. Looking at them at their most vibrant though, only reaffirmed the toll the past year had taken.

Vida swung her legs round and faced the rest of the bedroom. Everything was so neat and tidy, and she wondered whether Maggie had been one of those unnaturally tidy teenagers or whether someone had tidied up in here on her behalf. Bedside tables sat either side of the double bed; one hosted a white Sonos speaker while the other was laden with a bedside light and a small pile of books. Crossing over, Vida noticed there was a small heart shaped enamel bowl on the table too, full of stud earrings and oddments of jewellery. There were two Maggie Stiefvater books and then a thin Indian-silk covered notebook. Feeling even more like an intruder, Vida slid the notebook out and snapped it open.

"That's her journal." Vida jumped as a voice whispered from the doorway. She whipped round, half-expecting to see the teenager standing there, ready to gripe at her for being in her room. Instead, Jane stood there, looking whiter than ever.

"Can I?" Vida asked, gesturing with the journal. "I mean... do you mind?"

Jane shook her head. "No. That's why you're here isn't it? To read her words. To understand her mind."

"Well, not quite," Vida said awkwardly. "But that's part of it. I will need samples of her writing."

"I have more. Downstairs. Peter printed some of her emails and texts to us off last night. Will that be okay?" She seemed desperate for Vida's approval, desperate to help.

"Yes, of course. Anything that she's written is useful."

"I'll go get it now."

"Can I take this with me?" Vida asked, holding up the journal.

"Will we get it back?" Jane's voice was plaintive.

"Yes. Of course. As soon as I've finished my analysis I'll give them right back."

Jane nodded, seemingly approving, and then she left as quietly as she'd arrived, leaving Vida once more alone in the absence, with the written words of a teenager no longer alive dancing in front of her eyes. She sat down on the end of the bed, feeling overwhelmed.

A sharp buzz rang out, startling her again before she realised it was her mobile phone. She shook her head impatiently. What was wrong with her? Pulling out the phone, number withheld, she pressed to answer.

"Hello?"

"Ms Henrikson? This is DI Slater. I believe you were wanting to speak with me?" Her mind clicked over to the phone call she'd made this morning before setting off for the Donaldson's.

"Oh yes, thank you for calling me back. I'm a Forensic Linguist at Sheffield University. Perhaps your colleagues have mentioned me? I've been working with the force as part of the education programme?"

"Yes?" Rising intonation. He was curious.

"Well, it's about a suicide I believe you investigated, Maggie Donaldson? I've been approached by Mr and Dr Donaldson? They wanted me to look at her suicide note, maybe see if it is consistent with her writing style?" Vida mentally rebuked herself for the constant query.

"Yes." Falling intonation this time. Disapproving now.

Vida hurried on. "I realise that the coroner recorded a verdict of suicide, but obviously the Donaldsons feel quite strongly that their daughter didn't kill herself. I was just wondering if there was anything at all at your end to suggest that there might have been more to it than was recorded?"

A long pause. "Ms Henrikson... the coroner recorded a verdict of suicide because that's what it is. Of course, the Donaldsons are unhappy about it, but feeling guilty that they didn't know or protect their daughter doesn't change the outcome. Maggie Donaldson killed herself." There was no give in his voice.

"Right. Okay." She paused, wondering how to frame any further questions. Wondering whether there were any other questions she should ask.

"If that's all? I'm rather busy."

"Erm... no. I don't think so," she said, cowed. "Well, thank you anyway." The line was dead before she even had time to say goodbye.

Chapter 9

Slater hung up the phone and ticked off the task from his to-do pad on the right of his desk. He knew others mocked his list, but it helped him stay organised and an organised crime was a quickly solved crime. The phone call had been a speedy job, a quick win. Thinking about poor Maggie Donaldson brought back a small niggle though. He meant what he'd said to the Linguistics woman; Maggie had definitely killed herself. But he hadn't been able to get to the bottom of why. Why would such a beautiful, apparently vibrant young girl with her whole life in front of her kill herself? And in such a lonely and horrible way? Still, he'd done his bit, played his investigative part, closed the case to the satisfaction of his superiors. Trying to understand human emotions just over-complicated everything.

Slater joined the team, gathered around a conference table, all of them in various stages of exhaustion. Louise looked as alert as she always did, leaning forward in her chair, notepad on her knee as she looked around at the others. In contrast, the visual data analyst, George Davies, slouched in his chair, not bothering to stifle the yawns and periodically rubbing blearily at knackered eyes. Dawson was about as well put together as he ever was, neatened up by his wife as she pushed him out the door. Slater knew he'd deteriorate as the day went on, knots coming untied, crumbs accumulating and creases visibly emerging. It was a source of fascination to him; there was an art to being able to disassemble oneself without conscious effort.

Slater could never tell if Dawson was oblivious to it or recognised the developing deshabille and just accepted it. Slater's own functional suit remained neatly creased; he was punctilious about his appearance to the point of OCD. Hussain stood upright in the doorway, arms crossed, a crocodile in the water.

"So where are we?" Slater asked.

Louise consulted her notes. "All of the staff at Grey's have been interviewed. Nobody remembers seeing Kitty at all, let alone with anyone else."

"I don't think she was ever inside the bar," Davies offered. "We've tracked Kitty across a few CCTV cameras. Most relevant is this shot here." He fiddled with the laptop before casting a grainy image to the TV on the wall. "This is just at the entrance to the alley." He pressed rewind and cued the video. The team watched as Kitty and an unidentified figure moved across the screen and then disappeared out of view. They sat quietly for a few moments.

"There doesn't look to be any duress," Louise said.

"So why would she go willingly with someone into a dark alley at night?" Slater asked.

"Sex," Dawson offered.

"No," Slater said, vehemently. "She wasn't that kind of person."

"Wasn't that kind of person?" Dawson scoffed. "Did you see the dress she was wearing? No knickers? Bloody gagging for it!"

"No," Slater repeated. "Whatever she was, I don't think she was 'gagging' for it." He spoke with disdain. "She seemed to live a virtually monastic life. Faithful to her boyfriend. Out to work but then home to bed. Not your typical rock and roll lifestyle."

"What's with the spangly mini dress then?" Dawson asked, conveying his disbelief in what Slater was saying.

"Fashion," Louise offered.

"Maybe," Slater conceded. "Part of the image maybe. We still have the question though of why she went willingly into that alley. Can we tell anything about the person with her?"

"About five ten," Davies said. "Can't tell if it's male or female though. Could be either. The hoody obscures the hair and the face a bit."

"Have we got any clearer images elsewhere?"

"Nope. I've looked through all of them. The first sighting we have them together is at the corner of Holly Street and Trippet Lane. I can't tell if they arrived there together or met there. They walk up round the back of City Hall and then towards the Alley."

"How do they seem together?"

"How do they seem?" Davies asked, confused.

"Yes, I mean, are they friendly? Do they hold hands? Are they talking? Are there any signs that Kitty is being forced further down the route? A knife in the side?"

"They walk within about one foot of each other. There's no indication that Kitty is being forced to go anywhere she doesn't want to. Doesn't seem to be any talking."

"Drugs? Alcohol?"

Davies shook his head. "No evidence from the way she's walking. She appears to be sober as far as I can tell."

"Postmortem can confirm that for us."

"Press Conference is at ten," Hussain interjected.

Slater nodded. "That might produce some more leads. What have we got on social media?"

"After the press release confirming her death yesterday, everyone who ever met her, or was in the same room as her at some point or liked her or even had ever heard her name has tweeted something or other. We're trawling through all those at the minute. Not come across anything from last night yet," Louise offered.

"Keep at it. Someone must have seen her. That dress was noticeable. And they walked quite a distance through town. I know it was a Sunday evening and was pretty cold and miserable but there should have been someone out there." He looked around and nodded. The others started to collect their notebooks and belongings together. "Dawson, you ready for the PM?"

"No-one else you fancy taking?" wheedled Dawson.

"Nope, it's got to be us."

They took Slater's car; it was a quick ten-minute drive to the mortuary on Watery Street, a pleasant twenty-minute walk if the weather permitted but neither of them fancied battling the icy drizzle again.

Slater always found the mortuary an incongruous place. It was purpose built but attempts to normalise death and comfort families made it feel like some sort of weird office block. The rough carpet was an inoffensive navy, the walls a light grey. Potted plants were dotted around the place, an attempt to make it feel a little more homely he supposed. He wasn't sure why they bothered. Every pathologist he'd ever met swore blind that the morgue didn't smell of anything apart from that unique hospital blend of disinfectant and over-cooked dinners. His head told him that they were right, but his heart was sure that he could detect the scents of all the bodies who'd been through here. Real or not, the tang of iron and salt sat on his tongue. Charred flesh and waterlogged tissue made his chest thump. The unpleasant aroma of RTA roadkill swam round his head. Occasionally, if he was feeling particularly spiritual, he even fancied he could smell the souls of all those departed folk, as if they'd hang around the scene of their final ignominious stripping. Perhaps it was all in his head, but he couldn't help but keep nervously checking around his peripheral vision in case someone or something was hanging around out of sight.

In contrast, the noises of the mortuary were reassuringly human. Voices were kept low, out of a strange honour for the deceased, even though they had gone long past hearing. Distant chatter and occasional radio tunes accompanied them, the background melodies of office blocks up and down the country. Until the bone saw started up. The sound penetrated Slater's own bones, making him feel as though he were being sliced up along with the victim.

Dr Horace Ellison was waiting for them at the small administrative office at the entrance to the medical suite. A large, rotund man he didn't resemble at all the idea Slater always had of pathologists. A florid face and a handsome ginger moustache made him look more like some sort of Texan oil baron than a doctor of death.

"Ah, DI Slater and DS Dawson. On time as usual. Good to see. So many of your colleagues do not seem to have the same respect for my time," he said sternly, his voice short with clipped vowels.

"You know how it is Doctor. Cases seem to suck you in and spit you out without letting you look at the clock," said Slater, feeling personally targeted and obliged to defend his maligned associates.

"Indeed. Well, SOCOs have made a start. Fingerprints have been taken and photographer's in there at the minute."

"Great. Thanks for bumping this up for us."

Ellison raised his eyebrows. "Your Ms Hussain is not an easy woman to refuse."

"I think she prefers Detective Chief Inspector," Slater muttered to Dawson as they followed the pathologist into the mortuary suite. The room had been built with a specific viewing box for the police and any other interested parties, and Slater and Dawson took up position as Ellison bustled into the stark white room. SOCOs in white overalls busied themselves around the body, taking a last few snaps of the body. It was still clothed at this point, the sparkly dress even more starkly out of place on the metal bed than it had been in a Sheffield city centre alleyway. It seemed even tinier than before, stretched long on a frame that was designed to hold bodies much heavier than this one.

"Ready?" Ellison's voice boomed into the viewing gallery through the microphone hanging from the ceiling. Slater knew there would be a recording device attached somewhere to enable the doctor's words to be typed up at a later date. The SOCOs in the room nodded and the autopsy began.

Slater and Dawson sat back in awkwardly positioned office chairs, both silent in the face of the human horror in front of them. Slater knew the autopsy wasn't worse than the actual death. There was no fear or panic here. Just science. But there was something disturbing about the calm slicing open of what had been living and breathing just a short time ago. It was his first autopsy ten years ago that had led him to becoming vegetarian. Watching the ritual dissection of a middle-aged Jamaican woman, someone he'd known as a boy, had turned his stomach firmly from ever eating meat again, not because of the taste but because he couldn't bear to prepare it.

"Female decedent," began Ellison. The policemen watched and listened as the body lay, unprotesting, through the series of trespasses. Clothes were sliced off and dropped into waiting evidence bags, carefully numbered and passed on to more forensic officers. Fingernails and toenails were scraped. Gums and teeth wiped. Body washed carefully, the water running off into a gulley where any further detritus could be captured. Marks and wounds on the body were measured, photographed, casts taken of some of the deeper ones. Hair, scalp and pubic, was combed carefully into waiting receptacles. Vagina and anus were gently swabbed. And finally, the superficial completed, the knife came out and separated the skin with ease. An army of efficient ants, clambered over the body, taking it to pieces bit by bit and carrying each element off for further investigation in a lab somewhere. Slater sat, blinking slowly, determined to take it all in. He hoped when he died that he went in some immediately obvious way that didn't require this further scrutiny, just a quick check to make sure everything was as it should be. Finally, after what seemed like time eternal, Ellison nodded at them and switched the microphone off. Slater stood up and strode out to meet the pathologist, Dawson lumbering behind him, looking a little green.

"So, we've got a female, aged between 20 and 25. I believe you have an ID? Cause of death is the slash wound to her neck. Came from behind, assailant must have grabbed her head, pulled it back like so," he said, ably demonstrating with Dawson, "and then a single slice across. No hesitation marks so could be a confident killer."

"Would they need to have been tall to achieve that?" Slater asked.

"Not necessarily no. The victim herself was only five foot two and weighed just 44.5kg. A little on the underweight side. Pretty much anyone who was a little bigger than her could have achieved this wound. It's all about confidence really. I would say that the assailant is probably right-handed as the dragging on the wound indicates a left to right direction compatible with a right-handed action." Again, he mimed the actions on the ever-obliging Dawson.

"What about all the other wounds?"

"All inflicted at or just after the moment of death. Some of the wounds show oozing but equally some show no blood reaction."

"Seems like a bit unnecessary."

"I agree. I'm no profiler," he said, making it sound like a dirty word, "but I believe we would agree on the rage shown here."

"Any signs of sexual assault?"

"No penetrative injuries, no bruising around the genitalia. No semen or other body fluids detected. No condom lubricant. So no, no sexual assault. And no signs that the victim had had sexual intercourse within the past few hours."

"Anything else that we need to know?"

"Victim had been recently pregnant. There are signs of a D&C so she either miscarried or had an abortion. Also, toxicology indicates above average blood alcohol of 0.279%. That's a fair few glasses of wine there. Stomach contents indicate she ate about 8pm."

"That should help us pin down movements. Was she killed at the scene or dumped?"

"SOCO will confirm but I believe she was killed at the scene. There was a substantial pool of blood beneath the victim, on the rubbish bags and the ground below.

There was also evidence of arterial spray along the alley wall."

"So, there was a lot of blood?"

"Yes. I would hazard a guess that the assailant was fairly well covered himself. The arterial spray would have gushed away from him, but the number of stab wounds mean that there would have been a substantial amount of blood still, even though some are post-mortem."

"So, unlikely to have walked away with no trace on them?" The pathologist agreed. "Well, thanks Doctor. That's potentially some good news. We must be able to find a witness who has seen someone covered in blood walking through the streets."

"I'll email you the full report over as soon as possible." Slater nodded his thanks again and then left the scene, a pale Dawson following him. Outdoors, they both took big gulps of air. Even the grey city air was preferable to the bleached and disinfectanted air behind them.

"So, Kitty had been pregnant recently," Dawson said.

"Hmm. Text Louise and ask her to rush the medical records if she can. Interesting that Adam didn't mention anything about a pregnancy. Maybe because Kitty's parents were there. Maybe it's not the sort of thing he wanted to discuss in front of them. He told me himself that he's a private man. Still, it gives us some questions to answer, doesn't it? Miscarriage or abortion? Seems like the kind of thing that might upset a relationship balance though. Let's get him in."

Maybe the right questions and Adam could help him understand the enigma Kitty presented.

Chapter 10

Jane Donaldson made a swift call to Maggie's school, and Vida found herself trailing behind the head on a tour of the facilities within thirty minutes. It felt like sales pitch. It was clear that she wanted to cast the school in the best possible light, and who could blame her really? If there was anything to connect the school to Maggie's suicide, and Vida really didn't think there was, any more than there was to connect it to parental neglect, then it could do a great deal of damage to the school's reputation. Which meant losing large financial contributions in the long run. The parents who were wealthy enough to send their children here normally had options as far reaching as their wallets and Vida didn't think it would take many students being removed to create a downward spiral in the financial situation. Although private schools were largely immune to the financial threats facing the state education sector, they weren't financially blind to inflation and ever-increasing operating costs.

So Vida plastered a polite smile on her face and nodded approvingly as the headmistress showed her the gym and the pool and the music suites and the language library and every other amenity that the school was blessed with. This place was better equipped than the university. Her tour guide was much younger and more feminine than the heads of Vida's experience. Her own secondary head had been a burly man of dark eyebrows and long cigars. This one barely looked older than Vida herself and was stylishly dressed in a tight black suit with a pencil skirt. More Miss Moneypenny than Miss Trunchbull. She turned now and smiled at Vida, a red-lipsticked curl that didn't quite meet her eyes.

"So that's the facilities. Perhaps if you'd like to join me in my office for coffee, then we can chat a little further about...?" The head turned and gestured towards a large oak door adorned with 'Ms Heathcoate, Head.'

"Yes, of course, that would be helpful." Vida followed the head into a large and well-lit study; a traditional mahogany desk sat with its back to a large window, which was draped in velvet navy. Along one side were floor-to-ceiling bookshelves, groaning with what looked like traditional leather-bound classics. The books were clearly designed to be props rather than literature, and Vida wondered if anyone actually ever read them. The whole room was very stylised 'gentleman's library', and she knew that she'd never be comfortable in such an intimidating room. The head didn't seem to have the same insecurities though, as she sat confidently behind the behemoth of a desk.

"So, Maggie Donaldson," the Head started. She typed something on a MacBook in front of her, as though she were looking something up, but Vida felt sure that she already knew all of Maggie's information off by heart. Unless suicides really were that common here that there was a long list of girls who'd killed themselves?

"Yes. As you probably know, the coroner recorded a verdict of suicide. Maggie's parents don't have confidence in that verdict and so have asked me to look into it a little."

"And your area of expertise is..." she scrabbled with a pile of printouts on her desk

"Forensic Linguistics," supplied Vida.

"Not something I'm familiar with."

"It's a relatively new distinct area of science, although it has been used in many criminal cases over the years."

"Criminal?"

"Well, yes," frowned Vida. "A young girl's dead. That would be criminal, whether suicide or something else." She was beginning to dislike the woman's obfuscating.

"Yes, I see." Heathcote looked discomfited for a minute. "Well, I'm not sure that we can help here."

"My science is based on the written word, and what I'm interested in is procuring some samples of Maggie's writing."

"Her writing? Well, I'm sure we can find essays and some things like that."

"That would be helpful. But I am particularly interested in Maggie's informal communications. Emails, texts, letters to friends, that kind of thing. Perhaps it would be possible for me to meet with the girls she was close with and ask if they have anything Maggie has written. The more texts I can get my hands on, the better my linguistic profile will be and the more likely it is that I can put Mr and Dr Donaldson's mind at rest."

"I'm not sure I can agree to that. Of course, my responsibility lies with my girls."

"Maggie was one of your girls," reminded Vida, firmly.

"Of course, of course. But unfortunately, I can no longer do anything for her."

"This is me asking you to do something for her," said Vida, moving forward in her chair and appealing to the uncertain woman. She was very sure that whatever head teaching training course she'd been on, it hadn't had a module called What to do when your pupils commit suicide, and a Forensic Linguist comes asking questions. "Ms Heathcoate, I'm sure Mr and Dr Donaldson have been extremely generous to the school in terms of financial commitment. In fact, didn't I notice Mr Donaldson's name over the new IT suite? I know they've been very generous to my own university. I don't want to ask the girls any questions. You can stay in the room with us if you want. All I want to do is ask them if they have anything written by Maggie. Anything at all that I can use to help bring her poor parents some peace." Vida now sat back, unsure where her sudden bolshiness had come from. It wasn't like her to put pressure on anyone but this woman, in her ivory-educated tower was getting up her nose. She was happy enough to take from the Donaldsons but didn't seem to be interested in helping them when they were more in need of help than ever before.

Ms Heathcote looked contemplatively at the screen in front of her. Vida wasn't sure if she was actually reading something or just using the time to think about it. She rolled the fingers of her right hand across the desk, tapping with long glittery red nails. "I can stay with the girls."

"Yes, of course," Vida replied, breathing out gently, relieved that she wasn't going to have to ask the Donaldsons for more direct assistance. "All the time. It won't even take very long. I'll just explain to the girls what it is I want and then give them my email address so that they can contact me directly."

"Okay," she looked up as the secretary pushed open the door and entered with coffee in two china cups. "Ah, Jenny. Immaculate timing as always. Please could you find me Tamsin Jennison, Petra Komalov and Vanessa Barrington-Kennedy? They were Maggie's closest friends," she said to Vida as Jenny put the coffee tray on the desk and then left quickly. "How do you have your coffee?" She moved one cup, black to the other side of her laptop.

"White, two sugars," Vida said, sucking in her stomach in case this black-coffee goddess felt like passing judgement on her rich taste. They sat in uncomfortable silence waiting for the secretary to return with the girls. Vida's earlier bravado had dissipated quickly, and she was intimidated once more. She'd avoided ever getting in trouble in her own school days, a tight-lipped nerd as the others around her tried to goad and taunt her into stepping out of line. The weight of potential parental disappointment weighed heavily, even though she recognised as an adult that her parents probably would have liked a bit more of a spark. They'd probably have celebrated if she'd ever been called to the Head's office for some sort of ill-behaviour. Her conformity and meekness had made her an outsider in her own home, a feeling she still hadn't managed to shake off. Now it was her extreme Swedish blondness and Home Counties accent that marked her as different. She wasn't sure she'd ever be comfortable in her own skin.

They both looked up as the door was pushed open, Vida swivelling round in her chair to watch the entourage come in. Three beautiful teenage girls, redolent with that verging on the obnoxious self-confidence that only teen girls, supremely assured of their own allure, can have. Vida fought the urge to shrivel back. She was here as a professional and as superficially self-assured as these girls were, she knew that deep down they would probably be a mess of confusion and distress. They were practically clones of each other, tall, long-limbed, all with long glossy hair and liner-ringed big eyes. Varied skin tones and hair colours were all equally complemented by the maroon and navy uniform, knee-length pleated skirts, crisp white blouses and expertly tailored blazers.

"Thank you Jenny. Girls, sit down. This is Dr Henrikson. She'd like some information from you. About Maggie," her voiced dropped at this last point, as though she might wake the dead by incanting their name aloud. The girls sat down and then turned to face Vida.

"Maggie killed herself," said one of the girls, a brunette, her voice flat.

"The police already asked us about it," said another, a clipped Russian accent emerging from a pearlescent mouth beneath arched blonde eyebrows.

"Well, I'm not from the police. And you're right. The coroner did rule that Maggie committed suicide. But her parents still don't feel that they know everything, so they've asked me to take another look."

"What can you do?" the final member of the trio asked, sharply.

"I'm a Forensic Linguist. I examine language, written and verbal. One of my areas is looking at authorship and seeing whether it's possible to prove that a specific person wrote a specific letter or note. I'll be analysing the note that Maggie left and comparing it to her usual written style to see if I can maybe help put people's minds at rest and find some evidence to show that it is her writing."

"But... wasn't the letter... like... typed?" Brunette, brow furrowed.

"Yes, but that doesn't matter. I'm not a handwriting expert. I look at the words themselves, and how we make sentences, and that kind of thing."

"So, what do you need us for?" asked the Russian, suspiciously.

"Well, I've got samples of Maggie's writing from her parents, and school have said I can have essays from them, but I figured that she probably communicated with you, her friends, more than anything, and so I was wondering if you had any texts that perhaps you could let me have."

"Like... IMs?"

"Yes, exactly. Instant messages, texts, emails, anything at all where Maggie has written something to you."

"But that's all like private," said the third girl, her voice raised at the end in a typical teenage girl query.

"Yes, of course it is. And I don't want you to share anything that you're uncomfortable sharing with me. I'm not interested in the content of the messages at all, just the style. I barely even read them," Vida said reassuringly. "It's all about checking out how specific sentence types are formed."

The three girls looked at each other, obviously sharing some sort of telepathic discussion. Finally, the brunette nodded. "OK, what do we need to do?"

"Let me give each of you my business card. My mobile number and email are both on here. Anything you've got that Maggie wrote, that you don't mind me having, please just send it my way." The three girls each took a card. "Thank you girls. Anything you've got, anything at all. It could really help me find out what happened to Maggie."

"We know what happened to Maggie," said the brunette, in the same flat tone she'd used earlier. "She killed herself."

Vida frowned. "Why are you so sure of that when her parents aren't?" she asked. "Do you know something else? Something that you haven't told anyone yet?"

Again, the three girls exchanged those telepathic looks and then shrugged their shoulders in synchronisation. "No, not really," their spokesperson offered.

Vida's eyes moved between them. Two pairs of eyes stared studiously down at their laps but the third girl, the one who'd walked in last and had spoken last and least, met Vida's eyes steadily before dropping down. Not before Vida had recognised something in them: knowledge and fear.

Chapter 11

The Adam Marriott who sat in Interview One was an even more unprepossessing character than the one who'd been sitting at a dining table the last time Slater had seen him. Of course, the battleship grey walls and harsh fluorescent lighting of the room cast everyone with an unattractive pall, but the impact on Marriott seemed greater than usual. He looked almost ill, a wash of grief across his face, his hair dishevelled. He'd refused representation, stating that he had nothing to fear and that only guilty men needed lawyers. Slater never failed to be amazed by the number of suspects who felt that asking for legal representation somehow cast them in a worse light than blindly incriminating themselves. Still, he wasn't going to complain. On Marriott's head be it. He'd cautioned him, just to be on the safe side and they sat waiting for Dawson to set the digital recorder going and deal with the preamble.

"So, Mr Marriott, Adam. We'd like to ask you some more questions about your relationship with Kitty." Slater put his files meaningfully on the desk in front of him and moved his chair in.

Marriott looked at them, eyebrows arched. He didn't say anything.

"You'd been dating for how long?" Slater asked.

"Around two years," he said.

"And how would you describe your relationship?" Slater made a note in his notebook, knowing that sometimes, jotting things down, relevant or not, would psych out a witness more than any recording ever did. That simple act of putting pen to paper seemed to make innocent and guilty feel like they might be found out.

"In terms of what?" Marriott looked appropriately unnerved by Slater's notebook.

"Well, in terms of, were you happy? Was Kitty happy? Two years is quite a long time. Did you have plans for your future together?" Slater kept his tone light.

Marriott shrugged. "I would describe us as happy, yes. Like any relationship, there were good times and bad. Being in a relationship with someone living in the public eye was never easy. People used to think that they owned a piece of Kitty. Like she owed them something in exchange for their support. Download a track and own a piece of Kitty Wakelin's soul." Impassivity quickly turned to spitting bitterness. It was clearly a nerve for him.

"What was that like?"

"We could never go out in public together, never have dinner together without arranging something special. Kitty wanted to separate our private life with her public side, but there's no real viable solution. I mean, it's not like I wanted to go out with her every night or anything. Just occasionally it would have been nice to go out without putting in place a giant privacy operation."

"I didn't realise she was that famous?" asked Slater, injecting a note of doubt into his voice.

Again, Marriott bridled in response to Slater's needling. "She wasn't. Not really. Not yet. She was recognisable I suppose. People did see her in the street and come up for autographs. But that was only locally really."

"So she was paranoid?"

Marriott tilted his head. "Paranoid? That's quite an inflammatory word. Implies, I don't know, some sort of imbalance."

"You didn't find it paranoid? To behave like you'd be swamped if you stepped out the door but only be locally recognisable? Maybe she was ashamed of you then? Maybe she didn't want to be seen in public with someone so..." Slater tailed off, waiting for a reaction. He was disappointed this time; Marriott sat impassively. "Different from her," Slater finally finished.

Marriott smiled. "Kitty wasn't ashamed of me. Not at all. She was just a fiercely private person. She didn't want people invading my life, making it difficult for me. Didn't want her fame to affect my everyday existence."

"That must have been a lot of pressure on her."

This time, Marriott seemed to take the statement to heart. "Not from me. Look, I don't know what to say. Kitty didn't like being famous. All she really wanted was to sing her songs and be at home with me. She wasn't paranoid. She wasn't ashamed. She just wanted a quiet life."

"So why not quit singing and work in an office or something?"

"Without being melodramatic, that would have been like asking a nightingale to not sing. Singing was her life,

Inspector. And when she sang, people stopped and listened. And it helped her. She seemed, I don't know, more peaceful when she was singing."

"She was stressed? You didn't mention this yesterday? Yesterday everything was appropriately perfect."

"Not stressed no," Marriott said, emphatically. "More worried. And just sad. She was a very sad person."

"About?"

"I don't know. I presumed that it was to do with the new opportunities. Moving to London. It was going to be a big change, and I know she was worried about it."

"So how was that going to work?"

"What do you mean?"

Slater was sure that Marriott was being deliberately obtuse now. "I mean, how was your relationship going to change with Kitty going to London?"

"We hadn't discussed it yet," he said.

"So, you're expecting me to believe that your girlfriend of two years had this amazing opportunity that was going to take her to London within the next couple of months and you'd not even discussed what was going to happen? Well, what did you think would happen?"

Marriott looked thoughtful. "You know, I don't think I'd really pondered it. I think I just presumed we'd carry on as we were, Kitty coming over when she had the chance."

"So, her being in London wouldn't have impacted on your relationship?" Slater asked, disbelieving.

"We didn't live in each other's pockets. We've always had our own space. Kitty's space would have simply been a bit further away."

"See, if it were me, I'd've worried about all the temptations that would be waiting for her in London. I mean, it's a bit different than our little Northern city. All those people, all those attractions. Presumably a good deal more money to play with. She's gotten into trouble before, we know that. What's to stop it happening again?"

"Kitty's a different person now."

"How do you know? You didn't know her before," Slater pointed out.

"Well, no. But I know her now. I mean, I knew her. She wasn't a silly little girl. She was thoughtful and calm and introspective and kind. Fame wouldn't change her."

Slater nodded contemplatively, and then opened the files that were sat in front of him. Louise had managed to get the medical files faxed through and he scanned through the reports again. From childhood into adulthood. A broken wrist as a six-year-old. A prescription for Microgynon. And lastly, a surgical termination.

"Was it your decision to get an abortion? Or Kitty's?" he asked abruptly.

Marriott blanched but remained silent.

"It's a big decision," Slater offered. "What are you? Forty? Surely it's getting to a now or never point for you? The window for fatherhood is passing by. I mean yes, for us men, you could say it's easier. We can just keep going. But no-one chooses to be an older father if they've got an earlier opportunity. Nobody wants to be the dad who's mistaken for a grandad in the playground or at Parents' Evening. What happened? Did you even know? Did Kitty fall pregnant and see all her future dreams disappearing down the toilet? A baby now and that's it for her career. Just as it's about to take off."

"No!" Marriott balled his fist and pressed it firmly on the table, as though he'd wanted to punch it but couldn't bring himself to that level of violence. "That's not how it was," he said quietly.

"So how was it?"

Marriott looked as though he were about to say something but then fell silent again.

"Mr Marriott? You didn't mention this to us yesterday. In fact, you stated that everything in your relationship was good."

"It was good. We were good. The abortion... well, it was difficult. It wasn't Kitty's choice though. I mean, not hers alone anyway. It was a decision we made together. I didn't want to be a father. Not now, not ever. Your biological clock might be ticking, Inspector, but mine never got started. I have zero interest in being a father."

"Okay, no interest in fatherhood for you," Slater said, holding up his hands. "But what about Kitty? How did you describe her? Calm? Kind? Seems like a good fit for motherhood."

"She would have been a fantastic mother. But she understood. She understood that it wasn't what I wanted, and she didn't want to trap me into a loveless relationship."

"Loveless?" Slater asked.

"Not now, I mean," he flustered. "But if we'd had a child, it would have ended up that way. I'm afraid I would have grown to resent her and the child. That was not a situation that either Kitty or I would have wanted."

"You made her abort her child because you would have ended up disliking her?"

"It was the right thing for her too," said Marriott, squirming. "Like you said, she was destined for great things. A baby wasn't right for her."

"It's good of you to decide that for her," Slater said.

"I didn't expect you to be so women's lib," Marriott said, going on the attack. "The police are normally well behind the rest of the world in terms of equality and justice."

"I'm the exception to the norm," smiled Slater. Dawson shifted in his seat but didn't argue. "And I am extremely women's lib as you call it. A woman's choice."

"It was her choice. I just put my point of view across."

"So how did it impact on your relationship?"

Marriott sighed but didn't say anything.

"Come on Mr Marriott. You've already admitted you talked Kitty into having an abortion that it doesn't seem like she particularly wanted. You can't keep telling us that you had this picture-perfect relationship!"

"It's not like any of this is relevant."

"I'll decide what's relevant. You sat there yesterday and told us everything was fine with Kitty. Nothing was worrying her. That wasn't true. What else is not true?"

Marriott looked up from the table and met Slater's gaze. "I was telling the truth when I said that Kitty's move to London wouldn't affect our relationship. We'd decided to break up. I just didn't want to tell her parents. I didn't want them to think that Kitty's last days were anything but happy."

"And you didn't think this was relevant? Information we should have?" Slater was incredulous.

"Our personal life has nothing to do with her murder. It's personal."

"You complained about your private life becoming public with Kitty. That was nothing compared to how public your life has to become when you're the partner of a murder victim. You don't get any privacy. You're owed nothing. Everything has to go towards finding out who killed Kitty, the woman you professed to love. You've lied to Kitty's parents, you've lied to the police and you're still trying to pretend like this isn't important information?" Slater snorted. "Time to tell the truth, Mr Marriott. And if you keep insisting on this legendary right to privacy then I would point out that what we've got, in police terms right now, is motive and opportunity. Motive in that perhaps the abortion was Kitty's idea. Perhaps she aborted your baby without even asking you for your opinion. Maybe she knew you did want a family. You were furious. You killed her and tried to pass it off as the actions of some sort of madman. No confirmable alibi. Watching a boxset. Convenient. You knew where she'd gone, you knew exactly where she'd be, and you killed her to punish her for killing your baby."

Marriott's mouth fell open and he turned purple. "Bloody hell. That's quite an imagination," he spluttered.

"Not at all," Slater replied, calmly. "I don't think the CPS will have any problems seeing the truth in this scenario. As I said, motive, opportunity. All we need is a witness, something linking you with the crime scene and we've got our conviction."

"You won't find anything," he said. "Because it wasn't me. I loved Kitty. I wasn't lying about that. But our relationship had come to a natural conclusion. We'd reached an impasse. We wanted different things. Needed different things. Kitty knew that. She understood that."

"There seems to be a lot of things that Kitty understood when it came to you."

Another flash of something behind the eyes. Amusement? Anger? Slater wasn't sure. "She was an understanding girl. That was one of the things I loved about her. She knew I didn't want to leave Sheffield, my job. So, when she accepted the new London representation, she knew that she was closing the door on our relationship."

"It was her choice?"

"It was mutual." He fell silent. "I'd met someone new. Someone my own age. Someone in the office."

"Did Kitty know?"

"Yes. She...erm...came home unexpectedly one evening and encountered my friend."

Slater swallowed hard. Calm, thoughtful and kind; Kitty must have been regretting those choices when she'd caught her boyfriend with another woman. "And was this before or after she decided to accept the London offer?"

"Before," Marriott sighed. "About three weeks ago."

"And how did she react?"

"Amazingly well. She seemed almost resigned. Like she'd expected something like this to happen. Said she understood and wanted me to be happy."

"And where did the baby fall in all this?"

"She fell pregnant before I'd met Elaine. That's my friend. But I'm afraid the abortion came after I'd already started a relationship with Elaine."

"You're a real gent, aren't you?" said Slater, amazed by the audacity of the man. "So just to get this straight, you got your girlfriend pregnant, started a relationship with a new woman, convinced your original girlfriend to get an abortion, got caught screwing your new girlfriend and then tried to pretend that the breakup was Kitty's idea? Jesus Christ." He looked appraisingly at the man in front of him. Hardly Lothario material but clearly he had some sort of appeal that Slater was immune to.

Marriott had the grace to look uncomfortable. "I know I didn't behave well, Inspector. And well, you're right. I should have told you this yesterday, but it was just George and Vanessa were there, I couldn't very well admit that we'd broken up."

"We asked you about Kitty's worries directly though. Why didn't you tell us that there was something worrying her? You could have said something to the Liaison Officer?"

Marriott ran a hand through his hair. "I just couldn't. I mean, I was in shock. I didn't think. I just wanted to preserve Kitty's memory."

"This still isn't making me believe that you weren't involved in Kitty's death," Slater said. "More motive thanks to the cheating and still no alibi."

"I'm afraid I wasn't entirely honest with you about that."

Jesus! What had the man been honest about? How could he expect them to believe a single word that came out of his mouth after this debacle of an interview? "More dishonesty? I must say Mr Marriott, you're seriously trying my patience."

"Well, that's unfortunate, Inspector. But I do have an alibi. I was with Elaine on Sunday night. She'll confirm that we spent the night together."

Slater threw his hands up in the air. "Do you know how much time you have wasted? Answers need to be found quickly. The first 24 hours is vital. And we've spent that looking at you." He jabbed his finger towards Marriott, wishing he could make contact with the bastard's face.

"I just..." He shook his head. "Look, I know. And I'm sorry. I just didn't want her parents to think badly of me. I didn't want them to think she was unhappy. And I knew that I hadn't had anything to do with her death. I didn't think it would make any difference."

"It does make a difference. Because while we've been chasing up medical records, and interviewing you, other lines of enquiry have gone unchecked, unexplored. You've wasted our time Mr Marriott, and in doing that you've let Kitty's killer stay free for that little bit longer. I hope your precious reputation was worth that."

Slater nodded to Dawson who ended the interview and switched off the recording. Gathering the papers back into the folder once more, he stood and then looked down at Marriott. The man finally looked repentant. "Time we'll never get back," said Slater softly as he left the room.

Hussain emerged from the viewing suite as he moved past the door towards the office. "Clock's ticking. We're moving out of the twenty-four hour window," she commented.

"He looked like a good option," Slater said, defensively.

"Well, what now?"

"Still following up on the CCTV. Trying to track her movements through the city centre." He shrugged. It sounded weak even to his ears.

"Marriott said something about new representation," she said. She didn't seem disappointed in the lack of progress, merely accepting of the difficulty. He knew she was probably under a level of pressure from above though that would put lesser officers to the knuckle.

"What?"

"He mentioned that Kitty had signed new representation for London. Didn't you interview her manager yesterday? Did he say anything about that?"

"No," Slater admitted. He hadn't noticed the comment, although he was sure he'd have spotted it later when he was reviewing the recording. Nothing slipped past Hussain though; Slater reckoned she had more in common with God than you might expect from a female police officer in Sheffield. "Might be worth following up."

"Exactly." She nodded at him and then whipped round and left.

Dawson came up behind him. "Bet that didn't go down well."

"Wasn't our finest hour," Slater offered. "But Hussain reckons there might be mileage in re-interviewing Rashid Khan and maybe his sister this time. Something about new representation."

Dawson nodded in agreement. "Not now though," he said, looking at his watch. "If I don't get home, Sophie'll have my balls for missing another bath-time."

"What do you think about her?"

"I tell you, she's getting harder and harder to please. Can't do anything to suit these days. I come home early, and she wants to know what I'm up to, too late and she wants to know where I've been." He wore his best hangdog expression.

Slater looked askance at his sergeant. "Not Sophie. Kitty. What do you make of Kitty?"

Dawson looked confused. "She's just a girl that got murdered, Gabe. I don't make anything of her."

"I just can't get a handle on her," Slater said, more to himself than Dawson, who was checking his watch again and looking meaningfully towards the door at the end of the corridor. "She gets more and more confusing the more we find out about her. Some sort of saint? But reformed from earlier trouble? Apparently intelligent but a complete doormat and lets a bloke like that tosser walk all over her?"

"Typical woman," offered Dawson. "Never know if they're coming or going."

Slater rolled his eyes. "Thanks for that insight, Mark. Right, off you get. Bright and early in the morning."

"Are you heading out? Hot date?" asked Dawson, almost over his shoulder as he moved in the direction of the exit.

"Not tonight. Home alone." He watched his sergeant leave, sidling cautiously through the door as though he was worried that Slater would change his mind and call him back if he made any sudden movements. Sometimes Slater envied Dawson for his easy relationship with his wife and the obvious love that he felt for her and his children. But with those thoughts came panic and he would feel again the loss of his father in an almost physical wave of nausea and grief. Opening yourself up in that way was just too big a risk. He would keep himself to himself for as long as possible.

Chapter 12

Driving straight from the high school, Vida made better than usual time and was home before Simon. Her thoughts were preoccupied with what the third friend had been trying to communicate. She couldn't shake off the feeling that she wanted to share something important. What was stopping her?

Vida shivered as she came in. The house was dark, and she moved through the rooms switching on as many lamps as she could find. Simon complained about the electricity, but they were her bills to pay and she refused to sit in darkness in her own home. She slid the thermostat up another degree and went to boost the heating before sitting in the kitchen with her laptop, notebook and a mug of steaming hot chocolate. Today had drained her in a way that she'd never experienced before. Working in education, especially the lectures, she was used to being constantly 'on', performing for the gratification of all the students who were indebting themselves to be there. It had been a whole new level talking to Maggie's mother, with her undisguised grief and then being political at the school. She wasn't finished yet though, and as she opened her laptop, her email alert began to sound vigorously. Before her eyes, her inbox was populated with what looked like hundreds of messages, screenshots of WhatsApp, Snapchat, emails, texts.

She turned as the front door opened and Simon bustled in, arms conspicuously laden with a paper bag from another nearby deli.

"You're home early," he said. Vida tried not to bridle at the implicit criticism she read into the statement. He probably had hoped he could smuggle whatever delicacy he'd bought now in without her noticing. Truth was, nine times out of ten, he'd have got away with it as her interests were always more academic than culinary. Caroline often commented on how lucky she was to have not only a good cook for a husband, but also an experimental one. For the most part, Vida agreed. She'd sat through too many midnight meals because something had gone awry though to be totally on board with the experimental side of things.

"I finished speaking to some people about this Maggie Donaldson thing early," she said, "so came home."

"Oh yes? Anything interesting so far?"

"I've not really started properly, but look," she swizzled the laptop towards him. "Hundreds of texts for me to sort out!"

He cast his eyes over the list and then nodded sympathetically. "That'll certainly keep you going for a while. Any underlings you can get to help?"

"I might ask Jamie," Vida said, naming one of her PhD students. "I don't think I'm comfortable asking for anyone else's help really though. This isn't academic research, it's personal. I feel responsible for it, for better or worse."

"Martyr," he mocked.

"Just means a few late nights with my favourite spreadsheeting system. Hope you're going to keep me plied with strong coffee?" she teased, stroking his arm.

"My lady's wish is my command," he bowed. "Bit hot in here though, love." He reached round and turned the thermostat back down a notch. "That's better. Stuffed artichokes for tea?"

He made it sound like a question, but Vida knew better than to express a preference. Truth be told, she was more of a meatballs kind of a woman than stuffed artichokes but at least this would count towards her five a day. "I'll let you get on with it while I print all this off." She retreated into the tiny back bedroom that they used as a study and hunted around for the spare toner she was sure she'd bought a few weeks ago. Then, setting the printer churning out the hundreds of messages Maggie's friends had forwarded her, she sat down and started to read.

Forensic linguistics was never going to win any awards for slickest science. It was slow and painstaking, analysing texts at sentence and word level, looking for any potential linguistic tells in someone's writing. She'd seen examples before where someone had used negative contractions but never contracted the positive versions, times when someone had consistently misspelled words with the dis- prefix and another where someone had used precisely five exclamation marks after every other sentence. Unfortunately, there was no way to tell what someone's tell was going to be without sitting down and reading the lot. The first read through she would use a genuine versus simulated checklist to review the letter.

Researchers in the US had produced information about what might be found in a genuine letter over a simulated one. It was a surprising list really, including much plainer sentence structures and an avoidance of the topic of suicide. Then, she would note down anything that stood out to her as being slightly unusual. It wouldn't take her long to get a sense of Maggie's style. Then she could start to think about what it was that made up that style: sentence lengths, word choice, punctuation. That would give her something to analyse in more detail on a second reading.

She started back with the suicide letter.

Mum and Dad

Please forgive me. I know that you have always loved me. Do not think that this is because of anything you have or haven't done. It's really not. I cannot even explain what it is. It just is.

I have thought about this lots and I know I'm making the right choice. I cannot live with it anymore. It's always there. When I wake it is in my head and when I go to bed it is in my heart.

I've been thinking a lot about the dinner we had last Saturday. I looked at you both and you love each other so much. I will never have that now. It's all been taken away from me and there's nothing left for me to do. But please do not blame yourselves. You've inspired me for so many years and I wish that I could carry on for your sakes. But I know that's no way to live. You cannot live for anyone else. I cannot live just for you.

But I do love you. I always have and I always will. Please forgive me. Do not be sad forever. I've done what is right for me.

Always your loving daughter

Maggie

Working with suicide notes always upset her. Thinking about how these people had been feeling as they put their pen to paper and wrote of their desperation. When she'd spent time in the US looking at these letters, she'd felt wrung out afterwards. It had taken months for her to stop thinking about those letters. It was even worse this time. Talking to Maggie's parents, her friends, seeing the pictures of her, it all made it much more real, and she had to wipe her eyes quickly as the tears blurred. This had to be a job, nothing more. She breathed deeply.

Turning her attention back to the letter, she highlighted a few words and sentences. Short simple sentences. Key words underlined. Mainly declarative in tone. Repetition of words and phrases, like always. Lack of commas. Of course, a suicide note, written under the inevitable pressure of what was to come would probably have a different tone. But some of these things would have been so ingrained in Maggie's writing style that she would have used them irrespective of the event. That was what she was looking for; those links, style connections that underpinned the writing, no matter the occasion. She just hoped she could find enough to bring peace to her parents.

Chapter 13

Slater pulled up outside the small house that always filled him in equal measure with pride and annoyance. This had been his family home growing up and he was always immensely proud of everything his mum had achieved for him. He knew it had never been easy and was thankful for all the opportunities she had given him through sheer willpower alone. He was however annoyed by that same stubbornness now. Despite Slater's best cajoling, his mum refused to move to somewhere nicer now that he could afford something a bit better. She clung on to the days when the streets and streets of mill housing had been filled with bustling community and lifelong friendships. A time when people from all over the world blended into one big group of people doing their best for their families. The area still housed a big migrant community but now instead of pulling together, the people were disparate and suspicious parts of the whole. Too tired, too traumatised, too beaten down by whatever had brought them here to put any energy into anything beyond surviving. So, the streets around his mother's house fell apart, boarded up windows, the ubiquitous mattresses parked on the corners and colourfully artistic rubbish strewing the ground. From the outside, his mother's house looked no different but inside, she had somehow, miraculously in his opinion, created pure Jamaica.

It was no different this visit and as soon as Slater let himself in through the front door, the warmth and spice of a homeland he had never visited enveloped him. The heating was kept at a tropical level and whatever was cooking always released the most delicious coconutty, chillied smells possible. He nodded politely to the coronation picture and white Jesus that hung on the wall, knowing his mum would make him come in again and do it properly if he didn't acknowledge allegiance to country and God somehow. In truth, he didn't mind; nothing soothed and troubled his heart in such equal measure. Home was home. The memories of his father were never far away, in the imposing portrait of him in the hallway, stern and immeasurably proud in his police uniform, the same portrait that had been used next to his coffin at his funeral. His father had been kind but distant, a somewhat authoritarian parent to his mum's voluminous warmth. Slater had often wondered though how their relationship would have developed if his father had lived beyond Slater's eleventh birthday though. How would his life have been different?

"Gabriel?" Durene called, emerging from the kitchen door. As always, she was dressed in a riot of colour that made her a figurative giant, a metaphor of reds, oranges and greens, despite her diminutive size. "Where have you been, my boy? I not seen you since the new year!" The warmth of her Jamaican resonance washed over him and drew him in. Nothing made him feel more loved and more alone than that unmistakeable lilt. In the months after his father's death, the house had fallen silent, as though she could no longer find the words, or perhaps the reason to communicate. But her constant patter gradually restarted and now, as before, she needed no response or even any audience to chatter constantly. He suspected the cat was the most common participant in the conversation.

"Sorry, Mum. Been busy on a new case." He swept her into his arms and squeezed tight, pressing his lips onto the top of her head, feeling her wiry hair tickle his face.

"Will you be promoted?" she asked directly, when he'd set her down, appraising him with bottomless brown eyes. Slater shook his head. Durene's constant push for him to climb the ranks was another thing stemming directly from his dad's career being cut off before he ever got the opportunity to get higher than a Detective Sergeant. Slater also knew though that his mum was looking at it through extremely rose-tinted glasses and in reality it was very unlikely that a black man would ever have got any higher in the 1980s. His dad had had to work damn hard and put up with levels of abuse his mum would never hear of to just keep his job, whatever the rank.

Durene pursed her lips. "Is it safe?" was always her next question, suspicion laden. Slater knew it was inevitable. Here was a woman torn between pride in her son for achieving what he had done and bone-rooted fear that the profession that had cost her husband his life would do the same for her son. No matter how much he tried to reassure her, she never seemed to truly settle. Any event within the city that could result in harm to the police would always result in a slew of texts checking on his well-being and getting increasingly high-pitched if he didn't reply immediately.

"It's fine, Mum. Just your normal routine case." The same lie, softly told. In truth, policing seemed to be both safer and more dangerous than in previous decades. He braced himself for what he knew would be the third in his mum's unholy triptych.

"Have you seen your brother?"

"No, Mum," he sighed. It was a sore topic. His brother, Caleb had chosen the opposite path to him. Last time Slater had seen him had been in the cells after a drunk and disorderly call. Both had been resentful of the other's presence and it just seemed easier to ignore him from then on in. Durene however didn't see it that way and she was constantly trying to force them into some sort of happy-family scenario. Periodically, Slater allowed himself to be manipulated into a family dinner with his brother, but it always ended in a shouting match. Well, Caleb shouted while Slater sat impassively contemplating his water glass. For some reason, that wound his brother up even more and he'd eventually storm out.

"Come, sit down," she said, bustling him through to the kitchen. "You're lucky, I have enough dinner to stretch!"

Slater hid his eye-roll; his mum always made enough food for the entire neighbourhood. She and his dad had come over from Jamaica alone, fifteen years or so after the original Windrush immigrants, and had left all their family behind. Durene had made friends, her natural effervescence attracting people from all areas of life, all ages, shapes and colours. She'd joined the church and had thrown herself into hosting and enjoying feeding all those people, but Slater knew it was a poor substitute for the family they'd abandoned. His and Caleb's refusal to play

Happy Families just added to the problem. The bright side was that there'd be leftovers aplenty for him to take home to his own cold, dark flat.

He sat and watched as she piled his plate high with steaming jerk chicken and coconut rice, truly the food of gods. All the time she chattered away, telling him about the local community, people he might have once known and a fair few that he'd never met. He turned Kitty Wakelin over in his mind. He couldn't make sense of her at all at the minute. That didn't usually matter to him; he was a functional policeman, capable of dealing with cases efficiently and quickly, just the way Hussain liked it. But there was something bothering him about the dichotomies Kitty Wakelin presented. A beautiful and successful young woman who lived in a dingy little house with a dingy little man with as much charm as the average petty bureaucrat. A privileged upbringing but she wasn't a demanding individual. On the verge of immense success but nothing to show for it. Troubled by caustic messages but unwilling to involve the police. He had even less of an understanding of who she was now than he had when he'd never even heard of her.

He looked up to see his mum watching him eagerly, a bright smile on her face. "Delicious, Mum," he mumbled, his mouth full. The smile got even wider.

"Eat, eat," she urged. "It makes this mother very happy to see her son eating so well. You getting thin, I think. You eating properly?" Slater shrugged. "You need look after yourself. Or better yet, you need a woman," she finished gleefully. Another of her favourite topics.

"I've been busy, Mum, work, hockey."

She nodded sagely and then shifted around in her seat a little. "I know you said you not spoken to Caleb, but I thought he might have rung and told his news!" His mum couldn't hide the excitement from her voice.

Slater stifled a sigh. His brother always had exciting news; sometimes it was even something positive like a new job. They didn't tend to last past a probation period. All too often though, it was some sort of doomed money-making scheme that would cost his mum too much of her pension and push Caleb dangerously close to, if not over, the boundaries of legality.

"It's Sabryne! She pregnant!" Sabryne was Caleb's girlfriend and was as much trouble as he was. With viciously long nails, and a tongue sharp enough to physically wound, she seemingly kept Caleb on a short leash.

"What?" he asked. "Pregnant?"

"Yes, isn't it fantastic? Just imagine, I'll be a GramMa and you're going to be an uncle." She clapped her hands together.

Slater swallowed the horror that bubbled up into his throat. Sabryne pregnant. His brother a father. What a bloody disaster.

Dear you

I know what you did and I will make you pay, you faithless whore. I am your dark storm and I will have vengeance.

You probably think you're safe. You probably think that what you've done will stay in the past. I'm going to make sure it doesn't. I'm going to make you pay.

Chapter 14

Vida swore quietly under her breath as she struggled with the pile of papers she'd shoved under her arm and the key to her office door.

"Can I help?" Her PhD student and sometime Research Assistant, Jamie appeared at her elbow.

"Hmmhmm," she mumbled through a mouthful of purse. He grinned at her, disentangled the keys from her fist and unlocked the door. He pushed it open and stepped aside to let her through. "Thanks," she breathed, dropping a clatter of belongings on to the pile of papers already strewn across her desk. "Phew! That was a struggle. You got my email then?"

"Yes, sounded interesting."

"I didn't expect you to be here at the crack of dawn though. I thought you students liked to sleep in on a morning."

"You know me, Vida. I'd never miss an early morning meeting with you." He raised an eyebrow at her.

"Ha! You can't fool me. I know you're just here for the suicide letter."

He looked at her contemplatively. "Maybe you're right."

"This is what I've got so far." She handed the pile of papers to him. "Suicide letter is copied on top. I've highlighted what I've noticed so far. Underneath is what had come in last night. I've sorted it into piles for academic work, informal short messages and then longer informal sources. My phone was buzzing all night though, so I reckon we'll have a load more to go at. Can you review what we've got so far and then start with the unfinished texts at the bottom there? I'll print out the new stuff that has just come in."

"No problem. But before we get started?"

Vida looked up from her laptop as he rustled a paper bag. "Ooh, pastries? You know the way to my heart."

"A woman of sophisticated tastes," he smiled at her, evidently gratified by the way she seized the bag from him.

"Still warm," she mumbled through a mouthful of crumbs. "You are the best kind of assistant!"

"Anything for you." He kept her gaze before she looked away, her eyes falling to the screen in front of her. She could feel his eyes still on her, appraising. Finally, after what seemed to her to be an age, she heard the rustle of papers and dared a look up. He'd turned his attention to the pile of documents she'd collated, his youthful face earnest as he leafed through the texts. Being in a room with him always made her feel every day of the decade that separated them. He was always so generous to her, a kindly nephew to her ageing aunt. Bless him.

She returned to the laptop and started to open the proliferation of emails that were clogging up her inbox. It needed sorting quickly otherwise the university system would be complaining that she'd exceeded her maximum mailbox allowance and start bouncing stuff back. Open. Print. Open. Print. She quickly got into the swing of the action when a file of a different nature took her by surprise. A video file. She checked the sender. A rather intriguing sounding 'misstery@gmail.com.' Was this really meant for her? The subject line read 'The truth about Maggie.'

"What?" she said softly.

"Problem?" Jamie asked, alert.

"Someone's sent me a video. Sounds a bit sinister."

He got up and came to stand behind her. "The truth about Maggie," he read. "That does sound a bit sinister. Are you going to play it?"

"Do I want to?" she asked, seriously, turning to him.

"Someone else obviously wants you to. It's probably nothing," he reassured her. "Just a video. I can watch it first if you want?"

"Would you?"

"Of course." He lay a reassuring hand on her shoulder and she felt the warmth of his touch through her jumper. She patted his hand neatly.

"You're a kind boy. Just stay there and watch it with me."

The video was grainy, around three minutes long, and started silently. The camera was aimed at a brown sofa, a harsh overhead light reflecting off it in a way that suggested leather or at least an imitation. The walls looked to be lined with some sort of textured wallpaper, an inoffensive magnolia, peeling in places. An oriental rug covered bare floorboards in front of the sofa.

"What the hell is this?" Jamie asked, incredulously.

"Shh," Vida said, watching intently.

They both jerked back suddenly, surprised as caught voyeurs, as the screen was filled with two figures, carrying something between them. As the figures moved away from the camera, they transformed into two obviously male figures, both dressed in black with what seemed like hideously deformed faces.

"They've got stockings over their heads," Vida said, recognising suddenly what had made the men look like that.

"Why?" asked Jamie.

"I think we're probably about to find out."

As the two men became clearer, so too did the object between them. As they slung it onto the sofa and it sprawled along the length, it came horrifyingly into focus.

"That's a girl," said Jamie. Her skin was almost luminous against the dark sofa, so pale and delicate. One arm hung limply off the sofa. "She looks like she's asleep."

"I don't think it's natural," Vida said. "You'd wake up if people chucked you around like that. I think she's been drugged." Her head was wedged into her chin, pushed in by the arm of the sofa, but as they watched, one of the men almost tenderly lifted her head and slid a cushion underneath, bringing her face into the light. "Oh god, that's Maggie." She paused the video and turned to Jamie, feeling sick..

"That's Maggie Donaldson, you know, the girl," she said, gesturing to the papers littered around her smaller table. They both fell silent, contemplating the girl on the screen in front of them. "What should we do?" Vida asked, finally.

"Watch it."

"Shouldn't we just take it to the police?"

"Why? At the minute, all we've got is a girl being laid on a sofa. It could be nothing. P'raps they've just put her there for her own safety. Maybe they're going to find her friends to help her."

Vida arched her eyebrow at him.

"I know, it's not likely," he admitted. "You don't tend to wear a disguise if you're just helping someone. But the point is, we don't know. We're going to have to watch it all to know for sure."

The cursor hovered over the play button. Was Jamie right? Surely it was obvious what was going to happen? She heard again the dismissive tones of the police officer yesterday. She didn't want to look a fool though. Vida clicked.

The pillow under the head was the last kindness they saw over the next two minutes and 37 seconds. The shorter of the two men disappeared from view, while the taller, bulkier one lifted Maggie's hips and yanked her clothes off. The skirt and knickers came off easily, while her top was ripped in two. The girl lay naked to the camera now, still unmoving, laying on the detritus of her outfit. Vida wanted to look away or to reach in and pull a blanket over the girl or something and she felt Jamie shifting uncomfortably behind her. The smaller man re-entered, this time presaged by a tautly erect penis. There'd been no sound up until this point and Vida had presumed that the film had been recorded silently, but the guttural grunt that the man gave as he thrust himself into Maggie turned her stomach further. Maggie's lifeless form made no response, but the squeak of the springs in the sofa and the soft rubbery sound of flesh against leather accompanied the man's movements. If there was any mercy in this, it was that it was over quickly, his climax announced by a deeper groan. He withdrew, shiny wet and dripping. Vida hadn't even noticed the approach of the second man, and had to look away as the violence was repeated once more. In some ways though, hearing the groans of the rapists and obviously unconscious whimpers of Maggie made the horror even greater.

Jamie coughed. "I think that second man is Asian," he said.

Vida looked at him, uncomprehending.

"That one," he pointed at the screen, not quite making contact with the beast at the end of his finger. "His skin tone looks darker to me. Maybe it's just a tan but you can just see his hair through the stocking. That looks black maybe." Vida looked at where he was pointing.

"Maybe." It came out as little more than a squeak.

The second man finished, as similarly triumphant as the first. He hastily tucked his now limp penis back into his fly and turned to face his accomplice. They exchanged a high five and Vida could almost make out the grins under their stockinged faces. The two moved out of shot, leaving Maggie, still unmoving, exposed and brutalised. The video snapped to black. The end.

Vida sat back in her chair, resting her hands on the edge of her desk as though braced for some sort of impact. She took deep breaths to try and control the rising nausea.

"I wish we hadn't watched that," she said.

"At least we know now that we have to take this to the police. Do you know who sent it?"

Vida shook her head. "When you sort by sender, this is the only message from this source. The other messages have all come from recognisable accounts, with names and such in their addresses. I mean, misstery? What sort of an email address is that? Who the hell has sent me this?" The sickness gave way to anger. "Why did I need to see that?"

"Maybe they trusted you to do the right thing," suggested Jamie.

"But who? Why?"

"Why don't you ask them that? Reply to the email."

Vida looked at him for a moment. "That's not such a bad idea." She quickly pressed reply and then dictated as she typed. "'Who are you? Why have you sent me this? Have you sent this to the police?' Is that enough do you think?"

"What about asking when it was? I mean, if this was months ago then maybe it doesn't have anything to do with Maggie's death?"

"It looks recent. I mean, Maggie looks the same as she does in the pictures I've seen of her on her Facebook page."

"Well, still, you never know." He seemed stung by her rebuttal.

"No, you're right," she soothed. "When was this?" she added to the email and then clicked send.

"What do we do now?"

"Is there any tried and tested method for wiping our memories?" she asked bleakly.

"Neat vodka?" he suggested.

"Somehow I don't think all the vodka in the world is going to get rid of those memories. That poor girl, Jamie. That poor, poor girl. She was only sixteen. Why would anyone want to do that to anyone? What the hell is wrong with people?"

"Why didn't she report it?" he asked. "There must have been loads of evidence. Easy to get a conviction you'd think. Not like they bothered with condoms or anything. All that DNA." He sounded incredulous, judgmental.

Vida pursed her lips. "It's never that easy. It's not necessarily about evidence, is it? Maybe she was threatened. She's so out of it, maybe she didn't even realise. We don't know how she ended up in this situation. Maybe she was just too scared to say anything. There's loads of reasons why women don't report rapes."

"Maybe if more did, the conviction rates would be better."

"Oh yes, that's great Jamie," she said, her face furious. "Blame the girls. Blame those poor women who've been abused in one of the worst ways possible for the poor conviction rate. It's their fault. Not the fault of the police, or a justice system that isn't fit for purpose when it comes to examining and punishing violence against women. Blame the victims. You'll be telling me next that you think she bears some responsibility for getting raped in the first place."

He reddened. "Well, no but how did she end up in that state? She obviously wasn't paying attention. She'd probably had too much to drink." He tilted his chin at her as though daring her to argue.

"For gods sakes," she said. "Just listen to yourself. You're supposed to be part of the educated class. The bright new future. And you still think women are asking for it if they wear pretty clothes and have a drink? Have you never drunk too much? Never been on one of our infamous pub-crawls? Don't be such a hypocrite. One rule for you men, another for us women." She shook her head, horrified into silence.

"Look," he started, holding up his hands in mock surrender. "I didn't mean to offend. I was just playing devil's advocate a bit, that's all."

"I don't think you were," she said. "And if you want to look at why rape investigations don't result in convictions, look in the mirror. There's your answer. Too many people still think it's the victim's fault."

They both stared at the screen as though watching the video again.

"She was 16 though," Vida said, finally. "Sixteen, Jamie. A child still. How can that have been her fault?"

"You're right," he said. "I'm sorry. I didn't mean her. And I didn't mean to offend you." He reached out and stroked her arm. She moved it away.

"Maybe you need to learn to choose your words a little more carefully," she said. "As a linguist, I'd hope you could do that. And perhaps learn to think before you judge."

Her new mail alert broke the stern silence between them, and her rebuke was instantly forgotten and forgiven as they moved back to look at the email that had come in. "It doesn't matter who I am. Somebody needs to know what happened," Vida relayed.

"Not very illuminating," said Jamie.

"No," she agreed. "What do I do now?"

"Well, I think you need to take the video to the police. Whoever has sent it us hasn't said whether they'd sent it on, but presumably if the police knew about this, Maggie's parents would have known about it too."

"God, Maggie's parents," echoed Vida. "What am I going to tell them? How can I tell them that this has happened to their daughter?"

"Do you have to tell them?"

"What do you mean?"

"Well, you've been employed to look at the language in Maggie's note," Jamie pointed out, calmly. "We can do that. We've still got a pile of data to sort through and then we should be able to start to decide whether or not it was

Maggie who wrote the notes. Let's just do that. We don't need to mention the video to her parents at all."

"You think we shouldn't tell them?"

"Does it do any good? Their daughter's dead. Knowing this isn't going to make it any better for them."

Vida fell silent. She didn't necessarily agree with Jamie. The truth was, she didn't know what she agreed with really.

"All we've got here," he said, gesturing towards the computer screen, "is further proof that Maggie did commit suicide. We've got a reason. We just need to examine all the evidence and see if the forensic linguistics supports that conclusion. All Maggie's parents want is reassurance that the verdict was accurate. Well, realistically, what they really want is irrefutable evidence that Maggie committed suicide. And as no-one was on that bridge with her, they're never going to get that. All we can do is offer evidence one way or another. Let's do that with our texts. Forget the video."

"Altogether?"

"No, I mean, tell the police but don't mention it to Maggie's parents. After all, what they don't know, can't hurt them."

Vida wasn't sure that was true, but with the memory of Maggie's dead eyes staring out at the camera as she was violated, she wasn't sure she was strong enough to confront the alternative.

Chapter 15

Rashid Khan's apartment was directly beneath Kitty's. Slater remembered what Khan had told them about Kitty wanting him close, but he wondered how much of it had actually been driven by Khan himself. How many evenings had he spent listening for her footsteps above? The door was answered by a woman this time though, as professionally dressed as Khan was extravagantly, her business suit sharply pinstriped while his peacock suit had been replaced by equally loud tweed trousers and a tight red velvet waistcoat. "Officers, I'm Laila Khan," the woman introduced herself briskly. "My brother mentioned you wanted to talk to him again today. Of course, I didn't realise he'd spoken to you at all." She sent an arched eyebrow to Rashid Khan who looked away. "I wish you'd contacted me at the same time. I was an equal partner in Kitty's management."

"We didn't contact anyone the first time," Slater said, annoyed. "Your brother invited himself to a potential crime scene." This time it was Slater shooting eyebrows at Khan, who looked even more uncomfortable. "We do have some follow up questions regarding your relationship with Kitty, so it's good that you're here now." Slater moved past the Khans into the room, followed by Dawson. Apart from the identical layout and virtually identical view, this flat had little in common with Kitty's space above. In here, it looked a little like an IKEA showroom, a paint-by-numbers approach to interior design that looked comfortable and organised on the surface but would probably prove impractical in the long run. Laila Khan gestured towards large brown leather sofas that swallowed Slater whole as he sat down, despite his height. He edged back up, opting instead to perch on the edge to keep his equilibrium. Drinks were offered, declined by Slater and Dawson, a whiskey and water poured by Rashid Khan despite the morning hour. Laila Khan perched opposite the police officers, legs crossed neatly at the ankles, hands folded in her lap. Rashid remained lounging by the drinks trolley.

"So, questions about Kitty? Have you found something out? Have you caught the guy?" Rashid asked, eagerly. Despite the pristine outfit, there was something unwashed about him. A slightly stale smell and hair that was edging towards greasy made Slater wonder about how he was dealing with Kitty's death. Not as well as he was pretending to, it seemed.

"We're still pursuing a number of lines of enquiry," Slater said, smoothly.

"Tell us about your professional relationship with Kitty," Dawson started. The detectives had agreed that the sergeant would take the lead in the questioning to enable Slater to study the Khans' reactions. Dawson's gruff rugby-playing persona was bound to rub them up the wrong way and could result in some helpful fireworks.

Laila looked at Rashid, who'd turned his attention back to the whiskey decanter and then turned to look at Dawson, taking him in. Her eyes flicked back to Slater, as though deciding who it was he needed to communicate with.

"Ms Khan," Dawson said again, with a polite smile, "tell us about the relationship."

Laila shrugged. "It was good. We've been managing her since she first started performing publicly. I could tell she was going to be big."

"And that was when?"

"About five years ago now."

"And how did you feel when she told you that she was leaving for another management company?"

Laila looked confused for a minute and frowned. "Leaving?"

"Yes. We've had information that she was leaving for London and had signed with another agent."

"That must have been hard," interjected Slater, his voice smooth. "Seeing someone you'd nurtured right from the beginning, spread her wings and fly. Leave you behind."

The confusion on Laila's face slowly melted into comprehension and then acceptance. "That's what it was all about," she said. "Getting her to a point where she could spread her wings."

"It's easy to say that now, Ms Khan," said Dawson. "Benefit of hindsight and all. Must have been gutted at the time though."

Rashid turned round and pulled a flamboyant handkerchief from his trouser pocket to dab at his eyes. "We would have been gutted, yes," he interjected, roughly. "Not because it wasn't what we wanted, or expected, but just because... well, Kitty was special. The kind of person you only come across once or twice in a lifetime, let alone a career." He took a deep breath and fell silent again. Laila was watching him with annoyance. This seemed to be a road they'd trodden before.

"So, she was special. That must have made the loss even greater. And surely, you ask yourself just how much of that success is down to you? I mean, without you, she'd be nowhere, wouldn't she? She needed you to give her this break." Dawson sat back after his verbal en garde but then fell victim to the same sofa envelopment that Slater had suffered and struggled himself forward with a scowl.

"We had a role to play, yes," replied Laila, taking over the answers again as Rashid remained silent. "Kitty would have got there with whoever she was with but yes, we helped considerably. We'd significantly raised her profile and she had started to get noticed by producers and other musicians interested in collaborations. But the process of moving up is natural." She said it with a smile, but Slater could see the discontent. "It's a rare musician that makes their way these days anywhere outside of London. That's why it was time for her to move on. I'd done everything I could."

"We would have been the last ones to stand between her and the success that she so deserved." Rashid poured himself another drink, not bothering to extend an invitation again, and gulped it down quickly. "She was so talented, deserved so much success."

"So, you were happy that she'd signed with another manager?"

"No," Rashid said simply. "We would have been happy that she'd signed with a manager. But she didn't."

Dawson and Slater exchanged a glance. "You were unaware that she'd signed a new contract?" Slater asked.

"We were aware that she'd been offered different representation," Laila said, slowly as though she was explaining simple addition to the village idiot. "But she hadn't signed another contract. She didn't want to. She was determined to stay with us."

"So, she's on the edge of this great success, London and the world at her feet, and she turns it down?" This made no sense to Slater. Yet another string of confusion on the Kitty Wakelin fiddle.

"I know," Rashid said, forgetting the drink he had and sloshing its contents to the ground as he gesticulated. "Bollocks." He pulled out a handkerchief from his trouser pocket and blotted the spilled liquid carefully. Looking up at Slater through surprisingly long eyelashes, he said "I told her. I begged her, pleaded with her, did everything I bloody could to make her sign the bloody contract. I wanted her to go. Wanted her to be a success. But she just refused."

"We both wanted that," Laila jumped in. "Of course we did. We're good at what we do. Being that stepping stone and we've got loads of local talent waiting to make the same move. If anything, she didn't do us any favours, stopping around. Probably would have got a reputation for refusing to release artists when they asked. Nobody would have trusted us. Not like they'd've believed it was her choice."

"Did she explain why?"

"Said she just didn't want to. She wanted to stay with us. We'd looked after her from the start and she trusted us, she reckoned."

Who did Kitty trust more? Laila or Rashid, Slater wondered. Laila was obviously the business powerhouse, but Rashid was in love with her. Easy to manipulate and wrap around her finger, "No offence, but this is not sounding believable."

"We know," Laila scoffed. "I know. But it is. Look." She rummaged in the document laptop bag propped next to her chair. "Look, here. It's a new contract. Even if Kitty was insisting on staying with us, Rash wanted to adjust the terms."

"So you can make more money off the back of a talented little Yorkshire lass?" Dawson said.

Her face reddened. Was it shame or anger? "God, I wish. No, so we could take a smaller slice. Rash felt like being with us was limiting her. He insisted we cut our compensation percentage so that she had more. I don't know why I agreed. And Kitty argued with us over that too though. Said she didn't want any more money. Didn't need anything else to make her happy. Rash made this his sticking point though." It didn't sound like Laila felt the same way about Kitty as Rashid did. Had that caused tension? Could that be a motive for her death?

Slater observed the pair thoughtfully while Dawson flicked through the contract that Laila Khan had thrust at him. "Why did you care so much about Kitty?" Slater asked Rashid, finally. "You must have plenty of other talented clients. What made her special?"

Rashid paced up and down before slumping heavily into a chair next to his sister. "She just was," he started, hesitantly. "I don't mean her talent. She was amazing of course, but just as a person. I don't think I've ever met anyone so humble before. Someone who felt so strongly that they didn't deserve whatever success they'd achieved. She earned it, every accolade, every positive review, every bloody pound that went into her bank account. But she didn't want any of it. You know she gave a big chunk of her money to charity?"

"Do you know which one?"

"No, she never boasted about it or anything. I just know she did. Left herself enough money for essentials, her rent, some nice clothes, pay her bills, that kind of stuff and then the rest went to charity."

"So basically, she was a bloody saint," Slater said. "C'mon, Mr Khan, I'm not buying this. Nobody's that bloody perfect. Especially someone who ends up murdered in an alley. Well, not so much that," he backtracked, aware that he was edging towards victim blaming. "We've watched the CCTV; she follows her murderer very willingly into that alley. Those're not the actions of a saint."

Khan looked unhappy while Laila looked shocked. "She followed him?" Rashid repeated bleakly.

"Him, her. We're not certain of that yet. Tall woman, slight man. It's not clear."

"But she followed whoever it was. No signs of struggle?"

"Not a one."

"Fuck," sighed Khan. "How could she do that? Was she drugged?"

"No sign of any impairment like that in her toxicology report."

Rashid rubbed his face, pressed his fingers to his temples like he was trying to stave off a massive headache. "Fuck." Laila got out of her chair and went across to him, wrapping her arms around him. It was the first sign of any filial love.

They sat in silence. Slater felt sure that one of the Khans had something more to say and if they just waited for long enough, they'd break it out. Dawson was fidgeting beside him. Patience was not an interview technique he favoured, but he'd worked with Slater for long enough for a stern look to convey what he expected. Slater knew that he sometimes treated Dawson like a pet. Down boy. Wait. Take it then. But Dawson didn't seem to mind, and they'd built the rapport of a successful sheepdog and his master.

"She was bloody perfect," Rashid finally started, mumbling into the floor as his head hung down. "Bloody perfect." He looked up at them, met Slater's eyes. "In my opinion. She didn't feel the same way about herself though." Laila rolled her eyes and looked like she was itching to refute it. Not as big a fan of Kitty as her brother.

Slater's brow furrowed. "She was humble? That's no bad thing."

"It went far beyond that. She wasn't modest. I think she was probably clinically depressed to tell you the truth. Oh, there's no official diagnosis and I know I'm not a doctor, but it wouldn't have surprised me. She'd got this thing, this worm in her head, telling her that she didn't deserve any happiness. At times, it was fucking exhausting. Trying to be a cheerleader for someone who seemed to be waiting for some sort of catastrophic nightmare to begin all the time. When I first knew her, I thought she was just being cautious. I mean, most of them are so excited at the first sign of success that they feel a bit nervous. A bit fraudulent maybe. Like it might get snatched away. I'm used to having to do a bit of ego massage. A bit of there, there, you deserve it and all that shit." Once again, the bitterness that Khan seemed to feel about his non-Kitty clients seeped out.

"But it never went away for Kitty?"

"No. She was tortured by it all the time. Whatever measure of success came her way, she was always like 'I don't deserve this Rash.' If you ever saw her smile, it would last maybe a few seconds and then it'd be gone, and she'd look almost... I don't know ... guilty because she'd forgotten herself for a bit. It wasn't just her music either. It was her whole fucking life. You know, it really doesn't surprise me that she followed this bastard to her death. She was probably like 'Oh yes, Mr Murderer, I've been waiting for you my whole life.' And off she jolly well trots. Probably bloody smiled then." His jaw was clenched tight and he looked furious. But then he softened and said "Stupid bloody girl. Why couldn't she see how much value she had? Not just in music but to her family and Adam and me." The last pronoun was a plaintive breath, a bubble of sound capturing all the regret and despair he obviously felt at Kitty's death.

"Is that all?" Laila Khan asked, sharply, stroking her brother's head gently at the same time. "My brother's upset as you can see. If you've no further questions then I've got a lot to be getting on with. The PR doesn't stop when the artist is dead." She seemed to notice how cold her words sounded and sent a worried look to Rashid, but he'd not looked up from his hands.

"That's all, for the minute," Slater said, not entirely convinced they wouldn't be back to have another chat. "We'll see ourselves out."

"What do you reckon?" Dawson asked Slater, in a low hiss as they closed the door behind them. "Not sure I've heard such utter bollocks in an interview before."

"Me either," Slater admitted. "But I'm not sure that means he's not telling the truth. This is what I'm trying to explain to you. There's something off about Kitty Wakelin. She didn't behave in the way you'd expect her to behave. Nothing about this girl makes sense."

Chapter 16

The previous day's icy drizzle had given way to a crisp February day, which sat at odds with the dark preoccupations of Vida's mind as she made her way to the police station. Her mind had been toing and froing with questions of what to do and who to turn to. The thought of showing the video she'd found to Maggie's parents made her feel physically sick, but at the same time not telling them, not letting them know just what had happened to cause Maggie to take her own life also seemed unbearable. Which was worse? Knowing and not having to imagine, or not knowing and having to fill in the gaps?

Eventually, she'd made the decision to come in and show the policeman who'd been involved in the case and she now sat on the uncomfortable chairs in the public reception area of Snig Hill Police Station and waited. She'd given her name to the desk sergeant who was now trying to track down DI Slater for her. She'd never been in a police station before; she didn't know quite what she'd expected but this bureaucratic uniformity hadn't been it. Apart from the topics of the posters on the wall being law and order themed, she could be in her local council office or GP's surgery. Clearly, they all decorated from the same Keeping the Public Calm textbook.

She uncrossed and recrossed her legs, shuffling the folder she had on her lap from one knee to the other. As much as she tried to stop it, her mind kept flicking to the video she'd seen. Maggie's face, contorted in pain and fear, and those anonymous male attackers violating her.

She took a deep breath and tried to swallow the memory, focussing desperately on the Crimestoppers poster on the wall.

The door to the main station swung open and her eyes swivelled to see who had come in. A tall, black man strode into the room, his face serious, jaw tight. "Ms. Henrikson?" he asked, glaring at her.

"Dr. But yes." Vida nodded. She got to her feet and promptly dropped the file from her knees, sending printouts and annotations sliding across the floor. Falling to a squat to collect them, she didn't miss the eye-roll and barely contained sigh he'd given before bending and picking up the papers that had found their way to his feet.

"DI Slater," he said, offering her papers back to her. "I don't mean to be rude, but I don't have much time for this today."

It occurred to Vida how often British people used a mitigator before saying something that would be considered bad manners. Her mother-in-law was particularly fond of the line, 'you know I like to tell the truth' before launching into something rude and hurtful. Normally about Vida's waistline. It was simple as far as she was concerned. If you didn't mean to be rude, then don't be.

Of course, she didn't say this, being master of her own politeness features and so opted for "I understand. But I think I've found something you'd be interested in seeing."

He observed her for a few seconds with cool, dark brown eyes before nodding slightly. "I can give you five minutes." The tone clearly said that she should be immensely grateful for his indulgence.

"Thank you," she said. "Do you have a computer?" She held up the memory stick she'd copied the video on to.

As he took her through to a nearby room equipped with computer equipment and the internet, she filled him in on the linguistic profile that she'd built up of Maggie so far.

"So, you reckon Maggie did write the suicide note?"

"Probably," she confirmed. "As far as I can tell, the style in the suicide note is sufficiently similar to Maggie's normal writing style so as to be a match. But I've not finished yet."

"So, we got it right?" He logged onto a machine for her.

Vida frowned. Why the constant need for validation? What did he want? Her to bow down and admire his all-mighty policing ability?

"Probably," she said again. "But that's not why I'm here. It's something else I found. May I?" They swapped places and Vida inserted the memory stick and brought up the video. "I feel like I should... well... this isn't pretty viewing," she offered finally.

He looked at her, almost seeming insulted by the fact she'd felt it necessary to warn him. His male pride obviously took it as an invisible slight. "I've seen some horrible things before."

She shrugged. Couldn't say she hadn't warned him. She double-clicked on the file and immediately, the screen was filled with the horror she'd watched with Jamie. She span around in the chair and stood up, crossing to the window and looking out across the car park towards the canals and mills instead. Behind her, she heard the chair creak as Slater sat down. Thankfully, the sound was muted so she didn't have to rehear those whimpers of pain and fright again.

"This is Maggie Donaldson," Slater said.

Vida wasn't sure if it was a question or a statement, but she settled for "Hmhm," as a response. She kept her eyes fixed outside, as though she could cleanse her mind by concentrating on nature, the hard frost still lingering on the roofs in front of her, the sky a vibrant blue above.

"How did you get this?"

"One of her friends sent me a link to it. I think," she shuddered, "I think maybe this is why she felt she had to kill herself."

"Why the hell didn't anyone say something to us?" Slater asked, his voice low and furious.

Vida couldn't help but hear criticism of her and bristled but then bit back on a snarky response. She'd felt the same way and had asked the same question when she'd seen the video for the first time. Why had they not told the police? Why had they shared it with her?

"Perhaps they were worried that they'd get in trouble," she suggested, surprising herself with a relatively meek tone. "Perhaps they thought they could just forget about it but then found out they couldn't. I know I won't be able to," she said. "Forget it I mean." She sighed softly, her breath catching on the window and misting the view in front of her.

"No, me neither," he said. She looked up and for a moment, their eyes met in reflection in the window and the brusqueness and impatience were replaced by sorrow and regret, but she blinked, and it disappeared again. "The case is closed though. She committed suicide. Nothing you've shown me here changes that outcome."

Vida spun round to face him. "I know that," she said, failing to keep the exasperation out of her voice. "But I thought it might be something that you could look into further. The video I mean. That's rape. Surely you want to investigate that? That's what police do, isn't it? Investigate crimes?"

He scowled. "Yes, of course, but this doesn't alter the result for Maggie's parents. Of course, we will be looking into the video, the rape. Cyber may need access to your laptop and all the other files that have been sent."

"It's all web-based," Vida said.

"Yes, well, thank you for bringing this in, Dr Henrikson. I'll pass the link on and someone may be in touch with you for a statement and further information." Shared humanity forgotten, he stood, clearly waiting for her to leave the room.

"I could look into all the messages I've got and see if I could work out who sent me that video?" She stayed firmly at the window, leaning back into the icy panes.

"I don't think that will be necessary," he said, gruffly.

"Oh. Okay, well, thank you, I guess." She turned to go, sliding past him and setting off back down the corridor.

"Wait," he called after her. She turned round. "You need someone to accompany you out."

"Fine."

They retraced their earlier steps, the same uncompanionable silence surrounding them as had when they'd walked in. Vida sneaked her eyes sideways at Slater. He seemed to be chewing over something.

"Actually, Dr Henrikson." He stopped suddenly. "Can I pick your brains about something else?"

Without waiting for an answer, he doubled back on himself. She looked after him for a minute. Clearly, he was used to complete and utter obedience. She was torn between academic curiosity and a personal desire to stick her fingers up at him and walk herself back to the exit. The nerd won over the rebel, as it always did, and she trotted after him, pursuing him as he strode through a warren of rooms and staircases, eventually ending up on the third floor in a cubicled conference room. "Just wait here," he instructed, leaving her alone as he disappeared into a different room. She shrugged and pulled out one of the chairs around a round meeting table to sit on. Like the corporate bland downstairs, so too was this room like a thousand other conference rooms she'd been in: inoffensive, blue-cushioned chairs, white boards and oh-so-neutral walls. There weren't even the posters to alleviate the boredom. She pushed open the file she'd been carrying and looked once more at Maggie's words, traced them across the page with her fingers. There was something particularly intimate about getting into someone's brain like this

The door opened and she guiltily flipped the folder shut once more, feeling like she'd been caught doing something she shouldn't. DI Slater was back.

"As I said, I'm currently working on a case. It's quite a big murder investigation."

Bully for you, thought Vida. This man got right under her skin. He seemed so passionless in his approach, more of a corporate face than a policeman.

"In the course of this investigation, we've found some hate mail."

Now her ears pricked up.

"I just thought, seeing as you were here anyway, perhaps you'd be able to take a look at it for us."

"What are you looking for?" she asked, cautiously. One result and suddenly everyone thought you were a linguistic superhero.

"Well, it's more a question of what you can tell us?" he said. "I admit, this isn't something I'm familiar with. I haven't come across your science before. But well, one of the DCs in the team said she'd been to a lecture you'd done, and I reckoned we might be able to get something out of these letters." He opened the box file and a squashed pile of documents immediately spilled over the desk.

"Have you... I mean... have you fingerprinted these or something?" she asked, looking at the heap in front of her.

"Yep. They've all been scanned and printed. A couple have got identifiable prints on but most of them are just smudges or nothing at all."

Vida nodded contemplatively and tried to hide the excitement in her eyes. It wasn't seemly to get so excited about something so nasty. "I can certainly have a look at them for you. If there's common authors then I might be able to group them together."

"Is that it?" he asked, not bothering to hide the disdain.

"No," she bridled. "If there's a sufficient body of work from a particular author, I could perhaps offer some clues as to their identity." She added a mental so there.

He nodded, approving now. Vida fought the urge to be pleased by his approval and looked haughtily at her nails instead.

"How precise can you be?"

"Well, it's not like a fingerprint. I can't say definitely it is that person. What I can do is have a look at what's written and predict gender, education, age as the basics. Maybe city or county of origin if they're UK based."

Another flattering nod. "How does it work?"

Chapter 17

Slater watched as the previously nervy looking Forensic Linguist metamorphosed into a confident and passionate teacher, explaining all the nuances of her science to him. It was an interesting transformation. She was fairly bland looking in terms of colouring; he guessed Swedish ancestors somewhere along the lines with almost white-blonde hair and glacial blue eyes. Her enthusiasm for her work though fed through to a blush in her cheeks, and expressive intelligence behind her tortoiseshell-rimmed glasses. He was unconvinced by the science itself. Most of it could be put down to common sense and a few lucky guesses but as an advocate for the process, she was winning him round. The file she'd thrown all over the floor when they met had been reopened and she'd talked him through the evidence she'd found to support the fact that Maggie wrote the suicide letter.

"So, you can say that this person wrote this text?"

"We can say that it's likely that this person wrote this text," she corrected him. "The pattern of these negative non-contractions, these sentence styles, the way she addresses other people and signs off, they all indicate strongly that the author of the suicide letter is the same as the author of all the other texts her friends provided."

"How long does it take?" he asked.

She gazed steadily at him. "As long as it takes," she said with a tight smile. "It won't take me that long to ascertain authorship groups as that's quite superficial. But if you're looking for a linguistic profile for someone, especially if you've got more than one someone you want looking at, it will take me longer."

So, no quick fix for the investigation here. But on a case like this, surely it was worth throwing everything he could get at it. It was a bit unconventional, sure, but sometimes even he needed to try something new. It had nice deniability too. With a bit of luck and a fair-wind, they'd have this all tied up within the week and then he could pretend he'd never even contemplated such a bit of woo-woo science. Else, he'd be commended for using his smarts and taking a new approach.

"What do you need?" he asked.

"Just the texts," she said. She smiled at him broadly, clearly more relaxed since her specialist lecture. A woman who liked to share how smart she was.

"I can arrange for you to have copies of the originals, if that's okay?"

"Fine."

"Will the university be okay with this?"

"I don't know," shrugged Vida. "They might want to charge a consultancy fee. But I'd rather just have the option to turn this into a research paper." Slater grimaced. He wasn't keen on the idea of someone else's misery being turned into a spectacle for study. Grief and anguish were private affairs, to be managed within the confines of your own head. "It'd all be anonymous of course," she added, as though sensing his thought pattern.

"You read minds too?" he asked.

"No, but paralinguistics is a fairly well-established field. It didn't take a rocket scientist to recognise the frown on your face meant you weren't happy with something."

"I'd prefer it if this was kept private, anonymous or not."

"OK," she nodded. "Still could be useful to hone the science and build more of a base of linguistic ideas."

"I can live with that. I'll have the letters sent over to you this afternoon."

On his return to the office, having seen her out, he found Hussain waiting for him at his desk.

"Ma'am?" he asked.

"Who was the lady?" Her tone was curt. She liked to be kept informed, but she couldn't be finding fault with him for not informing her of something he hadn't even seen happening.

"Dr Henrikson. She's a Forensic Linguist at the university. I've asked her to look at the hate mail we found at Kitty's apartment."

She laughed sharply. "Forensic Linguistics? One of the Division Heads was talking to me about that the other day. Sounds like a load of rubbish. I expected better of you."

Slater's brow knit at her dismissal. But she was only voicing his own initial thoughts. So much for plausible deniability. "That was my thought too. But she's been looking into the Maggie Donaldson case."

"That's been to inquest and the case is closed," Hussain said.

"I know. And she knows too. It's just Maggie's parents still weren't willing to accept the truth. Dr Henrikson has analysed the suicide notes and she found that in all probability it was Maggie who wrote the letter. At least it will bring her parents some sense of relief. Release. I don't know," he shrugged.

"I'm sure," she said, miming someone at a seance. "I can hear a voice coming from beyond..." She laughed again.

"That as may be," acknowledged Slater. "But look at this. It's pretty unpleasant." He sat down at his machine and brought up the video Vida had shown him earlier. This time Hussain watched in silence, her eyes narrowed, her skin paling underneath her makeup.

"Turn it off," she barked. Slater looked round at her. It was a sign of how bad the video was to see how it affected Hussain. She was steely faced with the best of them normally but this film, this abhorrent visual reminder of just how low the human race could go was particularly offensive. "What are you planning on doing with this? Not showing it to the parents I hope."

"No," Slater said. "Case is closed. It's not our place to show anyone anything anymore. But I thought I'd pass it to the sex crimes team. They can perhaps find out some more details about who posted it and then maybe, who those bastards are."

Hussain's normal colour had returned as she nodded approval. "I still don't understand what you're hoping to get out of the language lady."

"Perhaps nothing, ma'am. But as you pointed out, it's a big case and perhaps it's worth giving it whatever we've got to try and resolve it."

"Right. I've got a further press conference at 2pm this afternoon. Are we any further forward?"

"Thanks to George's CCTV scouring, we've found the restaurant where Kitty ate her last meal. It's a tiny tapas bar called Lorentes just off Church Street. Uniform have interviewed the staff that were on that night. Just a couple of waiters in the front of house, chef out the back who didn't see anything. Both staff members remembered Kitty alright. Said she was pretty noticeable in that outfit, and one of them was a fan so he was a bit starstruck. Neither of them remembered much about Kitty's companion though. In fact, their witness statements are pretty much useless. Both said the person was slight, wearing black clothes, maybe. They thought maybe dark-skinned, but whether that was black, Asian or just a bloody Malaga tan they didn't know."

"They're in a tiny bloody restaurant and the murderer was invisible?"

"I wondered whether Kitty's clothes were a strategy to distract people from him. Maybe he'd told her to dress in a certain way, knowing that she'd almost provide a cover for him. Who's going to look at a dowdy companion when you've got a sparkly popstar to gaze at. People would probably just assume he was security or something."

"Is there any suggestion that Kitty knew him or her before this?"

"Not yet, but nothing to indicate not either. SOCOs recovered Kitty's laptop from her flat and that's with IT so maybe that will throw something our way but at the minute we've got no bloody idea about when they met, or why they met."

"Was it a chance encounter?"

"No. Restaurant confirmed that Kitty had booked the table herself for two. The staff remembered her getting there first, and then the companion arrived about ten minutes later."

"So basically, no progress, DI Slater? Day three and we still can't say anything apart from the murderer may or may not be human." Slater winced at the scathing tone of voice. "We're well outside of that golden twenty-four hours. The press is going to be asking difficult questions about what exactly we are doing, and I have absolutely nothing that I can tell them."

"We've been following up every line of enquiry," replied Slater equably. "It was never going to be one of those cases that was solved within the first few hours. The body of a famous singer in an alley? Clearly not a domestic, which is what most of these cases are going to fall under. Clearly not a random attack as she'd been following this person around all night. It must have been someone she knew. We've ruled out her partner and her manager. We're currently waiting on further evidentiary information from her laptop."

Hussain glared at him with those cold brown eyes. "That still sounds like absolutely bloody nothing. All you can tell me is what it isn't, nothing about what it is."

Slater stayed silent. She stared at him a little longer before turning and marching away with her usual regiment. It didn't feel anything like victory, but at least he was still alive to carry on the search for justice for another day.

Chapter 18

"Hello stranger." The voice startled her as she approached her office door. She couldn't shake out of her head the idea of what Maggie had suffered. Taken together with the vile words she'd scanned on the letters from the murder case, she was beginning to question the ongoing humanity of anyone around her. The irrational thought skipped through her head that perhaps someone had seen her at the police station and followed her here. Someone who didn't want her to find the truth. Maybe a rapist. Even a murderer.

"Caroline," she breathed a sigh of welcome as she recognised her friend emerging from the shadows.

"Sorry, my lovely," Caroline said, moving forward and enveloping Vida in an embrace of perfume, hair and expensive angora wool. "Didn't mean to startle you. Not like you to be so jumpy."

"No," said Vida, ruefully, thinking back to just the start of the week when everything like rape and murder seemed like a jolly good Sunday-afternoon crime novel. "It's been a surprisingly rough few days." To her surprise, she suddenly felt like she was on the verge of tears and drew in a shaky breath before smiling brightly, if fraudulently, at Caroline.

The older woman studied her carefully, clearly not missing the tremulous voice and slightly over-full eyes. "What have you been doing to yourself?" she asked, her eyes dark with concern.

"Nothing really. More what other people are doing to each other," Vida admitted. "Were you coming to see me?"

"Yes, of course. Why else would I be in this godforsaken building?" Caroline was a Landscape Architecture lecturer, working out of a much more stylish block, overlooking the manicured park Vida hankered after so much. "It feels like it's been an age since we caught up last."

In fact, it was only a couple of weeks ago, but Vida felt the truth in Caroline's comment. "Come in, let's have a coffee."

"You don't want to go downstairs?"

Vida shivered. "Not if you don't mind. I just want to be surrounded by my four walls at the minute, really."

Caroline's expression once again was flooded with concern, but she nodded compliantly and followed Vida in.

"I've not quite got the range of hot drinks unfortunately," said Vida. "Peppermint tea, dead-people tea or black coffee?"

"What a selection! And dead-people tea?"

"Well, green really. It always tastes like dead people to me. Not that I know obviously, just in my head. Supposed to increase my metabolism or something like that though and I'm willing to give anything a go apart from cutting down on the cake!" Vida knew that she was babbling. Maybe that was the downside to her career choice, an ever-present recognition of her own language weaknesses. Right now though, she was just desperate to keep the chat light to try and distract her from the case.

"Dead-people tea for me then please," smiled Caroline. Not that she needed to increase her metabolism. She was the fittest person Vida knew, always spinning or yogaing or undertaking all the other sorts of physical activity that brought Vida out in an uncomfortable sweat just thinking about them. The pair stayed silent while Vida boiled the kettle and poured the hot water over teabags in chipped mugs.

"Sorry," she apologised, as she handed the drink to Caroline. "Not got the same finesse in serving as the cafe either."

"Never mind that. Just tell me, what on earth is going on?"

Vida took a deep breath and unburdened herself, appreciating the way her friend sat patiently listening to her, never offering fixes, or anything beyond small supportive noises. This is what she needed; just someone to listen and take it on board. A problem shared and all that. It was a shame that she couldn't do that with Simon. If he listened properly at all, he was always ready to offer solutions. It wasn't solutions she needed, just an ear.

"You poor thing," Caroline offered when she'd finished and again Vida welled up.

"Thank you," she said, softly. "I mean, I know what I'm doing, it's nothing like what has happened to those poor girls. I mean Maggie and now Kitty, this murder victim. I feel a bit selfish really, feeling upset over it. It's not happened to me. It's not even happened to people I knew in real life."

"Oh sugar, that doesn't mean you don't have the right to be upset. Damnit, we all have the right to be upset that this kind of thing is happening to people, to women, no, to girls, in this day and age. I mean, doesn't it just make you furious? It's the 21st century for fuck's sake. How can we still be driving victims like Maggie to kill themselves? What sort of a society is that?" She looked incensed but then the anger passed, and she reached out and put her hand carefully on Vida's knee. "I'm sorry, love. I got carried away. You are completely allowed to feel sad. And to feel traumatised. And to feel exhausted. All of that is completely natural."

Vida felt a weight leave her shoulders. To be given permission to feel bad was a powerful thing. "Thank you," she said softly. "Honestly, that is a load off my mind. Just being able to talk to you. I tried to talk to Simon, and then there was Jamie who was helping me with the Maggie thing, but they just didn't seem to get it."

"Hmmm," Caroline said, her mouth pursed.

"What?" asked Vida, expecting to hear some sort of defence of Simon. Caroline seemed to worship the ground her husband walked on, forgiving him all his fecklessness in exchange for a good ravioli. Although, a good ravioli did go a long way towards making her feel better too, she admitted to herself.

"Jamie."

"What about him?"

"Love," Caroline started, tentatively. "I've heard rumours about you... and Jamie?"

"Rumours?"

Caroline's gaze fell to her drink and she looked a bit sheepish. "About you two perhaps having a relationship beyond student and teacher?"

Vida stared at Caroline, uncomprehending, before the clouds cleared and she burst into laughter. "Oh Caro, me and Jamie? That's the funniest thing I've heard! Jamie and me!" She wiped her eyes of tears of hilarity rather than the trauma of the past few days. "That's just what I needed."

Caroline remained looking sombre and slightly uncomfortable. "Well, I'm glad there's nothing to it," she said, "but you need to be careful, love. People are talking and in this climate, all it takes is for a complaint in an ear and you could find your academic career scuppered. We've all heard the noises about some restructuring coming your way and all they need is an excuse. Irrespective of whether it's supported or not, it could give them enough ammo to cut your linguistics all together."

"Honestly, Caro, there's nothing between Jamie and me. As if there ever could be! Have you seen that boy? I'm old enough to be... well, not his mother maybe, but certainly a worldly-wise aunt. As well as the fact I'd never let anything like that happen, he'd never want to be with me like that. Yes, he's sometimes a little bit flirty, but that's just because he feels sorry for me. It's very clear I don't get much flirtation directed at me. My bottom's the size of a small country and the most positive thing anyone could say about my looks is inoffensive," she scoffed, taking a swig of her peppermint tea.

"You do yourself a disservice, Vida." Caroline's gaze was unflinching. Vida shrugged, a little uncomfortable, more unconvinced.

"Honestly," she repeated. "I mean, thank you, lovely, for watching out for me but there's nothing true in it. Now," she changed the subject briskly, "what am I going to do about this Maggie thing? Do I just let it go?"

"Can you?" asked Caroline after a pause, seemingly trying to decide whether she should pursue the Jamie thing anymore. "I mean, that poor girl, Vida. And it doesn't exactly sound like this policeman is any sort of hero. Are any of them anymore? Who's got the time to be a hero when your budget's been slashed and you're doing the work of ten regular men?"

"But what can I do?" Vida meant the question to sound thoughtful, but it came out as a little whine instead.

"Do what they can't," Caroline suggested. "Get those girls to talk to you. You're good with people, Vida. They like you, trust you. There's a reason one of them reached out to you."

***

Vida checked the website for school hours and was waiting by 3.45pm. Still a while before students started leaving but she got herself into a prime position just around the corner from the school gates. Close enough so that she could see people coming and going, far enough away so that hopefully no paranoid parents would spot her and phone the police. She pushed her seat back and opened up her laptop, making a start on how she was going to phrase her report for Maggie's parents. Just how much was she going to give away?

The temperature in the car dropped rapidly, the falling darkness forcing its frigidity into the enclosed space. She grabbed a blanket from the rear seat and folded it neatly around her lap, giving up on the report but using the laptop to keep her hands a little warmer. At about 4.15pm, parental Mercedes and BMWs started amassing, ignoring the warning zigzags on the road, to park haphazardly on pavements and crossings. Five minutes later and a stream of teenagers emerged, melding into a mass migration moving away from the building. She wished she was a bit closer now, as all the teens disappeared into one uniform facade, especially in the dimness of the light. Maybe that damn dog would have been a good idea after all, an excuse as to why she was walking up and down outside. Packing the laptop back away, she got out of the car, preparing to move closer to see if she could get a better look. What if she'd already missed them?

It was the tall Russian blonde who caught her eye first, her blonde head a beacon through the grey. She'd obviously left before the other two and was strolling rangily away from the main entrance. As Vida watched, she was joined by the tanned brunette and then finally the mousy one. The trio was complete. She moved quickly now to try and intercept them before they got too far.

"Girls!" she shouted, waving. About a hundred female heads turned to face her. Thankfully, 97% of them turned away, disinterested. The three she wanted looked at each other, shared one of those silent messages and then crossed the road to meet her.

"You're looking for us?" the Russian asked.

"Yes. I wanted to thank you for the messages you all sent me."

"You were able to use them?"

"We were able to make enough of a match to suggest that it was Maggie who wrote the note, yes."

"I am glad for her parents." The three turned to walk away.

"Wait," Vida said, reaching out to them. "I wanted to ask you about the video."

"Video?" asked the brunette, the picture of innocence apart from the tiniest twitch of her eyebrow.

"Yes, you know, the video?"

They exchanged glances again. "We don't know what you're talking about," said the blonde.

"Yes, you do." Vida was sure they did. They weren't the masters of subterfuge they thought they were. Tiny tells, a hurried blink, a refusal to meet her gaze and a tightening of the mouth, told her that they definitely did know something about a video. "Don't make me spell it out, girls. You know exactly what I'm talking about."

"What did you want to know?"

"I don't know who sent it to me," although the sidelong daggers being cast at the pale girl in the middle told her that the others had their suspicions, "but I wanted to know if you knew who the men were? Or where it was filmed?"

"It shouldn't have been sent to you," the brunette said. "We'd agreed that we wouldn't tell. Maggie killed herself to try and stop people seeing it. It wasn't fair for us to send it on to anyone, Ness," she said pointedly at her mousey friend. "We decided that together."

"I know," muttered Vanessa, "but it was her parents. For her parents I mean. They needed to know, Tamsin. You know they did. I just wanted to help them."

The blonde, Petra glared at her for a moment before she shrugged and said in her short Slavic tones, "What's done is done. We don't know where it was filmed or who the men are," she continued. "We were at a party, a house party. One of our friends has a cousin and his parents were away for the weekend, so we were at his house. There were loads of people and we just lost track of where each other was. We found Maggie in a guest bedroom when people had started to go home. She was still unconscious. Someone must have spiked her drink. She swore she'd only had one glass of punch. We rang Tamsin's brother, and he came and got us, and we took Maggie back to Tamsin's. She came round by the morning and couldn't remember what had happened. But she was sore, and there was blood and we figured out that she must have been raped."

167

"Why didn't you phone the police? There would have been DNA evidence. They could have caught him." Vida found herself echoing Jamie's questions from yesterday.

"Maggie didn't want to. She felt ashamed. We tried to tell her that it wasn't her fault. But she didn't want her parents to find out."

"And then she got sent the video," Vanessa said, tearing up. "And so did everyone else. And everyone knew. And she felt so bad."

"So why not go to the police then?"

"She didn't want her parents to know that she'd let them down," Vanessa said. She was crying freely now, attracting the glances of a few nosy teenagers and some concerned parents. Vida tried to smile reassuringly at everyone, dismissing unspoken questions with a quick shake of the head. "We told her that they'd want to know, and she hadn't let them down and they'd love her still, but she didn't listen."

Tamsin moved to comfort her friend. "Everyday someone new seemed to have the video. Upper school first and then the juniors too. Mags felt like they were all judging her. People were whispering behind her back or they were calling her a slut to her face. And they would message her on Snapchat and send frames of the video. She couldn't see any way out," she said, desperately, seemingly pleading with Vida to understand them.

"Mags texted us that night," Petra said, taking up the story. "She told us that she loved us."

"We should have known what she was planning," sobbed Vanessa. "We should have guessed. We could have stopped her."

"She didn't want us to," Petra said, simply. "We had to respect her wishes."

"Did you not think her parents would have wanted to know? They've wondered for a year about what happened to her." Vida fought to keep the judgement out of her voice. These girls were still just children, faced with an impossible choice between loyalty to their friend and betrayal of her deepest desire.

"That's why I sent you the video," Vanessa said. "I'm sorry Tamsin, Petra, I know we said we wouldn't, but I just couldn't face the thought of Mr and Mrs Donaldson wondering still. They're such lovely people, they deserved to know the truth. It's been keeping me awake. Every night. And I just thought... I told myself that if anyone asked me again, I would tell them what happened. And then the inquest said she killed herself and it seemed like that was it. But then you came, and I knew... I knew it was time."

"You did the right thing," Vida said, feeling the superficiality of her words but unable to help herself. "It will help her parents, I promise you. They just want to understand what happened."

"Come on." Petra moved to huddle her friends away and back to school. "We'll be late."

"Wait, just one more question. This party, where was it?"

There was a final questioning glance between them before Tamsin pulled out her phone. She scrolled through screens before reaching a message and showing it to Vida. It was an address.

"Thank you," Vida said, taking a photo. "Thank you girls." She looked at each of them earnestly in turn before they turned and left.

She returned to the car and talked to herself for a few minutes. She should give the address to the police. Maybe DI Slater had sent her the documents by now. She could just reply to one of those messages and say by the way, I found this out. But she saw his stern gaze and that downturned mouth, remembered the feeling of powerlessness she'd felt as he'd so smoothly passed the horror of that video onto someone else. She didn't want just to hand it over to someone who didn't seem to care. She wanted to find out for herself.

Programming the GPS in her car, she set off, following the directions to take her to an address across the city, around thirty minutes away. The sun, weak in its efforts all day, had finally dropped below the skyline of the buildings. As she approached, the sky lit up with the strobing blue of a police vehicle. The road she needed was cordoned off, so she pulled up further away and walked back, muttering "Oh god, oh god, oh god," all the way. She could see more than one police car, an ambulance and a forensics van. "Please don't let it be number 28," she whispered, crossing her fingers behind her back.

"Damn it," she exhaled as the recognisable figure of DI Slater stepped out of a house and pulled the door shut behind him. Number 28.

Chapter 19

The blur of blonde frizz caught his attention and for a second, he couldn't place where he recognised it from. It was one of those out-of-time-and-place moments where he knew he knew the person but couldn't quite work out who they were.

"Bugger," he said, as the puzzle resolved itself.

"Isn't that your pet Professor?" snapped Hussain as she swept out of her car and towards him. "What's she doing here?"

He shrugged. She wasn't going to like it but all he could offer was "I don't know."

"You'd better find out then, hadn't you?"

"She looks like she's leaving," he said, optimistically.

Hussain cast her eyes back over in the direction of Dr Henrikson. "Walk me through what we've got and then you," she jabbed at his chest with a manicured finger, "find out what the hell she is doing here."

"Yes, ma'am." That urge to salute again. He stepped back into the house, taking a final look at the Forensic Linguist, before Hussain followed him in and closed the door. He briefed her as they both gowned up. "Victim is Ashaz Khan, forty-five years old. He was found by his nephew, Raheeq, when he came home from school. Both men live here along with Raheeq's parents and his maternal grandmother. Parents and grandmother are currently out of the country in Pakistan, visiting relatives there. Raheeq stayed behind as this is his A-Level year and his uncle agreed to stop with him." Slater led Hussain into the living room.

Despite the fact he'd already seen the body, he was taken back again by the brutality of the scene. Just like Kitty's murder a few days previous, where the congruity of her beauty juxtaposed against the rubbish heap had struck him, here the domesticity of a family living room was set against a spray of blood that arced across the walls and ceiling. The room with its ostentatious patterned wallpaper and gaudy gold coffee tables seemed to be fighting that domesticity, but the sideboard crammed with a thousand family faces put it firmly back in that sphere.

Ashaz Khan was sprawled in a cream leather armchair, facing the open doorway. His head was slumped forward, but it was easy to tell from the red bib stained into his t-shirt that he'd suffered some sort of wound to the neck. The bright lights that the SOCOs had brought with them to scope the scene reflected off the bald spot on the top of his head. It was an unflattering angle. "Knife wound to the throat," Slater said. "As far as the doctor's concerned, it was a single slash, a cut made left to right from behind."

"Any sign of restraint? I can't see a man just sitting there and letting his throat get slashed."

"Nothing visible. Doc thinks perhaps some sort of drug was given to subdue him. Raheeq says he heard no disturbances last night so there must have been something that knocked him out."

"What do you make of his positioning?"

Slater looked at the victim. He hadn't thought anything about the positioning truth be told but as he studied him he noticed what Hussain must have spotted immediately. "The chair's been moved from over there," he pointed to a space in front of the bay window. "He must have been posed in the middle of the room like that."

"But why?" Hussain asked. "What's the point of it?"

"Display?" hedged Slater. Hussain looked at him, her brow oozing disappointment.

"Entry point?"

"No sign of forced entry. Looks like he could have let his murderer in willingly."

"If he came in through the front door, there's a good chance someone around here spotted him. Twitching net curtains and all that." She surveyed the scene again. "What's the connection with the previous murder?"

"This," said Slater, pulling a see-through bag out of the evidence crate. He held it out to her, and she examined it without touching.

"More hate mail? How very old-fashioned."

"It's got some of the same language I think as the ones Kitty had received though," Slater said, tracing the words with his gloved finger. "I think it might have been written by the same person. And honestly, what are the odds of two murders happening within a few days of each other where hate mail is found at both of them and they're not related? Like you said, it's old-fashioned. There must be a connection.'

"Hmmm," she said, sounding unconvinced. "Dissimilar victim type, looks like a different MO altogether, no links as far as we're aware between the two victims. I think you're grasping, Detective Inspector. Surely one set of hate mail is always going to sound like the other. I hate you, blah, blah, blah." Her eyes narrowed as she stared at him.

"Perhaps," he conceded. He didn't agree with her. He was virtually certain that the letter writer of this hate mail was the same as someone who'd written to Kitty. Luckily enough, he knew just the person to ask to confirm. Hussain had made her opinions of the Forensic Linguist clear though and his career was too precious to him for open admittance that he was... not disregarding direct instruction but perhaps bending its interpretation a little. Hussain watched him for a little longer and he was worried for a moment that she really could read minds but apart from a slight huff through her nostrils, she made no more comment as she turned and left the scene.

Dawson emerged from the kitchen as she departed. "Oh, just missed the boss?" he asked, his voice innocence verbalised.

"Yes. Funny that. SOCOs turned up anything else of interest?"

"Two empty glasses in the dishwasher, clean unfortunately."

"We need to ask Forensic Science to examine the blood on Ashaz's neck to see if there are any traces of anyone else's on there. If the same weapon was used then we might have some transference."

"Who are we comparing it to?"

"Kitty Wakelin."

"Do you think they're connected?" Dawson sounded surprised.

"You don't?" Slater was beginning to feel like perhaps he was seeing unicorns when everyone else saw rhinoceroses. "Knife wounds, this letter?"

"Well, I suppose it might be. Seems like they've got less the same as is different though. This feels very different to me," he finished, seriously.

"I'll be sure to take your intuition into account when I'm deciding how we proceed," Slater said.

"Vic's nephew is waiting in the dining room still."

"Any indication he could have been involved?"

"He's a big lad. Certainly would've had the oomph to do it."

"Anything else of interest here?" Slater asked.

Almost immediately, he heard Tony Fairbright call his name from somewhere towards the back of the house. "Slater, I think you'll want to see this." Fairbright emerged and beckoned him towards the back garden.

"Anything in the house," Slater asked, as they crossed a gravelled garden towards what looked like a large summerhouse at the end.

"Nope. Officers are processing the rooms but there's no indication that anything happened beyond the front room. It's out here that I thought you'd find interesting."

The garden structure was bigger than Slater had first thought. A single door brought them into the narrow hall, darker than anticipated even though it was still dim outside. It barely seemed to have any natural light.

"Look at the door," Fairbright instructed him.

Slater obeyed. He'd taken it for any other uPVC door, but closer inspection showed him an impressive locking system. He swung it closed: bolts, a chain and two separate locks. Someone had wanted to keep this place secure.

"I wish criminals would realise that the quickest way to make something look suspicious is by making it look anything beyond ordinary," Tony said. "May as well take out an ad in the small pages."

The narrow dark hall ended abruptly, a blank wall with a door on either side.

"The right's the big room, left the little," Tony said, cryptically.

"And which would you recommend I see first?"

"Let's take this magical mystery tour to the right. I'd be interested to see what you think." He clicked open the door and stepped aside to let Slater through.

The room was instantly recognisable. The sight of the black leather sofa sat squarely in the middle, laminate flooring and bright lighting made his stomach lurch. He knew this room, had seen it in his waking and sleeping consciousnesses as he relived the rape of Maggie Donaldson.

"I've seen this place before," he said to Fairbright.

"You're ahead of the game then. Looks like a fairly bland living space. Not sure what the value of having a garden room with no windows is, but I guess they're aiming for a different view here. Up there and there," he pointed, "are a couple of high-end cameras. This lighting rig is pretty high spec as well," he said, nodding to an ugly set of lights. "This is not a cheap operation. Want to tell me where you've seen it before?"

"Rape of a fifteen-year-old. Filmed and the video was used to drive her to her death."

"Bloody hell," Fairbright said. "Our next stop on the tour probably won't surprise you either, then."

They left the large room, stepped across the hallway into a much smaller room. "Digital recording suite," Fairbright offered. "Again, high end equipment. Whatever these guys were up to, they were doing it with quality in mind."

"Any sign of what they were up to?" Slater was beginning to have a sinking feeling about this. A single brutal rape of a teenager was about to get a whole lot worse if they found what he thought they would find.

"External hard-drive, connected up to this machine." The screen had looked dead, but Fairbright ran gloved fingers over the mousepad and it came instantly back to life. "No password, would you believe? Guess these guys went in for physical security rather than technical. Maybe they didn't want any number-letter combination to get in the way of their porn." He smiled and looked to Slater.

Slater didn't return the smile. He was looking in horror at the screen which had filled now with an image that was both familiar and unfamiliar at the same time. The setting, the room next door, looked exactly the same as the last time he'd seen them on screen. What horrified him was the fact that it wasn't Maggie Donaldson's body lying limp on the sofa. This girl, perhaps woman, Slater wasn't sure, was very surely fighting back. The picture was frozen, but he could see the force she was putting into pushing away the heavy-set man who was pinning her down. Her top had evidently been torn in two, baring skinny breasts and even skinnier ribs to her attackers. A second man stood on the edge of the shot, clad all in black, a pink and swollen penis jutting out towards woman and her attacker.

He felt sick all over again. Maggie had died over a year ago. Perhaps if he'd done his job properly then, this woman might not have been raped. And how many others? How many crimes had he failed to stop because he hadn't got to the bottom of Maggie's?

"Sick bastards, eh?" said Fairbright, cheerier than Slater could have been. Maybe he was more accustomed to seeing this level of hell.

"Is this the only one?" Slater asked, trying to keep his voice level. He was praying that Fairbright said yes. Only one more girl had suffered because Slater hadn't done what was needed to stop this abuse.

"As if. All this equipment, they needed to be making a pretty penny to cover the costs. We're talking a hundred at least, Gabe. Looking at the dates, maybe fifteen years of recordings."

Slater couldn't stay in the room a minute longer. He pushed past a slightly bemused looking Fairbright and burst into the back garden, gulping the air. Mist still cloaked the roofs, but anything was preferable to that dark, hot, sticky scene of depravity. He took another deep breath. Shit. Bollocks. Damn them to hell. What had his screw-up cost all those women?

"Gabe?" Slater looked up. Dawson hovered over him looking nervous. "You alright?"

"No, I'm bloody not, Mark. I'm bloody well not." His eyes scanned over the house. You'd never know from the outside; it looked like any other semi-detached in Sheffield. He wondered whether the neighbours knew, whether they'd seen the women, the men, going in and out. Twenty years ago and you wouldn't have been able to get away with these things without the complicity of all your surrounding houses. Everyone knew everyone's business. Nowadays though you probably didn't even know your neighbours' names. His eyes lighted on a figure at the downstairs window.

"Raheeq Khan?" asked Slater, nodding towards the figure. Dawson turned, checked and confirmed with a nod. "I want him cautioned and taken the station. Neighbours might not have known but there's no bloody way you'd not know if you lived in the same bloody house."

"Cautioned for what?"

Slater's phone buzzed suddenly with an incoming text. Number unknown. *Maggie was at a party at the house the night she was raped. Vida x.* He didn't want to know how she'd got that information. Another example of her succeeding where he'd failed.

"Let's start with rape," Slater said, showing the message to Dawson. "With this new information and the biological certainty that there's no chance that a teenage boy living in this house didn't sample the wares so to speak. Somewhere on those files, we'll find him."

He glowered at the figure until he saw it turn as Dawson entered the room. He'd failed to help Maggie; he wasn't going to let these women down too. Whatever it took.

Chapter 20

All the caffeine in the world couldn't wake Vida up from the terrifying loop her brain was stuck in. The functions of her job were completed perfunctorily, but if her students had noticed her absent mind, they were kind enough not to comment on it. These late-afternoon lectures were always a struggle against falling energy levels, and the truth was that an hour's seminar on the changing use of adjectives between a plagiarist and the original sources was one of her less interesting topics. That, together with everything she'd seen over the past few days, meant she was unable to keep her mind on the material.

"Vida, a word please." She'd been so caught up in thinking about Maggie and the new letters that she'd not noticed Myfanwy sidling into the room as the students left. She'd shut the door firmly behind her. This didn't bode well. "I've had an interesting conversation earlier today. Can I call it a conversation I wonder? Maybe complaint would be more accurate? You're the linguist, you can tell me," she said, baring her teeth. She was tapping her foot impatiently, impossibly high stilettos adding a few inches to her height and also doubling up as a threatening weapon.

Vida remained silent, waiting for whatever it was. She could think of a thousand reasons why a student might complain about her at the minute, although she felt aggrieved about how quickly appreciation had turned to annoyance. It had only been a couple of off days. Surely that wasn't long enough a deterioration to generate student complaints? Her brain turned over the Jamie issue a little; could there be some truth in Caro's warning?

"A phone-call from DCI Hussain. It seems you've been over-stepping the mark in terms of your relationship with the police. Turning up at murder scenes?"

"Oh, for god sakes," Vida sighed. "None of this is my choice. Do you honestly think I'd insert myself into the middle of a murder scene?" So there had been a murder. Could it just be a coincidence that it was the same property where Maggie had been raped? Had her giving the film to the police precipitated some sort of murderous action. She breathed in shakily, suddenly feeling overwhelmed. "This is horrible, Myfanwy, absolutely horrible."

Her boss looked sceptical. Her red lips pursed and relaxed as though she were chewing over Vida's protestations. "Your choice or not, DCI Hussain was very clear on the fact that you need to be steering clear of the police going forward."

"But I've been asked to review some letters. Some hate mail."

"By someone who out-ranks DCI Hussain?" Vida's eyes fell to the floor. "Then their requests are irrelevant. You are to stay clear," she said briskly.

"I'm just following your instructions, Myfanwy. You're the one who got me involved with the Donaldsons." She tried to keep the accusatory tone out of her voice.

"I understood from the Vice-Chancellor that that was resolved now?"

"In the immediate, yes. I mean, I can demonstrate that Maggie did send the letter and I also found out why. But that's just opened this whole new can of worms that needs looking into it. You can't really expect me just to leave it, Myfanwy. Girls are getting abused and raped. Maybe girls that we know. And there's a murderer on the loose." She could hear the volume of her voice increasing and she took a breath. Losing her temper at her hierarchical superior was going to do her case for the future of the Forensic Linguistic course no favours. "I'm sorry, Myfanwy." She forced a smile onto her face. "It's just something I feel very strongly about. I don't think I could live with myself if I just dropped it now. What if I can find out something really important about the killer? My profile could help them find someone who's murdered two people."

Myfanwy looked contemplative.

Vida pushed on. "It could be great publicity for the Forensic Linguistics course, for the department as a whole, if we can play an instrumental part in solving this crime. Perhaps we could use the win to apply for more funding to research in this area. It would probably help attract more students too. A real jewel in the university's crown, so to speak."

Myfanwy's cool grey eyes met hers and for a minute Vida wondered if she could sense the lie in her words. Who knows? Maybe it wasn't a lie. But as soon as she'd said the words, Vida could hear the falsehoods. She wasn't interested in the case because of any reasons of publicity and promotion. It had gone past the point where she was interested for scientific reasons too. She couldn't pretend that it was all academic to her. This was real and she was as involved as it was possible to be. She couldn't just walk away now; it would feel too much like she was betraying Maggie and the poor girl who'd received all that hate mail. She needed to be involved to hear their stories, perhaps to learn from their stories if she could.

"You say a policeman involved has asked for your assistance?"

"Yes, DI Slater. I've got photocopies of all the letters he's asked me to look at in the office."

"Well, perhaps you may as well finish your research into those," Myfanwy conceded. "But I would suggest that you steer clear of interacting with DCI Hussain. The university has a close working relationship with the police force, and I could not countenance any action which put that at risk. If there was to be any such risk, I would of course have to make it clear that you were acting against my advice."

So, she'd be a sacrificial offering if anything went wrong. It felt like that was pretty much to be expected in today's results driven society. As any football manager could tell you, you're only ever as good as your last match and even in the supposedly cloistered world of academia, one bad student appraisal could have you on the short road to competency proceedings. "Of course," she said. "It's my decision to continue." What else could she do?

Chapter 21

Slater sat opposite Raheeq Khan. Although he was just eighteen, Slater would have pegged him as being substantially older. He was a well-built man, muscled not fat, nearly as tall as Slater himself but bulkier. Only the soft facial hair gave away his true age, a straggly beard and wispy moustache. That and the fear in his eyes. Interesting. Slater wondered what he was afraid of. He'd seemed easily confident at the scene, not particularly bothered by the murder of his uncle. Perhaps that had been for show. Or perhaps something had happened in the intervening time that had caused the change in confidence. Some dawning realisation of the potential trouble he was in perhaps. He sprawled in his chair, knuckles practically dragging the floor like some sort of neanderthal throwback. In contrast, his solicitor sat to his right, a tightly wound Asian man in a sharp suit and spectacles.

"Raheeq, I just wondered if you could take me through the details of what you found this afternoon when you came home from school?" Slater wanted to start softly. The man had to know what they'd found at the end of the garden but perhaps he'd be lulled into some sort of retreat if he thought that Slater wasn't going to mention that.

"You know what I found, man. I ain't describing it. It's in here, burned on these." He pointed to his eyes.

"You don't have to describe the scene. What happened this afternoon, before you found your uncle's body?"

"Nothing, man." He shrugged.

"There must have been something, Raheeq. At some point, you must have started home from school?" Slater kept his voice patient, his tension travelling through to a tapping foot.

"Well, yeah, man. I came home and found Ash like that." He paled suddenly.

"What time?"

"About half-four?"

"That's quite late, isn't it?"

"Nah man, I got intervention after school." He made it sound like a fate worse than death.

"Was there any sign of forced entry?"

"You mean like was the door broke? Nah. I used my key, like normal."

Slater leant in closer to the man. "Our pathologist believes that your uncle was killed in the night Raheeq. You must have seen him in the morning? You must have known he was dead? But you went merrily off to school like nothing had happened."

Raheeq shook his head, violently. "Nah, I didn't. I was late in the morning. I just ran out of the house. I didn't see nothing. I wouldn't have left him like that."

"And what about last night? What were your movements? Did you see anything? Hear anything?"

"Nah. Not a thing, man. I'm working hard, revising for my A-Levels so I was in my room studying all night. I went to bed at about two. Didn't hear anything from Ash."

"Was that normal?"

"Yeah, man. We're not friends or anything. That's it."

"You don't know if he was intending on meeting anyone last night? Seeing anyone?"

"Nah, man." Slater felt his eye twitch at another broad dismissal. The vocal tic was getting on his nerves. "His private life is private. I know nothing," Raheeq continued, sitting back in his chair, legs splayed, arms dangling to the sides. Another interesting change in emotion.

Slater watched him carefully. Raheeq met his gaze at first but then began to withdraw again. His legs closed slightly, and he pulled himself up in his seat. Slater leaned forward. "Tell me about Maggie Donaldson, Raheeq," he said, quietly.

The reversion to fear was instantaneous. There was something here worth picking at. Something that Slater could find out. He wasn't sure if it would give him any answers for the double murder he was looking at, but it might give some further resolution to the Donaldsons.

Raheeq looked panicked and started shaking his head. "Nah, man. I don't know no Maggie Donaldson." He looked to his solicitor, who was frowning.

"Is this relevant, Detective Inspector?" the solicitor asked, consulting a notepad he'd been scribbling in since they arrived. He wasn't someone that Slater was familiar

188

with and he wondered whether the solicitor's area of expertise really was crime or if he'd been co-opted in to help at the last minute.

"Yes, it is. Raheeq?" He looked back at the man. He was fidgeting on the chair now. "We know you knew Maggie. We know quite a lot about it really. We've seen the video." Grenade detonated, Slater leaned back in his chair and watched panic turn to dread.

The solicitor was looking at his client with a similar level of fear on his face, although Slater felt it was probably professional out-of-his-depth fear rather than anything more sinister. Raheeq still squirmed, sending panicked looks across to the solicitor. Was he afraid of him? For him?

"Raheeq?" Slater said again. "We know you went to the Boy's School. You must have known Maggie?"

"I know lots of girls, man. I'm the Party Master. They flock to me." He gestured widely with his arms. The words were confident, but the fear was still hanging in his eyes.

"Well, this one didn't have such a good time at your party."

"Nah, man. My parties are legendary."

"This one went down in the history books for another reason." Slater pulled out a picture of Maggie and slid it across the table. She looked indistinguishable from every other teenage girl, wide smile and eyes that spoke of the future. Slater sent up another prayer of regret. "Ring any bells?"

"Nah, man." Raheeq swallowed, looking still whiter. The solicitor didn't look like he was in any hurry to intervene on his client's behalf. If anything, the glazed expression in his eyes suggested he was barely even paying attention.

"You know, Raheeq," said Slater, deciding suddenly to change the angle again, "we've got a lot going on right now and much of it seems to centre around your address. We've got Maggie. This was her when she was alive. Perhaps it might jog some memories if I tell you that she died, shortly after this video was shot." He slipped a freeze-frame from the rape video. Maggie lying unmoving, the dark-set man looming over her. "Maybe you'd find it easier to remember her like this."

Raheeq's fists clenched. He shook his head.

"You might not know," Slater started conversationally, "but recognition technology is improving every day. You might think that we need to see someone's faces to compare against but that's just not true anymore. We can look at different body parts, if you see what I'm saying, Raheeq, to get a match." He fell silent. He'd got no idea if that was true. If it wasn't, he didn't fancy the role of hard-on comparison-maker. It might get far enough under Raheeq's collar though to get something useful out of him.

Raheeq remained silent. Had he pushed hard enough? Time to up the ante a little more.

"So, that's the rape of Maggie Donaldson. Who was the other boy by the way? No? No answer. That's fine. Same applies to him. Perhaps you need to think about that.

When we go talk to him, he's going to think you've grassed on him. Maybe you want to get your side of the story out now, before we find him, and he blames you. Your house, your recording equipment..."

"It's not mine," Raheeq said, urgently.

"Whose is it then, Raheeq? You obviously know how to use it." Slater tapped the picture of Maggie's rape again.

Raheeq shrugged.

"So, not yours, at your house, used by you, but you don't know who owns it. What about the rest of the films we saw, Raheeq? Seems to be hundreds of girls and women on those videos. How many are we going to find your dick playing a starring role in? How many women have you raped on that sofa, Raheeq? Was Maggie the first? In the middle? One of hundreds?"

Raheeq was shaking his head violently now. "No. None of them. I ain't like that."

"This says different," Slater said, eyes glancing again to Maggie's video shot.

"That was different," Raheeq finally said, his voice low. "That was just two mates messing around."

Slater felt bile rising in his throat and pushed his hands hard against his thighs as a physical reminder to not hit this pathetic human being as hard as he possibly could. Dawson looked at him, shook his head slightly. When Slater finally spoke again, his voice was under control. Dangerously so.

"You drugged her. You carried her to the place, and you raped her. Multiple times. And if that wasn't degrading enough, you filmed it and shared that film with the kind of people who would judge a girl for being brutally raped rather than judging the bastards that did it. And you will pay for that, make no mistake Raheeq. We will gather sufficient evidence and you will be sent to jail for what you have done."

To his surprise, Raheeq started to cry. "Nah, man. I didn't share no video. That weren't me. I wouldn't have done that."

"Rape is fine, sharing the video's not?" Slater let his incredulity show.

"They'd've killed me," the boy said, his voice low.

"Who?"

"Them," Raheeq said, gesturing widely.

"Raheeq, you're going to have to be more specific than that. We need names."

Raheeq buried his head in his hands. Slater wondered whether his solicitor would step in, but the man still seemed out of his depth. To continue hard or to go on softer? He looked again at Maggie's picture. The man had as good as confessed to her rape. Was that enough? Not even close.

"The equipment is at your house, Raheeq. Your uncle must have been involved. Your father too, I'd guess. They must have been running this operation for years. All those women raped, attacked, filmed and yet they've never been caught. Not even questioned as far as our records can show. That must have taken a supreme level of control and management. And then you," he said, jabbing towards

Raheeq, "come along with your stupid teenage hormones and no ability to control yourself or your pathetic desire to fuck someone who obviously wouldn't have given you a second glance normally. I'll tell you what I think happened. I think your uncle found out about you raping Maggie. Maybe he already knew? Someone must have shown you how to use the equipment." Slater pulled out a picture of the lighting rig and video cameras. "So, the initial rape, that was with your uncle's loving permission. Make you a man, my lad?"

Raheeq sat still, seemingly listening intently, the tears still falling sporadically. One fat droplet had got caught in his beard and glistened wetly.

"Rite of passage," suggested Dawson.

"Exactly," Slater said. "But I'm guessing your uncle was not behind the publicity that came after. All those years of secrecy and you blow it with a moment of madness. I bet he was furious. In fact, Raheeq, now we're going along these lines, I'm liking this more and more as a viable answer to the question of what happened in your living room last night."

"P'raps he just found out last night," chipped in Dawson, helpfully. He'd warmed up to his side of the pairing now.

"I think you could be right, Sergeant. I think Raheeq thought he'd got away with the Maggie thing. After all, it's been a year. Done and dusted. Suicide verdict delivered and nobody had found out. If I were Raheeq..." As if he ever could be such a sick little pervert. "I'd be thinking that I was home free. Then if I found out that someone was poking around again, I'd be feeling panic. Maybe that someone would find something out this time. Maybe this time, that someone would find his or her way to your door and finally let your uncle into your secret."

"I think he found out," Dawson said, proudly as though he were a child proudly showing his parents his first correct sum.

"I think you might be right again. Your uncle found out, Raheeq, didn't he? He found out and he was furious. You'd put everything in jeopardy. Everything he'd built up. Years of investment and you'd blown it in an instant. I'm sure the CPS can fill in the rest themselves. A fight and he ends up dead. You remember reading something about a murder in the newspaper and stick that pathetic letter on top and job done. You've framed the Sheffield Stabber." Even as the words were falling from his mouth, Slater knew they weren't true. Dawson seemed to have bought into the story and was nodding excitedly but Slater could hear the gaps. The only person looking into Maggie's story was Vida, and she hadn't turned up at the Khan's house until this morning, after the murder had already taken place. And this man, looking more like a boy every minute, wiping his nose on his sleeve, didn't have the gumption to murder anyone, nor the intellect to try and frame anyone else.

"It wasn't me, man," Raheeq said, desperately. "I didn't kill him. He knew about the video already. I told him when Roberts first sent it out."

"Roberts? The second starring role in the film, I presume."

Raheeq looked shocked for a minute, as though he hadn't realised what had just come out of his mouth. "Yeah, man," he sighed. "Leon Roberts. It was his idea. We'd watched a couple of the clips together and he had this giant hard-on for Maggie. He planned his move at the party, divide and conquer." The accompanying hand gestures were lewd. "But she turned him down. We taught her a lesson. Then he took it too far and sent that clip round. I didn't want that to happen, man. I didn't want her to die or nothing."

How many times had people looked at Slater with pleading eyes since he'd started on this investigation? How many times had people told him they hadn't meant something to happen? Like that made it okay.

"She did though," he said, coldly.

"I know, man. But that wasn't my fault."

Slater felt the anger rise again. Nothing was anyone's fault anymore.

"And your uncle?" pushed Dawson.

"I didn't kill him either. It's like I said, I was in my room all night. At school all day. I didn't see nothing." His tears had dried up now and he sat up straight in his seat.

"You expect us to believe that?" Dawson said. "He died last night when you were in the house. You seriously expect us to believe that your uncle didn't scream when someone was cutting into him?"

"He didn't, man," Raheeq said, wild eyed. He stopped suddenly.

"Raheeq," prodded Slater, sensing some sort of capitulation.

The boy looked to his solicitor who was looking a bit green and closely examining the margin on his notepad. As much use as a bloody chocolate fireguard. "I saw someone. Skinny. Shorter than my uncle but taller than my mum."

"Any identifying features?"

"I didn't see his face."

"Voice?"

"Didn't hear anything. I weren't lying about that. I saw him when I went upstairs and then I didn't hear anything else."

"You didn't want to see what he was up to?"

"Nah man, I assumed he were a new client. I didn't need to see no more." The boy's bluster had resumed. The teenager emotional gamut was knackering to follow. He must have felt more secure.

"So a man, no identifying features, no idea what he sounds like. Not much help, Raheeq. Anything else?" Slater's voice was laden with scorn. Irrespective of his involvement in his uncle's murder, he was directly responsible for Maggie's death; Slater didn't want Raheeq to forget that for a minute.

"Nah man. Nothing else. He was dressed in black with a hoody. Mebbe dark hair but I only got a glimpse through the bannisters so it might just have been his hood up."

Slater sat back and thought. The description matched the figure they'd seen on the CCTV, leading Kitty down that dark alley. It was another connection. He needed confirmation though, that the two cases were related. At the minute, he couldn't for the life of him work out what a girl like Kitty might have had to do with a gang raping and abusing women. Had she been a victim? Was that why she lived such a reclusive life? Fear? It made sense to him. It wasn't the sort of thing that was easy to recover from; Maggie's tragic choice showed that. Maybe Kitty had just taken a more passive approach to stopping living. But then why the hell would she have ended up murdered by the same person who murdered the perpetrator of the abuse? There was still a missing link here.

"If you think of anything else, Raheeq, you need to tell us immediately. There's someone out there murdering people like you. Rapists, I mean Raheeq."

For a minute, the boy looked like he was going to object to the label, but he subsided quickly as he took Slater's words in. "You think I'm in danger, man?" he asked, his voice with a slight edge of hysteria.

"I couldn't really say, Raheeq." Let the little bastard squirm. He didn't deserve to feel comfortable ever again. "But the sooner we catch the killer, the better for everyone. Now, my sergeant here is going to take you along to the custody desk where you will be charged with the rape of Maggie Donaldson. I suggest you give us Leon Roberts' full name and address to make sure that we can share the burden between the two of you."

Raheeq nodded. Slater turned the recording off and then led him back to the custody sergeant to lock away while they waited for a charging decision from the CPS on the rape. He didn't think it would be long. At least that was one little bit of this nightmare closed down. Now he needed to get that positive link between the two cases. Time to find out just what a Forensic Linguist was good for.

Chapter 22

It was dark when Vida got home, and for once she was grateful for the aromas that told her that Simon was home and concocting some kind of culinary marvel. The house smelled like roasting peppers and tomatoes, the warmth of a Tuscan summer enveloping her as soon as she shut the door to the February chill. She leaned heavily against the door for a minute, closing her eyes and breathing deep. If she'd found it tiring being out in the field yesterday, the horror of today had tripled that exhaustion. After her encounter with DI Slater and Myfanwy, she'd returned to her office and continued trawling through the texts she'd got from Maggie's friends and family, trying to add greater probabilities to the pretty much already certain. Jamie had turned up but had thankfully kept his thoughts to himself for the rest of the day and they had worked in companionable silence. They'd processed nearly all the texts and she felt like she was ready to report back to the Donaldsons. She just still wasn't sure exactly what she was going to say to them.

"V? Is that you?" Simon called.

"Yes." She followed the smells into the kitchen, knocking the thermostat up a notch as she went to try and heat her bones through. Simon was sitting at the table, laptop in front of him, soup bubbling on the hob and what looked like fresh bread waiting to go into the oven sitting on the side. She slung her bag onto the chair and then sat down opposite him. He glanced up and smiled a welcome at her but seemed oblivious to her slumped shoulders and grey eyes.

"I've had the most amazing idea," he said. "Check it out."

He spun the laptop round to face her. On the screen was a picture of a dog. She looked at him questioningly.

"It's a dog."

"I can see that," she frowned. "I just don't see how this matches up to an amazing idea."

"It's a Lagotto Romagnolo."

"Are you sure that's not a car?"

He looked bemused for a moment. "No, that's a Bugatti. This is definitely a dog. Listen, I was thinking earlier about that truffle that I bought. I mean, that was expensive. And for what? A little lump of fungus. Don't get me wrong. I think it was worth it and you said about it bringing out the flavours but then I thought...what about hunting for my own truffles? These guys are experts in the field. Italian water dogs who've been retrained as truffle hunters. I rang a bloke earlier and he was telling me about all the spots that you can find truffles around Yorkshire. It's not as rare as you might think."

Vida stared at him. She rubbed her forehead. "You want to get a dog?" Her tone conveyed disbelief and extreme disappointment. Simon failed to pick up on either.

"Yes, don't you think it's a great idea? We can get one of these little guys and then when I'm not working on my PhD..." Which was all the time, Vida thought. "I can take him up into the known truffle hunting spots. He can ferret out some good Yorkshire truffles. Maybe we can sell them on. Local produce is really popular right now; I bet we'd be able to sell them at a premium."

Vida looked at the dog and then returned her gaze to her husband. He wore a puppy dog expression himself, eyes pleading, slight pout on his mouth. She shook her head, stood up and went to pour herself a glass of wine.

"Have white, not the red," he said to her. "It'll go better with the dinner. I've already opened a bottle in the fridge."

She ignored his instructions and poured herself a big glass of merlot. He watched her, silently.

"I presume you're not on board with this idea," he said, slightly haughtily, as though her objections had grievously offended him.

She snorted. "I haven't even got my head round what this idea is, Si. I have had the worst day imaginable and I'm tired and I'm upset, and I come home and instead of seeing that perhaps I might need some comfort and support, you launch straight into another one of your stupid plans. I mean, a dog? A dog, Si? How are you going to ever finish the PhD when you're running around after a labradoodle?"

He looked hurt, but she couldn't tell if that was because of the PhD jibe or her mislabelling the dog. "Well, excuse me for having ideas and looking for ways to maybe save a bit of money and improve our lives."

"We wouldn't have to save money if you didn't keep spending it all on stupid ingredients." This time he physically recoiled as though she'd dealt him a blow.

"I lead a stressful life, Vida," he said. "It's important for me to have an outlet for that stress. I seek solace in my cooking. And don't pretend you don't benefit from it. You certainly eat enough of it."

"Wow," she said, shaking her head. "So many insults, where to start? A stressful life? You want to know what I've been doing, Simon? I watched a video of a girl being raped. That girl who killed herself? She was raped and they recorded it and they sent me a video and I had to watch it and I took it to the police and they're going to look into it, but I can't get it out of my head, Simon. I can't stop seeing her." She took a deep breath and looked at her husband. He was watching her, warily. "She was drugged. She couldn't do anything to stop them. And I had to watch her. And I wanted to stop it, but I couldn't." She took a shaky breath and a gulp of wine. "Don't talk to me about stress, Simon. You have no idea."

"Vida," he started, getting to his feet and crossing over to her. He placed his hands gently on her shoulders and looked down into her eyes, before enveloping her. "I didn't realise. And of course, you're right. I should have noticed when you came in just how tired you were. I was just...well, I got carried away. You know what I'm like." It was as close to an apology as she would ever get from him. He pressed his lips to the top of her head and then released her and led her gently back to the table. "Let me get the bread in. Twenty minutes and it will be done and then we can eat soup. Will you tell me about it? I mean, tell me about what you want to tell me about."

Nothing. She wanted to tell him nothing. She wanted to shut her mind and never have to see it again. Talking about it wouldn't help. He just wouldn't be able to say the right things. But if she didn't talk to him, he'd take it personally and use it against her next time they argued. He would accuse her of being secretive, she would accuse him of being demanding and then they'd be back in their usual cycle. Maybe now was the time to break it. Tentatively, she began to tell him about the video, her research and the visit to the police station. He put the bread in the preheated oven and then sat down opposite her, earnest eyes on her as she filled him in.

"They wanted you to look at some more things? That sounds promising."

"I don't know," she admitted. "I was really keen at first, but now I'm not sure. Within the space of two days, I've moved from fiction authorship queries to investigating suicides and murders. How did I get here? I mean, that video Simon. Seriously."

"But you're helping them," he pointed out. "You're not part of the problem. You could be part of the solution. How would that make you feel? Knowing that you were helping solve crimes. Helping the victims."

She thought about his words. "Maybe. But if it means more days like today, I'm not sure I can cope."

"You know what would help?"

"More wine?" she asked, swinging her empty glass.

He grinned and topped it up. "Well, yes of course. But I was thinking about something else really. Something warm and loving. Something that would always be happy to see you. Tail wagging when you come through the door. No matter what kind of day you've had, he'll always be ready to welcome you home and make the day feel better."

She sighed. "For god sakes Simon. You wonder why I don't share things with you? I'm trying to explain something to you. Telling you about my worries and concerns and you just turn it right back round to you. What you want." She downed the wine, grabbed her bag and made for the door.

"What about dinner? I've spent all day roasting the peppers for this soup."

She glared hard at him, running a range of witty comebacks about roasting through her head before simply growling and slamming out.

She didn't go far. A few roads down, a new wine bar had opened up. It probably wouldn't be there for long; businesses tended to pop up and disappear just as she was getting to like them. It certainly wasn't doing much business currently. Two besuited businessmen propped up one end of the bar while a pair of women in their mid-forties huddled round a small table, speaking in low tones and the occasional outraged gasp. After ordering herself a large gin and tonic, she retreated to a corner table, put her back to the wall and opened up her laptop. She wanted to do something to help. Feel like she was making a difference. She googled rape charities and organisations, reading story after horrific story of abused and traumatised women. Everyone pretended that they lived in a civilized society, but how could it really be that when all this was going on just below the surface?

She tried to think back to her own childhood, being a teenage girl. How would she have felt if one of her friends had been raped like that? And somebody had videoed it? That technology hadn't really existed when she was a teen; maybe she was looking back with rose-coloured glasses, but everything seemed to be much simpler then. Maybe it was just better hidden. Maggie's story represented the curse of modern times. There was no escape from any minor indiscretion, let alone the horror of something like this. Vida could all too well imagine the humiliation that Maggie would have felt. It wouldn't have mattered to her that it wasn't her fault. That she was a victim and the only person to blame would have been the rapists. Teenagers were brutal, especially teenage girls, and if Maggie had been beautiful and popular and smart then Vida was sure there'd've been a queue of bitchy girls waiting to tell her that she was a slut, and it was her fault for wearing that skirt or getting herself drunk. And these days, Maggie would never have been able to get away from it. It wasn't like the noughties, when a single copy of a video might have been ripped to disc. Films these days were copied, multiplied like a virus and you could never be sure that someone hadn't seen it. How long would it have been before one of Maggie's peers decided she was too big for her boots and posted the video to a site like Pornhub, where lecherous men could masturbate over it to their penis's content?

Vida shivered and took a long draw of the G&T. She was glad she'd opted for the double as the sharp tang of the gin strangely settled her stomach. She thought back to her meeting with DI Slater. He was not what she'd expected from the soft Sheffield accent on the phone. Tall and elegant, long-limbed and even a little beautiful, he wasn't making the best of his natural assets though. Tight black curls rambled a little long over his collar, his natural grimace had done nothing for his face and the suit he'd been wearing looked like the budget-end of Marks and Spencers' range. Someone that shape deserved more sartorial elegance than the boxy shoulders and baggy trousers of the ill-fitting clothing, as neatly pressed as they were. The biggest shame of all though had been his brusqueness and the disdain with which he'd considered her science. She thought she'd talked him around a bit, and at least he'd been willing to think about how he might be able to use her on the current case, but she suspected he was grasping at straws and just trying to cover his bases a little. Still, the thought of analysing the hate mail was an interesting prospect. The files hadn't been sent over to her yet, so she turned to YouTube instead and did a quick search for Kitty Wakelin.

There were hundreds of results; videos of the girl herself singing, interviews, karaoke versions of her songs, hopefuls covering her music. Vida wasn't particularly familiar with her music, being more of an eighties classics type of girl, but she'd heard enough on the radio to recognise the tune of the first video as she plugged her headphones in. Kitty, looking incredibly young and innocent, stood alone on centre stage. She had a guitar and a microphone but nothing else as she sang a simple ballad. Vida felt goosebumps shiver down her back; she often had this visceral reaction to good music but thought that this time it was probably more a physical recognition of the tragedy of the young girl. Such talent and such a loss.

Chapter 23

Slater pressed play on the video of Kitty Wakelin's last recorded performance. She stood in a spotlight on an empty stage, just a young girl and a guitar. The light bounced off her hair, super-shiny, her cheeks rosy, and skin flawless. She nodded virtually imperceptibly, a personal countdown before strumming the first chord on her guitar. An introduction, her face studied as she looked down at her guitar, foot tapping, before her voice joined the accompaniment, soaring a melody. Rashid Khan had been right when he'd talked about emotion; here it was raw and untamed. The song was a ballad, the usual schmaltzy lyrics of love lost and found, but while her voice was pure, Slater noticed that her eyes were cloudy. He'd been hoping that watching her perform would somehow convey something to him that he'd missed so far. He was disappointed. There was nothing to add to his understanding of her. The more he worked his way down this rabbit hole, the less he understood anything about her. He was still missing something.

Shutting his laptop, he checked his watch. If he left now, he'd make it to the arena in time for training. He'd been playing ice hockey with a local team for three years now and found the ruthless beating his body took each week cathartic. The chance to take his frustration and rage out on a padded opponent and a puck was too good to miss. He knew some of his colleagues drank their annoyances away; others had a line-crossing approach to reasonable force when arresting suspects. It was pathetic really, to be so weak-willed that you would lose control in that way. There were plenty of routes to working out your anger without resorting to things that would bring the force into disrepute. Two hours on the ice would relieve his tension and give him some valuable thinking time. Maybe focusing on something else would let him see the whole Kitty thing with more clarity.

***

"Well, well, well, what do we have here then?" the voice caressed him as he fumbled with the key in his lock. His body was aching with the brutality of the training he'd just finished, but he felt himself respond despite that. He rested his head on the door, feeling her hands snake around his middle and slide up along his chest. She pushed her body against the length of his and the smell of her intoxicated him. It always did.

"Sabryne," he groaned, before spinning round to kiss her hard, forcing her back against the hallway wall. She retaliated in kind, talons clawing in his curls, tightening painfully, lips meeting so forcefully that teeth clashed. "Sabryne," he said again, this time a soft mutter as he almost flung himself away from her. "Bloody hell," he spat. He turned and stomped into his flat, leaving the door open for Sabryne to follow him. He poured a large measure of rum and ignoring the bottle's instructions to sip, downed it in one swift movement. Another quickly followed before he had the courage to turn and face her again.

She was sitting languidly, feline, on the sofa, one arm across the back, drumming neon pink nails while observing him with one perfectly arched eyebrow. A beautiful woman with soft curves and endless legs that were only marred by the look of disdain that seemed to have settled permanently on her face. Even when she smiled up at him in bed, there was calculation, a sum weighing up possibilities and probabilities. He wondered whether she'd always had it, and he'd just not noticed. He'd been twelve when he first saw her. Fourteen when they'd started going out. Sixteen when she'd decided that his brother was the more appealing option. And not much older when she'd realised she could have her cake and eat it. Caleb by day, Slater when she wanted him. He was helpless before her. The feeling of getting one up on his brother was constantly tinged by a sharp shame that he couldn't resist. She knew him better than anyone else. He hated her for that.

"You're pregnant," he said, pointedly.

For a minute more she contemplated him, head on one side, a slight smile playing on her lips. "And you're worried about playing daddy," she pouted. "Might interfere with Mr Policeman's big important career?"

In a second he was in front of her, gripping her wrists tightly. "No," he hissed, his face close to hers. "I'm worried about my brother, my mum."

"You're hurting me," she said, wounded and wriggling. He glared at her before releasing her and going back to the rum once more. She was Caleb's girlfriend and he... what even was he? He'd been manacled to her for as long as he could remember, desperate to quit the betrayal, unable to find the courage to do it. It was nothing more than punishment now. An open sore he couldn't stop picking at. The pain kept him alive.

"What the hell, Sabryne?" he said, eventually. "I thought you were using protection."

"Always the woman's fault," she drawled. "So many men just wanting to stick it in without any thought and then just assume that it's the woman's job to stop anything happening."

"No," through gritted teeth, he tried to keep his temper. "You told me you were on the pill. You told me."

She smiled, benignly. "Nothing in this world is infallible. Not a man's heart, not a woman's memory and not any kind of contraception." She crossed her legs and switched the angle of her head, as if daring him to comment further.

He scowled. "Is it mine?"

"Eeeny meeny miny moe," she said, counting on her fingers, swinging her free leg. Slater balled his fist. It was a good job he'd already been to hockey practice and had wiped out the aggression of the week in the rink. It made it slightly easier not to physically explode. Whether he'd be taking it out on Sabryne or his own stupid self he wasn't sure yet.

"You must have an idea."

"It's Caleb's," she said simply.

He watched her. "Are you sure?"

One shoulder rose and fell. "I have an idea."

"They can never know."

"They won't from me. Why would I trade what I have with Caleb for this?" She gestured sneeringly at his sparsely furnished flat. "That man worships the ground I walk on." Her tone was mocking, and he felt a surge of anger towards her. She treated his brother like shit. Then a surge of anger for himself. He let her treat his brother like shit. He let her treat him like shit.

"We can't see each other anymore," he said, firmly.

Smiling, she beckoned him over. He resisted before yielding and sitting next to her. She uncrossed her legs and moved to face him. "My Gabriel," she said softly, tracing across his cheeks and around his chin, down his neck and into his shirt with her fingers. His eyes never left hers as she pulled his head towards hers and their lips met again, this time sweet and gentle and full of the promise both of them knew would never come to fruition. It was always like this; the self-loathing, the anger with his lack of control and then the quiet surrender into her embrace. As she stood up and pulled her dress over her head, leaving her tautly naked in front of him, no sign yet of a swelling belly or growing breasts he moaned and pulled her down on top of him, resigning himself once more to the greatest mistake of his life.

Dear you

I know what you did and I will make you pay, you faithless whore. I am your dark storm and I will have vengeance.

You probably think you're safe. You probably think that what you've done will stay in the past. I'm going to make sure it doesn't. I'm going to make you pay.

Maybe you don't think of it at all. I see you and I think that perhaps you've forgotten it. Is that the only way you could live with yourself? If you pretended that it had never happened. Pretended that she had never happened. I can't do that. I can't wipe her out of my memories. She's there every day, every minute in my brain, living with me, reminding me of everything she was and now will never be.

Chapter 24

Vida groaned herself upright and checked her watch again. 5.10am. Probably late enough now that she should just concede defeat and get up. She'd barely slept all night; since getting in from the bar she'd made her bed on the sofa. The thought of getting back into bed with Simon, which he would take as her capitulation, had kept her uncomfortable on the two-seater, propped up on cushions, the fabric itchy beneath her skin. Well, that and the dreams she'd endured all night where ghostly female figures had morphed between Maggie and her own reflection. Tortured faces and tragic eyes.

A hot shower and a hotter cup of coffee brought some semblance of order to her brain. She didn't bother tiptoeing around like she usually would. Let him wake up. Let him suffer the same all-round exhaustion she was feeling right now. Of course, her banging the kitchen cupboards didn't even make him stir. Maybe she should throw his pans around the kitchen instead. How much force would she have to use to shatter his precious Le Creuset casserole dish? The anger still roiled in her stomach as she slammed the front door behind her, and she stepped into the frozen February air. She strode towards her work, barely registering the dampness in the air beyond shrugging the hood of her parka up over her hair. Each footstep rang with either anger or horror, her dual emotional state fuelling the march.

The university was still shadowy and felt abandoned as she swiped her entry card and slipped inside. A young woman was stocking the cafe counter and gave Vida a friendly smile and wave. Vida managed a tight nod in return. The statistics she'd googled the night before ticked through her brain. Over twenty percent of women would be victims of sexual assault in their lifetime. Was that girl one of them? Had she suffered? Would she have suffered? Was Vida just ridiculously naive living in her bubble of safety?

Her office felt reassuringly safe. High in the building, with a lockable door. It had the smell of papers and dust and sunshine streaming through the windows. The heat was dry and cosy, and for a moment, it felt like home. What did that say about her and the life she'd chosen? She felt more at home here, in this messy little office, than she did in her own house with her own husband. She rubbed her eyes and ran a hand through her short hair. This investigation, even though she was only skirting round the edges of the horror, was draining her. She needed to get her focus back.

She logged on to her email and started the trudge through her inbox. Her undergrads needed to spend more time sleeping, less time submitting work at 3am. Absent-mindedly she opened work, reading but not taking anything in. No matter how hard Vida tried to concentrate on the words in front of her, she couldn't keep her mind on the task.

A knock at the door brought her out of her trauma-filled reverie once more. A smiling Jamie peered through the glazed panel on the door. Begrudging him as another obstacle, she waved him in.

She'd tried hard to not give any credence to Caroline's warning. She liked Jamie. Not as anything beyond a research assistant of course, but he was normally a damn good research assistant. Now she felt like maybe her judgement had been clouded. Or worse, her judgement was fine, but other people's opinion of her was now unfairly tainted. The worst thing was, there was very little she could do to convince people of the truth if they just weren't willing to listen. The truth, the whole truth and nothing but the truth was just not enough ammunition against gossip and sly whispers. She wondered if Jamie had heard the rumours.

"Hi," he said, brightly. "I've got those undergrad essays you asked me to initially review. I've popped on first comments and have sorted into rank order. There's some really interesting work here. I like the one who's looking into language of power in police interviews. Maybe the police would let us have a bit of interview recording to analyse."

Given Myfanwy's warning and Hussain's obvious antipathy yesterday, Vida doubted very much that anyone in the police force would be rushing to give her the tapes. She wasn't even sure that her module's place on the police's education unit would be secure after this. And that was the last thing she needed.

"It's a bit early, isn't it?" she asked, looking deliberately at her watch.

His smile faltered slightly, and his head cocked to one side. "Just before eight. Not that early. And besides, I've got some work to do in Leeds later, so I thought I'd come in and talk this through with you." His head switched to the other lean, looking like a dachshund puppy trying to understand its owner. "Do you think the police would let us have interview footage?"

"Possibly," she acknowledged, noncommittally.

"So, do you want me to look at these letters you've got?"

Vida frowned. "We've finished Maggie's investigation, Jamie. I took the findings to the police and they've opened a case into Maggie's rape."

"I didn't mean those ones. These other ones the police have asked you to look at."

Vida frowned. "I didn't realise it was common knowledge."

"You know how it works round here. Someone knows someone who knows something about someone. No secrets." He wagged his finger at her with a cheeky grin.

For the first time, she felt uncomfortable in their relationship. She had always assumed he was nothing more than a friendly research assistant. But what if there was more in it?

"I don't think that it would be appropriate of me to share confidential police information," she said, sternly.

He looked crestfallen. Literally, his crest had fallen. Vida fought a small and equally inappropriate smile as the image of Jamie as a bird of paradise danced through her head. She felt better for her deflation of him though. If anything, it had shown her that, even if no-one else was sure of her feelings for him, she knew he was just her research assistant.

"Why don't you work on your study?" she asked him. He was looking into the impact of Urdu on standard English in different regions of the UK. It was an interesting topic and amongst other things he was building a rich data set for others to draw on.

He shrugged. "I've just got one set of interviews left to do in Exeter. I'm scheduled to go there later next week."

"Have you analysed the data you've got so far?"

"Not really."

He was not making this easy. "Well, why don't you start there. Even if you've not got the Exeter data yet, you've got seven other dialectal centres to start with. The sooner you get started Jamie, the better. I don't want this running into the summer."

"OK. Can I send you the findings as I crunch it? I'd like to get your feedback, in the early stages at least, about whether you think the approach I'm taking is valid."

"Of course," she conceded, feeling magnanimous.

"Great. Thanks." He'd recovered some of his earlier bounce and turned to leave the office with the same light step he'd come in with. "Oh, nearly forgot." He waved a waft of papers at her. "Picked up your post from your cubby."

She took it from him and nodded her goodbye. Not much to look at here. Junk mail maybe, a couple of requests for information, information about an authorship case she was consulting on. There was one envelope that was different though. Smooth, white and high-end, it bore only her name, none of the address. She turned it over, looking for some sign as to how it had been delivered. Nothing.

A prickle of unease touched her neck. Her eyes went to the piles of vitriol on her desk. She shook her head. She was being ridiculous. Sitting back at her desk, she ran her finger under the seal. It came up easily, like it hadn't long been sealed. Carefully, unconsciously mindful of potential trace evidence, she pulled the contents out. It was a single side of printed text. Plain black serif font, double spaced. She started to read. It didn't take long for her to recognise her own words. It was the transcript of a video she'd done for a Mooc course the university had signed her up to deliver. An Introduction to Forensic Linguistics. Much of it mirrored the introduction she did for the police course, but with less focus on police procedure. Four words had been highlighted in pink in the middle of the page. 'Justice must be served.' At the bottom of the sheet, in the same pink highlighter, but in block capitals it read 'Let it be served.'

Vida's brow wrinkled. It felt like a threat. It didn't read like a threat. There was nothing particularly ominous about the words and there was nothing particularly sinister that could be read into someone accessing a freely available online resource about her. So why did it feel like a threat?

She studied the envelope again, and looked inside to see if there was anything else. Nothing. She pushed her chair round and looked out of the window, sighing hard. Was she being ridiculous? But why else would someone send her this unless they wanted her to feel threatened.

Another knock at the door caused her to spin round, her heart beating faster. Now she was definitely being ridiculous. Threatening people didn't knock politely on the door.

"Caroline," she smiled, letting the breath out that she'd been holding despite her acknowledgement of silliness. "Twice in two days. I'm a lucky girl."

"I just thought I'd pop in and bring you these. Great accompaniment to dead people tea." She offered Vida a packet of lemon thins.

Vida looked at her sceptically, taking the proffered biscuits nevertheless. "I don't think you came all this way, to this hideous example of brutalist building that you loathe so much, to bring me biscuits. I don't need feeding up."

"No, you got me," Caroline said, flopping into the armchair that sat in the corner of the office. "I did want to give you the biscuits. I picked them up at Hardwick Hall at the weekend and meant to give them to you the other day. Knew they're one of your favourites."

"They are," Vida said. "And nice distraction technique. But what are you doing here?"

"I just wanted to check on you." She leaned forward. "After yesterday, I mean. You seemed pretty upset. And then went haring off back to those girls."

"You told me to."

"I know. But then I thought maybe I shouldn't have. You're right to worry, Vida. This isn't our everyday life."

"It just got even less every day," Vida said. "Look." She gave the letter to Caroline. "What do you make of that? It's a printout of an online video transcript I've done."

"Is this all there is?"

"Yes," Vida confirmed.

Caroline looked up with what Vida took to be her attempt at a reassuring smile, but there was worry behind her eyes. "Good job I bought those biscuits up. Looks like we might be needing them."

Vida opened the packet and offered her one, before taking one for herself. "So, what do you think?"

"Well, I don't know," Caroline admitted, after taking a bite of her biscuit. "It doesn't look like anything really. I'm sure it's fine."

"That's why we broke out the biscuits?" Vida said, wryly.

"Well, I was taken aback, I supposed. But there's nothing really threatening here. And anyway, what would they be threatening you about?"

"The Maggie thing? These new letters?"

"But you're trying to do justice," Caroline pointed out. "Surely that means you should keep doing what you're doing."

Caro was right. Vida hadn't considered it in that light. Maybe it was just encouraging her to keep going. It didn't feel like that though. "What if it's not?" she asked, unable to keep the fear out of her voice.

A sharp knock on the open door caught both the women's attention and eyes swung to the doorway. It was like Kings Cross in here this morning. Vida blushed as she recognised the stern DI Slater. How long had he been standing there for? How much had he heard? Probably enough to tell that she was a woman on the edge.

"Can we help you?" asked Caroline, her voice a little sharp.

"DI Slater," he said, moving forward without waiting for an invite. "I need to take Dr Henrikson with me."

Panic rose in Vida's throat. She hadn't been doing anything untoward at the scene yesterday. Nothing that could constitute interfering with an investigation or anything. It was just a coincidence that her research had taken her there. "I haven't done anything wrong," she stammered.

Slater frowned. "No," he said. "I'm here to take you with me to see the Donaldsons. We need to tell them about the developments in their daughter's case and I thought you might appreciate being there. After all, it was your research that has led us here. Unless you've already informed them?" His tone was brusque.

"God, no," Vida said. "I've been struggling all night with how I'm going to tell them the findings of my research."

"Well then. Let's go."

"Hang on a minute," intervened Caroline. "You can't just come in here and expect her to drop everything like that and set off with you. She has responsibilities."

Vida winced at the headmistress tone in Caroline's voice, while simultaneously appreciating her friend sticking up for her. In truth, she wasn't certain she really wanted to go with him. Not to see the Donaldsons anyway. She didn't like his hard tone and the way he dismissed her earlier; she didn't really want to be there to see the Donaldsons' life shattered again.

"I could go alone later."

Slater shook his head imperiously. "No, it must be a representative from the police. I was the SIO on her suicide and so I should be doing it now." That was a lot of deontic modality in those sentences Vida thought. A great sense of duty. "I would also appreciate you looking at another text we found yesterday." He met her eyes meaningfully. "At the scene that you seemed to have followed us to."

"I didn't follow you," protested Vida. "I found that address on my own. It was just a coincidence," she repeated, vocalising her earlier belief.

"Hmm," he said, sounding unconvinced. "Well, perhaps you would be able to tell me more about how exactly this coincidence brought you to the same street as a murder investigation." In the same way Caroline's eyes had interrogated her earlier, Slater now refused to yield, his stare reaching into her and uncovering all the untruths and minor fibs she had ever concealed.

Caroline coughed deliberately and Vida looked at her. Vida met Caroline's raised eyebrows with a wan smile. "I'll be okay, Caro. Perhaps we can continue this later."

Again, the traction beam of her friend's look stripped her bare. She hadn't realised she could feel so emotionally and physically laid bare by the pure power of competing stares. "Really," Vida said, firmly. Breaking away, she collected her belongings, sliding the photocopied documents back into their file, along with the letter she'd received this morning. "After you, DI Slater. Shut the door behind you please, Caro, when you go." Head held high, belying the fact she felt like she was potentially marching herself straight into the lion's den, she swept out of the room.

Slater stopped her as she walked mindlessly down the stairs. "Before we go, I'd like you to have a look at this letter please."

"I thought we were going to the Donaldsons?"

"Well, we are, but I'd like you to look at this first. It doesn't need to be in any great detail, but I just want to know if this letter could be connected to one of Kitty's letter writers?" He dug around in a file wallet clasped to his side and brought out another photocopied sheet.

"Why couldn't you ask me this in my office? It's a lot more comfortable than on the stairs."

"It's confidential," he said. "I didn't want anyone watching what you were doing. This is an active murder investigation; I can't have all the world knowing everything."

Vida was about to protest on her friend's behalf but then realised that Slater was probably right. Gossip could easily be Caro's middle name. She took the photocopy and scanned it quickly. "I don't know," she said, shrugging. "There's not much to go on."

"I know. But can you, you know just get a sense or something?"

She studied him. There was a note of desperate urgency in him. Something has lit a rocket under his bum since yesterday. "Well, maybe yes then," she conceded. "I think this is probably written by one of the writers of Kitty's letters. But without sitting down and following the data properly, that's just an instinctive reaction."

Slater nodded, relief on his face. "Would you be able to tell for certain?"

"Not with only one alternative sample, but with a degree of certainty yes. I can do that."

He seemed like he wanted to say something else and she waited for him to spit it out. "I think the case yesterday is connected to Kitty's murder," he said, finally.

"And other people don't?" She read between the lines from the emphasis he'd put on the personal pronoun.

"No. The two deaths look quite different, but... I don't know. They feel the same to me, even if they are different. Does that make any sense?" There was doubt now in his eyes as he looked at her. It made a change from his normal close expression.

"Yes," she said, softly. "Sometimes when I'm looking at texts that are supposed to be from different people, with completely different features on the surface, I can see that really they've got the same author. Before I even really study anything. It's just a gut feeling."

He cocked his head to one side, appraising her. "I don't believe in gut feelings," he said, nodding, before pushing past her and carrying on downstairs. She breathed one of her imbued-with-patience sighs, fought the inclination to ignore his assumed obedience and return to her office, and carried on behind him. At the bottom, he turned suddenly. She bumped into him.

"Sorry," she started.

"No, sorry. My fault," he said. His eyes were cast down, obviously unaccustomed to apologising. "I just wanted to say, well, thank you."

"For what?"

"The text message you sent me yesterday. It gave us just what we needed to put pressure on Maggie's rapist. We caught him, Dr Henrikson." He stared at her. She wasn't sure how she was supposed to be reacting. An immediate relief and feeling of victory was followed swiftly by the bitter memory of Maggie's death. She'd never know the justice they'd sought for her. He nodded, apparently acknowledging her conflicted emotions. He was pure efficiency once more as he turned on his heel and strode out of the door, leaving her to scamper behind him.

Chapter 25

The car was silent. Occasionally, Slater would sneak a look at Vida beside him, but she was always staring resolutely out of the window, obviously determined to not engage in conversation with him. He'd occasionally heard little sighs and wondered whether he was supposed to interpret these, but her lips had remained tightly closed. He knew he wasn't a good conversationalist himself; not enough outside interests and a life focussed on his job made his small-talk rather boring. Every minute they drew closer to the Donaldsons', he was also questioning the wisdom of his actions. This was not proper police procedure. He shouldn't have asked a civilian to accompany him. In fact, even paying a visit to the Donaldsons was not proper police procedure. He should have just left that to whichever police officer was picking up the rape case. For some reason though, he didn't feel like he could just leave it there. Whether it had been Dr Henrikson's impassioned plea, or the horrible video, he wasn't sure. But something had stirred something in him.

"She's obviously involved," he murmured to himself.

"Pardon?"

"Sorry. I wasn't talking to you. I wasn't really talking to anyone."

"Okay."

They fell back to silence.

"It's just... I'm not really sure why I'm taking you to the Donaldsons or even going at all," he admitted.

She huffed. "You've taken me out here, marching into my office like the gestapo and dragging me out of there like I was a criminal and you don't even know why."

"I hardly dragged you," he said.

"Not literally now, but metaphorically. I don't get police officers appearing at my place every day. Well, I didn't used to," she muttered.

He paused. "Well, I'm sorry if you felt like that."

She huffed again. "What a non-apology. That's such a male thing to do. Apologise but not for actually what you've done, only for someone's misinterpretation of event. What about being sorry for dragging me out of there like I was a criminal."

"Fine," he snapped. "I'm sorry I dragged you out of there like you were a criminal." She was bloody infuriating.

"Hmm."

"Hmm? Is that it? And anyway, I didn't drag you out of there like you were a criminal. That's why I can't apologise for it. I just asked you to come with me."

"You don't get it." She frowned at him. "I've never had any dealings with the police before. Well, outside of the classroom. And suddenly, there are police everywhere I go. Worse than that! It's you, everywhere I go."

"That does lead me onto an interesting question."

"Don't bother," she said, holding up her hand. "I know what you're going to ask. And fine, I'll tell you. I'd've told you anyway. You didn't have to drag me out here."

"Bloody hell. Do not start on that again. I did not bloody drag you out here. If had bloody dragged you out here, you would bloody well know it. I promise you that." His fingers drummed angrily on the steering wheel, teeth clenched together. The rage was obvious bubbling too close to the surface.

"Don't threaten me!" Her voice rose.

"Well, stop bloody accusing me of something I didn't bloody well do!"

The car fell quiet again. Bloody woman. He mentally scolded himself for thinking that too. He was proud of his feminist leanings, proud to be a supporter of women's rights. Bloody Vida Henrikson, he changed it to in his head. She got under his skin for some reason. Probably all her pompous professoring and arrogant know-it-all attitude.

"Did you know that the etymology of bloody as a swear word isn't really known."

"Did I know that something isn't known?" he asked, exasperated.

She scowled at him; he could feel it burning his cheek despite not looking at her. "It's been used since 1676 at least and they think perhaps it evolved from the way the aristocracy, the young bloods if you like, would behave."

"Is that an apology?"

"No," she said firmly. "I was just sharing a little fact that I thought you might find interesting."

"It wasn't," he said, bluntly.

229

"Fine. I apologise for accusing you of something you didn't do. I was trying to explain that I've not been involved with the police before and I suppose I find it a bit frightening. That makes me sound silly, but it's true. I've encountered more horrible things this week than in my entire life and they just keep coming."

"OK. And I am sorry if I made you feel threatened." He congratulated himself on the mature and calm plateau they seem to have reached. Unclenching his jaw, he rolled his shoulders to try and release the tension he stored there.

"You want to know what I was doing at the house yesterday."

"The question had occurred. Either you're some sort of detecting genius who is able to get to a scene before the police, or you're incredibly prone to stumbling into criminal matters... or perhaps you're the murderer."

"Wow!" she said, exhaling loudly. "I never even thought of that. Well, I wouldn't, would I? Not being the type of person to be a murderer, of course it didn't cross my mind that you might think I was the murderer."

"There isn't a type of person to be a murderer," Slater said, softly. "In my experience, it could be anyone, for any kind of reason."

"Well, I'm not. The murderer I mean. I don't think I'm the type either, no matter what you say."

His jaw went again. His dentist would have a lot to say about this. "No matter what I say? It's my bloody job. I know what I'm bloody talking about."

"There you go with the bloodies again."

He breathed out, hard. It was a good job he was driving. He might have proven himself to be the type of person to be a murderer by throttling her in a minute. "Look, I don't really think you are the murderer. I can't exclude you, but I can't see any motive at the minute."

"I've probably got an alibi too," she offered.

"Probably. That wasn't my point though." She was extremely efficient at distracting him from what he was trying to do. A woman who not only understood the English language but could use it as a weapon too was clearly a dangerous combination. "My point is," he said, carefully, "that you seem to keep popping up in unlikely places. Finding the film of Maggie was one thing, but then I find you at the scene of a murder?"

"I didn't find the film," she pointed out. "Someone sent it to me."

He fought the urge to drive the car at the nearest lamppost in frustration. "Okay," he said, trying to strike a picture of controlled cool. "Someone sent you the film. Would you be so kind as to tell me how that led to you being at the scene of a murder this morning?"

She filled him in.

"So, the girls told you about the address?" he asked, trying to disguise his grudging admiration. He'd interviewed the girls several times and had never got anywhere close to any useful information.

Maybe she sensed that, as her next words were appeasing. "I think it was just right time, right place.

Perhaps because I'm not police too, they felt less threatened by me?"

He bristled at the suggestion that he was threatening, but then nodded, begrudgingly. He had to be threatening; it was part of his police officer role. But it didn't always work for the best.

"So, now I've shared mine, will you explain why you're taking me with you on this mission of shouldn't really? Are you hoping that my presence will butter the Donaldsons up a bit? That they'll be more forgiving if I'm there? The equivalent of dumping someone in public so that they won't make a scene?" Her voice was growing higher pitched again. "Well, let me tell you; I am more than capable of making a scene in public!"

"I don't doubt it," he said, wryly. He could picture it. She wasn't that far of the mark really though, and he didn't want to antagonise her. He was hoping that her presence would help defuse any potential anger the Donaldsons were feeling. Not that their anger would be justified. He'd done the best job he could, working with the limited facts that he had been given. They could hardly blame him for the crisis of confidence that had led to the girls blurting all their secrets to Vida. "I was just thinking that I want you to be able to take credit for the opening of the new investigation. It's thanks to your relentless search for the truth that we can finally answer the questions surrounding Maggie's death." Was that preaching too much? Would she read insincerity in his words? Even though he knew that it was the truth, to his shame.

It didn't seem like he'd gone too far though, and as they pulled into the Donaldsons' drive, she fell back into silence. Drawing the car to a stop, he looked over after her. Her knuckles were white, and she looked pained.

"Are you alright?"

"How are we... I mean, how am I going to tell them what their daughter went through. How can I possibly explain to them what's on that video?"

"You don't," he said, simply. "Just be there to answer their questions. Let me talk to them."

He'd not seen the Donaldsons since the inquest a few weeks ago, but he was shocked by the changes that had been wrought in Jane. She looked more wan than ever, almost skeletal as she greeted them in the doorway. While they'd been looking for answers, fighting for their daughter, despite the physical signs of grief, her eyes had burned with white energy. Now they were dull.

"Have you found something?" Jane Donaldson's eyes flickered between the two.

"Can we come in?"

Jane hesitated. Slater thought that she must be stuck in some sort of Schroedingen nightmare; she probably had been since the first knock at the door over a year ago. To be torn between wanting to know for sure but also not wanting to know because knowledge bought certainty and pain. His mind flickered briefly to Sabryne and the baby. He was convinced that that was a cat that needed to stay firmly in its box. There was no benefit to checking its vital signs.

He noticed Vida frowning at him and realised he must look a bit spaced out. He turned a gentle, non-threatening smile onto Jane. "We have news, Dr Donaldson, to give you both."

Still, she hesitated. But finally, she gave a virtually imperceptible nod and led them through to the kitchen. Slater hadn't been here since he'd delivered the news to the Donaldsons that they considered their daughter's death to be a case of suicide. He could still see the horror on their faces and their certainty that there must have been something that he missed, something that would account for how their perfect daughter had died. They had been right though, and he felt ashamed of the fact that if they hadn't kept pushing to find the truth, they would never have uncovered what had happened to Maggie and her rapists might have got away with it. They still might, he knew, but at least the odds were slightly more stacked against them now.

"Peter?" Jane called up the stairs, her voice wavering. She gestured towards the table for Slater and Vida and they sat down. Jane joined them and they sat in silence, waiting for Peter Donaldson to emerge. Slater looked around the kitchen; it was virtually identical to the one he had been in last year, but the pictures of and references to Maggie were now time-capsules. Her exam timetable pinned on the fridge, destined to be unfollowed. A trio of tickets to a play at the Crucible dated after Maggie's death, destined to be unwatched. He shivered. It was like a modern mausoleum. Maybe now he'd got some answers, some explanation for them, they'd be able to move on and start rebuilding their lives.

They all looked round as Peter came down. Slater stood up, wincing as the chair screeched along the kitchen floor. "Mr Donaldson."

Peter nodded curtly before standing behind his wife, his hands hovering over her shoulders as though wanting to offer comfort but being afraid to do it.

Slater sat back into the chair, lifting and dragging it in this time to avoid the noise. "We've got some news. About Maggie. About what happened to her."

Peter Donaldson's hands finally sank on to his wife's shoulders and she reached up and gripped one of them. They were ready to open the box.

Chapter 26

Vida had to admit that despite DI Slater's brusqueness in dealing with her, his approach to the Donaldsons was spot on. His approach was calm and measured. He laid out the facts for them, keeping the details light but giving them the information they needed. Vida found her own role reduced to supportive nods and offering a tissue as the Donaldsons huddled together, tossed together in a storm once more but this time with an end in sight. They'd taken the news in very different ways; Peter Donaldson had been angry, his face furious whereas Jane had looked faint with horror. Both had looked gratefully at Vida though when Slater had told them about the part she'd played in getting the new case open. It had made her feel a bit sick; like she was profiting from uncovering such a horrible truth. But by the end, while there was pain still in their expressions, there was also relief. The inexplicable had become explained and with it, their hearts settled just a little bit.

A phone-call summoning them elsewhere interrupted their meeting, but in truth there was nothing else that either she or Slater could offer them. She had confirmed that Maggie had written the letters and Slater had confirmed that her attackers would face long sentences for rape. It wasn't enough, but it was all there was. And when was the right time to leave people whose world you'd just shattered?

Vida wasn't sure what the phone-call had been about. Slater had excused himself and left the room, his voice low, his face dark, and all he'd told her was that he needed to stop off to see someone he knew because she had information for him. The hairdresser's salon they'd pulled up in front of was the kind of place that terrified Vida for its glamorous women and complicated menu of highlights and lowlights. Who was she kidding? All hairdressers petrified her for their unutterable glamour and ability to blow-dry their own hair without getting the brush tangled in it. This one, Jessie's, had made her feel nauseous as soon as they stopped. It was obviously the kind of place where the clientele never changed; generations and generations of the same families had been coming here for decades. They all knew each other. They all loved each other. And they all viewed outsiders with suspicion.

Slater obviously didn't have any of the same qualms. Perhaps he was part of these generations. The way he greeted the woman in the doorway suggested knowledge, but Vida couldn't help noticing that the paralinguistic features were a little skewed from how one might normally greet a friend. Slater had told her not to move, but she leaned forward, curious to see what was happening.

The woman in the doorway was most definitely glamorous and almost definitely could blow dry her own hair. It was a hard glamour though; she was edges and lines like a fine cut diamond. She met Slater with a kiss of brightly coloured lips, but Vida noticed that Slater averted his mouth at the last minute to land her on his cheek instead. The woman gripped the tops of his arms tightly, and he struggled slightly to bring his hand up to wipe the smear of lipstick from his cheek. Her eyes narrowed leaving Vida in no doubt that she was the kind of woman who would batter you to death with a stiletto if you bumped her drink in a club.

Suddenly, the woman looked over Slater's shoulder and caught Vida looking at them. Vida moved back quickly. It would be mortifying to be seen spying on them. Her heart pounded as she pushed herself back into her seat, aiming for invisibility.

When she dared to look again, the hairdresser's doorway was empty, the door shut firmly. She wished she'd asked Slater to leave the engine running, or the car keys in so she could start it herself at any rate. Once again she found herself trapped in a freezing cold car in the bitterest winter the city had known in ten years. This field work was playing havoc with her comfort levels. She'd got no idea how long Slater was going to be. She pulled her coat tight around her and then reached back for the file of photocopied letters in the back seat. Perhaps keeping her brain occupied would override how cold she was feeling. Her eyes caught on the letter she'd received, but she slid it back out of sight. She couldn't think about that now.

She roughly sorted the letters into different groupings. It was a hasty, gut reaction rather than the detailed analysis that would follow and prove, but she'd been able to determine that there were three senders of regular mail, based on their greetings and signoffs, and then a few one-offs. Of the three regular senders, two favoured hand-written notes whereas the last opted for typewritten communiques. Given that the letter found at the second murder scene was also typewritten, she'd start there. She flicked quickly to the picture of the letter they'd found at the scene of the second murder. Why the killer had left a letter this time? If it was the same killer. What did the killer hope to gain by signposting the connection?

The letter wasn't very long. If it was a match to one of the others she'd already got, it was much shorter than them.

I know what you did and I have made you pay, you fornicator. I am your dark storm and I will have vengeance. Your punishment will be witnessed by a party of believers. I took your future, the way you took hers. Everyone shall taste death. The Messengers are waiting to take you beyond to taste the penalty of burning.

I promise.

Some of the language was already reminiscent of one of the other writers she'd read. She wasn't religious herself but could recognise the language of someone who was. Believers, fornicator, vengeance all sounded like they'd been lifted from the nearest Bible. She pulled out a notebook from her handbag and, resting it on her knee, jotted down some of the key terms. The declarative sentence at the end was identical to the one set of letters she'd been particularly interested in. Again, why had the killer signposted themselves in this way? They'd made it really easy to connect the dots. Perhaps they wanted the police to connect the dots. But why would you want to make it easier for the police to solve the murders? There must be a point to it all.

A rap at the window made her jump, the papers scattering into the footwell. Slater pulled open her door and the cold wind immediately rushed in, further rippling all the pieces of paper around her. She scowled at him.

"Sorry, didn't mean to startle you. I need you inside."

"Need me?"

"Yes." There was still no please but he did pull the door open further for her. She rolled her eyes, gathered the papers back into the file and then got out. He locked the car and then marched her into the salon. Inside, it was everything that she'd feared; wall to wall mirrors and the kind of equipment that brought her out in a rash. Wefts, weaves and hair extensions hung from racks on the wall, looking to Vida like the scalps of victims. Slater spoke quickly to the woman she'd seen outside; Vida was surprised by the rhythmic cadence of his voice. The rise and fall of a Jamaican lilt now softened his Sheffield accent. It was fascinating really. She'd expected his accent to diverge. He was such an uptight ninny that she'd thought he'd maybe ham up a received pronunciation element to his voice. Instead, he'd converged towards the woman's accent. She must be important to him, despite the awkward doorway encounter earlier. Vida wondered if he was aware of it. She'd once dated a man who adopted the accent of every county and country they visited, even though he'd never visited before. It was a strategy that had limited success and in some places had resulted in the necessity of a quick exit from the pub they were in. Some of the locals appreciated his effort, most of them felt like they were being mocked. She tried to avoid staring at the woman, but the woman barely seemed to register Vida watching her. She was obviously used to the attention.

"This is Sabryne," Slater said. Sabryne flashed Vida a cold smile. "She runs this salon."

"This is Anna," Sabryne continued, taking over. She gestured to a petite and wan blonde girl in the corner. Age was indeterminate but whether fifteen or fifty, pain hung exhaustedly in her face. "She has information about a case you're working on."

She was talking directly to Vida. "What case? I'm not a policeman." Vida looked questioningly at Slater.

"She know that. Both us know that. But she want talk to a woman. She won't talk to no man." Sabryne interjected again. "She got information about that Kitty Wakelin woman. Only she weren't Kitty when she knew her."

"Is this alright?" Vida asked Slater directly. It seemed that Sabryne was about to answer but he quelled her quickly with a look. "Shouldn't we wait for a proper police officer? There must be someone you can ask?"

"It's not perfect, but it's time-sensitive. This killer is out there and might strike again. I can't afford to wait. And she won't sign a statement or anything anyway so it's the best we can do."

"What do you want me to do?"

"Just listen. I'll be listening too but from behind this curtain." Vida turned and noticed the kind of beaded curtain she thought didn't exist anymore. "Anna just doesn't want to see a man."

"Why doesn't she tell Sabryne?"

Sabryne sighed dramatically. "What you not getting about this, Doctor," she said with disdain. "She already tell me. Now Gabriel," her tongue caressed his name, "wants the story in his own ears. He said you ask Anna the questions and he would only listen."

Vida remained unconvinced. "How will this help?"

"You a maddening woman," said Sabryne, hand on jutting hip. "It will help."

"Fine," Vida conceded.

"At last. Now sit here." Sabryne wheeled her an uncomfortable looking stool over and pushed her down on it. Anna sat huddled in a client chair. Vida perched obediently and then shot alarmed eyes at Slater. He merely shrugged, turned and disappeared behind the curtain.

Feeling too much like Alice to contemplate, Vida turned back to look at the girl in front of her. Now Vida could see better, she realised that the girl was older than she'd first thought, mid-twenties perhaps rather than the teen she'd first taken her for. The close angle didn't make her look any the more healthy though; the girl was gaunt with angular cheekbones and hair that looked like it'd been messed with a few too many times. She observed Vida now, large grey pools that seemed to both encourage and rebuke in the same gaze.

"So, Anna," Vida began, cursing Slater for putting her here and cursing herself for going along with it so meekly. She should have refused to get out of the car.

Refused to go along with this ridiculous scenario. Refused to ever get involved. Refused to work with this pompous and domineering idiot; every time he showed a flash of humanity, he would undo it ten seconds later by being a complete boor. But, as her mother would always tell her with her soft Spanish consonants, the road to good intentions was paved with should've's. Whatever that meant. She sighed softly. "Will you tell me your story?"

For what felt like an eternity to Vida, they sat in silence, contemplating each other. She could hear Slater shifting around behind the curtain. Some covert operative he'd make. She was just about to prompt the woman again when she started speaking.

"I came to England when I was thirteen," she began. Her voice was barely above a whisper, but Vida could hear an Eastern European accent. As though, hearing Vida's thoughts, she continued, "I moved from Hungary when my mother met an English man and set up a home here with him. She had been working here for a few years, maybe since I was seven or so, and we had been apart for a long time. I lived with my grandparents in the country outside Debrecen. It was very remote?" The rising intonation made it sound like a question, so Vida nodded supportively. Anna's voice had become stronger as she continued, her story unfolding almost by itself.

"It was a nice life I had, with my grandparents. But I missed my mother and when she sent for me, I wanted to come. I was looking forward to seeing her and making up for all the time that we had missed. And people had told me some wonderful things about England and all the opportunities that waited for us. But when I got here I found out that it was all a lie. There is nothing wonderful about this country." She cast a guilty look at where Sabryne and Slater were standing, their shadows looming.

"Don't worry," Vida reassured her, startled almost by the sound of her own voice. It felt like talking in the library for a minute and she felt as though someone would scold her. Probably Mr Ego hiding in the back. "Nobody thinks this country is perfect. But why was it so bad for you?"

"My family in Hungary had money. We had a farm and a house and there was so much land around us. We owned all the land we could see. And I was free. Here, we lived in a tiny house in the middle of the city, surrounded by dirt and dust and so many people. I was not free. My mother had forgotten that I was now thirteen and still treated me like I was seven. I was not allowed out on my own and she had to know where I was all the time. This was not so she could spend time with me though. I was made to sit in my bedroom. Only it was not my bedroom. My bedroom was big and bright and had colours on the walls. This was like a prison room," she spat the words bitterly. "The house was not the worst though. I had spent many years learning English but still they were cruel because of my accent and the way I spoke."

"Who's they?" asked Vida. "Other children?"

Anna's lips tightened. "Yes, but not at first. It was my mother and her husband. They made me repeat words until I had the same accent as him. Over and over and over. The children, they laughed too but I did not mind that. That is what we do, young people. We attack those who are different."

"Your English is very good now," offered Vida, hoping to salve the woman's distress but merely earning a derisive snort.

"I hope so. For months I was drilled like this. Say sausages," she said, putting on an RP accent, "and I would. And the funny thing is that, at first, I thought that was the worst bit. But the worst bit was when they stopped caring. Eventually they got bored of training this human parrot and I was just ignored. My mother lost interest. She fell pregnant with his baby and I became not part of her family."

"Couldn't you go back home?" Vida asked.

"No. She did not love me, but she did not want to bring shame on herself. She would pretend she was this perfect mother and everyone believed it. If she had sent me home, she would have proved to everyone that she didn't really care about me at all and they would have talked about her."

"You must have been terribly lonely." Vida wanted to reach forward and touch the woman's knee, offer her some human comfort, but she wasn't sure it would be appreciated.

"I was, at first. But then again, the worst thing stops being the worst thing and just becomes the normal thing. I got used to it, to being ignored. I got very good at being invisible, at home and at school. I think if you showed a picture of me to my classmates now, none of them would even remember my name." She stopped suddenly and looked at Vida with eyes full of appeal. "I want you to understand that the next bit of my story, which sounds so horrible, it didn't feel like that at the time. When I was living it, it was the most loved I'd ever felt. I know that it was wrong. I know that they took advantage of me and my loneliness but sometimes I think it was worth it."

"Tell me," Vida urged, this time laying a hand on Anna's leg.

"I was maybe in Year 9 at school. No-one saw me. I heard about this girl in Year 11. She is called Katie and I cannot describe how magical she seemed to me." She gave a bitter laugh. "I know now that it was not magic that made her like she was; it was nothing better than money. But then...when a girl like that notices you, it's like you have won the lottery." She appraised Vida with cool eyes. "Perhaps you know what it is like to feel that way."

Vida didn't ask whether she meant the invisibility or the lottery, but tugged her top down over her middle and tried not to scowl. It was a fair call, in truth. The invisibility bit anyway. Simon sometimes felt like her lottery; she wasn't so shallow so as to be attracted purely by his good looks, but it had made an impression on her that someone like him might be interested in someone like her.

Anna nibbled her fingernails before continuing. "She saw me, she knew my name and it was like my world was better. At first, she would just talk to me at school. But then she would invite me to go to the park or the shops with her after school. I didn't have any money, but she taught me how to steal things." Both Anna's and Vida's eyes flicked to where Slater stood, looming behind the bead curtain but there was no movement. He'd obviously mastered the ability to stand still and just listen now. It was an underrated skill in Vida's book, especially amongst men. "First just sweets, but then we moved onto lipstick and eyeshadow. And then I would start to wear what I'd stole. And it wasn't just makeup, then it was clothes."

"Didn't you get caught?"

"Not me. I think afterwards... after I'd gone I mean, I heard that Katie had been caught."

"And didn't anyone notice you had all this new stuff?"

"Who would notice? My mother was wrapped up in her new family. I didn't have any friends. The teachers at school couldn't care less. I could have walked around with no clothes at all and I don't think anyone would have seen me. Katie always noticed though. She would say how pretty I looked." She stopped talking and looked sickened. "I tell you all this now and I feel so angry with myself. How did I not see what was happening?"

Vida's heart began to fracture. It was easy to see the child Anna must have been and there was a feeling of inevitability over what she was being told. You couldn't be a present member of society at the moment and not know what had been going on around the country. "You were a child, Anna. It was not for you to see what was happening. Those adults around you should have seen. I'm so sorry that they didn't."

"I was not stupid. I could have known," Anna said, angrily.

"It's not a matter of stupidity, Anna. You were vulnerable and they took advantage of that."

"It is kind of you to say so, but I know it is not true. They say it is my fault, and I know it is," she said, firmly.

"Who's they?" Vida asked.

"Everyone. The police, the people in the newspapers, my mother."

Vida's fists clenched as she thought about how innocent and unprotected Anna must have been as a thirteen-year-old. How could anyone blame a child for what had happened to them?

"It's okay," Anna said, reassuring Vida. "It was bad. But now it is better. I do not talk to my mother anymore and Sabryne has helped me find a job and a home." Vida tried to hide her surprise; she hadn't expected the hard-nosed woman she'd been introduced to to be as caring as she was being painted. Anna must have noticed. "She is much softer than she pretends," she said, sending a friendly smile towards the back area. "And she has helped me more than anyone else. That is why I am telling you this today. She says a friend of hers needs some information. That it will do me good to share my story and help him."

Vida nodded. "Thank you."

Chapter 27

Slater looked at Sabryne, who was studiously avoiding his gaze and keeping her eyes on Anna. He wanted to ask her whether she'd meant that. Was he really a friend? He'd never thought before about how she might view their relationship. The assumption was that she thought she was using him to get one over on his brother. It suited him to imagine that actually he was using her for the same reason. Hearing himself labelled as a friend he couldn't tell whether he was hurt, flattered or indifferent to it.

Sabryne was giving him nothing back though and he filed the questions at the back of his mind, turning his attention back to Anna and Vida in the main salon. He was grudgingly admiring of how Vida was handling the woman. He could understand why the girls had felt able to confide in her. There was something warm and welcoming about her; perhaps it was the fact she was so imperfect that people were at ease with her. She wasn't anyone to compete with and it felt like she would never judge you. Just nod, maybe a small head tilt and encourage you to continue in a soft voice. As soon as the positive thought had crossed his mind though, he met it with a self-rebuke. This kind of interview was going to lead to nothing but trouble. He needed to get it formalised.

Anna continued her story and Slater looked at Vida looking at Anna. "I was stealing, and I was wearing what I stole. It was not me, but Katie said how nice I looked in these short skirts and big eyelashes. I would have done anything for her, and the praise made me feel very happy.

Then she started dropping these names into conversation I thought they were boys that she knew. I am a girl; I liked the idea that a boy might like me. She kept saying that they couldn't wait to meet me. She would tell me they would be somewhere, and I would go but then they would not be there for some reason or another and I would feel disappointed." Anna gathered her skirt into her fingers and kneaded it nervously. "She was very clever. I was wanting so much to meet these boys that I did not really notice that they were men. And if I did notice, I was flattered that grown men would show an interest in a skinny nobody like me. They would take us for rides in their taxis. Sometimes they would ask for a kiss. I did not like it but it made me feel like I was wanted and so I did it. Then after a few weeks, I was picked up and Katie was not with them. I felt afraid but I told myself that these men were friends, and they would not hurt me. I was wrong." The tenor of her voice had changed and now all emotion had been stripped from it. Slater clenched his jaw together, bracing himself for what he knew must be to come. It was an uncomfortable feeling too because he had the rising of excitement of finally finding a motive for Kitty's murder. He was glad he was behind the curtain now and out of sight because he would have hated it if Anna could see the thrill in him of the answers finally arriving.

"They took me to a house. There were other men there. I became very frightened and told them that I wanted to leave. They laughed and said that I was theirs now. They owned me, they said. Then they held me down and they had sex with me. Not just one man but many. All of them. At first, I tried to fight them, even though they were stronger than me. But then I realised I could not stop it and I lay there. Afterwards I could not move. They ignored me, like I was just a thing, a toy that they had used. I heard them though and they said that Katie had been paid triple money for me because I was a virgin. And then I realised what she was. I thought she had been my friend. Even after this had happened, I thought that she had been tricked by these men. Then I knew that it was I who had been tricked. By her."

"How could she?" Vida burst out.

The younger woman looked at her and Vida recoiled slightly. Slater wondered what she'd read in Anna's gaze. "I cannot answer that question. I know I was not the first and not the last. She made lots of money selling us to these men."

"What happened afterwards?"

"One of the men told me it was time to leave. He gave me some baby wipes to clean up with and then threw me out. I walked home. My mother had not noticed I had been gone and scolded me for looking so awful when I got home." She began to softly cry, but when she looked up, it was anger that glowed in her eyes. "I see her in the newspapers, and hear her singing on the radio and she has everything. Now she is this Kitty singer. And I am still nobody. Nothing."

There was a sudden clatter of the curtain beads and Sabryne hurried out from the hide before Slater could stop her. "That's enough now. You don't need to hear more."

She rushed to Anna's side, wrapping an arm around her. "You are not nothing."

Slater would have liked to have heard more, but he didn't feel capable of challenging Sabryne's insistence that it had gone far enough.

"That was really helpful," Slater said, slipping the curtain back neatly behind him. "Thank you Anna, for telling it to Vida. Can you remember anything else about the men involved?"

Sabryne looked like she might slap him. "No questions, Gabriel. That was the agreement. Anna has told you what she knows."

Slater grimaced. "Well, if you do want to give us any more details Anna, please just call me. It could really help other girls like you. Any time." He slipped out a white business card. "Anything at all. Even if you think it's not important."

Reluctantly, Anna took the card and tucked it into a breast pocket on her shirt. He smiled at her, hoping it was encouraging and thankful rather than threatening. He needed her to take this further. Needed her to make it more than just hearsay and proposition. Vida clasped her hands and hurriedly wrote her own number on a receipt she found in her pocket. She murmured something to Anna, but he couldn't make the words out. He led Vida back out to the car, avoiding Sabryne's farewell kiss and piercing stare.

Vida seemed sombre in the car and for a moment he felt a pang of guilt. While he'd been admiring her easy way with the witnesses, she'd been hearing the sort of story you normally only read about in the newspaper. It was different when it was being told directly to you, he knew. It made you a part of the story in a way that just reading about it in the paper never did.

"Was there a point to that?" she asked, once they were underway. "If she won't make it official, then does it do anything at all for your case?"

"Motive," he said simply. "I'm not making a case against Kitty Wakelin. The chance to do that has long gone. I'm trying to find her killer and stories like Anna's give me the clearest motive we've got. You heard Anna; she's not the only one that Kitty abused in that way. There must be many girls. If we can put them together with the videos we found this morning then perhaps we can find some people who would want to make Kitty pay." He fell silent. The windscreen wipers pulled stickily at the windscreen, smearing rather than clearing.

"Videos?" she asked, prompting him.

"You don't miss much, do you?" She had an analytical mind he noticed. She reminded him of Hussain really in the way that she could pick ideas out.

"We found some videos this morning that would illuminate the tail end of Anna's story, shall we say," Slater admitted.

"Videos like the one of Maggie?" Vida asked, her face blanched.

Slater nodded, swallowing down the anger at himself again.

"You think one of the girls that Kitty groomed might have murdered her?" Vida seemed contemplative.

"It's the best reason I've heard so far." It was the only reason he'd found so far. He contemplated the horror of what Kitty had done, driving on autopilot as he wove his way through the town to Vida's home address. Was it made better or worse the fact that she'd only been a teenage girl? Better or worse that she'd obviously learned a lesson at some point? Better or worse that she'd lived her life seemingly trying to repent for her actions?

"I don't understand how this can happen," Vida started suddenly. Slater jumped slightly, his hands twitching on the wheel; he thought they'd both agreed to fall into a companionable silence. He kept his side of the bargain and said nothing in return. "I mean, I knew it did happen. Of course it did. But here and now?"

"What bothers you most?" Slater said, finally realising that her question was waiting for an answer. "That it happens at all? That it happened then? Or now? Or that it happens here? Or that it has happened and now you know that it has happened? That it's crossed the line into your safe little world?" He wasn't sure where the harsh words had come from and knew as soon as he'd posed the idea that he was being unreasonable. He was taking his own guilt out on her. She'd had a lot thrown at her over the past four days. She wasn't police, wasn't trained for this. The only thing she'd trained for was looking at dusty documents in dusty offices; of course, she wasn't coping. He'd heard it before. Heard it, and felt the burden of not stopping it. He shook his head a little. He needed to stop this introspective navel-gazing. He wasn't responsible for everyone else. He closed his cases. He looked into them. He solved them. He didn't leave them with unanswered questions. Except for Maggie Donaldson, his conscience whispered.

He didn't need to look across at her to hear the frown in her voice. "That's unfair. I mean that it happens at all. How could you think I was so shallow as to care that it's touching my world? Honestly, I'm horrified that I didn't know. This stuff is going on under our noses. People like me, teachers, and we don't know about it."

"If we did know about it, it probably wouldn't be happening," Slater pointed out.

"But people must know," she insisted. "Something that's going on on this scale, how can people not notice?"

"Maybe they do. Maybe they look the other way. Our society is broken I think. We all just want to look the other way."

"But you're a policeman," she pointed out. "Surely, you don't have that option."

"No, I don't, that's true. But I think there are still other policemen who think they do. Not so many now maybe, but then yes and still a few now. Anna went to tell the police the day after the rape. But I probably won't find any record of it anywhere; it certainly didn't come up when I put Kitty's name into the system and Kitty's parents didn't mention it. Whoever she told just didn't care."

"That's awful! That's even worse than neighbours ignoring things. You're the police; you have to care."

"Most of us do." He could sense Vida looking at him but didn't want to take his eyes off the road; no doubt it would be another reason for her to accuse him of dereliction of duty. "I'm sure you've got fellow academics who don't give a stuff about academia. It's the same in policing. Much better now than it was when my dad was a policeman, but it's still true. There's a hard core of people who join the police because they want to be in charge; that's the worst reason imaginable for joining the police."

"I didn't know your father had been a policeman."

"No reason for you to," Slater said, simply. "He was a career policeman, I'm a family policeman."

"He must be proud of you for carrying it on."

"He died when I was young."

"Oh, I'm sorry." The words were automatic, but Slater was sure he could hear genuine regret in her voice. "Oh... this is me!"

Slater pulled the car to a smooth halt, reversing easily into a nearby parallel slot. He looked at the piles of documents on the back seat. "Would you like a hand with this?"

"Yes please. If you wouldn't mind just grabbing the pile on the left." He followed her out and then down the path of a well-kept little front yard. "Just come into the kitchen and then put them on the table, please," she called out, leading him down a narrow hall and into a light and bright galley-style kitchen. It was clearly a culinaire's space. His attention was immediately grabbed by the impressive range of shiny silver pots and pans together with a butcher-worthy collection of knives.

"Are these just for show.."

"You bastard!"

Slater wasn't sure whether he was more surprised that she'd interrupted him or that she'd sworn so vehemently. "Sorry." He held his hands up. "I didn't mean to offend."

"Not you," she said crossly, turning to face him. He noticed she was waving a bit of lined paper. "My stupid husband. He's only taken himself off to Bologna to buy a dog."

"Bologna? Italy?"

"Yes, Bologna, Italy."

"A dog?"

"Yes, a flipping dog. Sorry, sorry," she said. "Not your problem. Thank you for your help carrying the stuff." She gave him an effortful smile. "I'll make sure I look at the letter you found at the scene this morning first and compare it to the others that we have from Kitty."

"Thank you. Look, are you sure you're alright?" Slater asked. She seemed like she was either about to kill someone or break down in tears. He wasn't sure which was the optimal outcome.

"Yes, I'm fine," she said, shortly. "Don't worry. I've had many years training to deal with my dear husband's idiocies and vagaries. He'll ring tonight, safe in the knowledge that he's out of the country and we'll pretend to

257

have a discussion and then he'll do whatever it is he wants to do. Bastard," she repeated softly.

"Have you got a friend who could come over? I don't like the idea of you being here alone after the past few days you've had. It was hard listening to Anna earlier." He was surprising himself with his unusual sensitivity. Maybe he'd been more affected by Anna's words earlier than he'd imagined. Either that or he was just more tired than normal. Between work, and Sabryne it had been an exhausting week.

"I'll be fine," she said, firmly. "I'm a grown up. I only had to listen to it. Not experience it."

"Well, you have my mobile number if you do need to talk to anyone." She looked at him, an eyebrow raised, and he found himself blushing. "I mean, I might be able to refer you to someone professional."

"Of course. Yes, thank you, but I'm sure I'll be fine." There was nothing that he could do but take her at her word. He nodded once and then left, leaving her looking more forlorn than he thought she'd looked all day.

Chapter 28

Whether out of a sense of guilt, or the hope that feeding her up would appease her when he returned, Simon had left the fridge amply stocked. More than enough macaroni and cheese to last her for the next two weeks, not to mention the tiramisu he'd whipped up. Vida did feel slightly better about her wayward husband while enjoying the creamy pasta and cheese, but as soon as the last mouthful had been swallowed, she felt the anger bubbling back up. Why did he always get it so wrong? She felt attacked on all fronts; Myfanwy obviously wanted her professional head on a stick and Hussain clearly wasn't her biggest fan either. More than anything she wished Simon was there to curl up with and forget the day. Instead, she was sitting at her desk, looking at the hate mail once more. Another evening of bile seemed to await her.

Her phone rang. "Vida Henrikson."

"Hi? Dr Henrikson? I've been given your name by Pip Lacewing."

Pip, Vida noted. Clearly a much closer relationship with the Vice-Chancellor than she had. "Yes?" she said, cautiously. Was giving out staff numbers allowed?

"I'm a journalist with the Sheffield Star. I hear that you've been working on some cases with the police. Pip thought I might be interested to talk to you as part of a wider piece I'm doing on community links."

All sounded perfectly plausible, so Vida murmured an understanding and let the journalist continue.

"I wonder if you could just outline how you got involved with the police and what you're helping them with?"

"Erm, well I'm not sure how much I'm allowed to tell you. Basically, I've been looking into some hate mail sent to a murder victim, with a view to perhaps helping the police narrow the suspect pool."

There was silence at the other end, broken only by the sound of shuffling papers. "A murder victim?" she finally repeated. "Is this Maggie Donaldson, Dr Henrikson? Are you saying that you've discovered that she was murdered?"

"Oh god, no," rushed Vida. "Sorry, crossed wires I think. Sorry, I didn't realise you were asking about Maggie?" Damn it.

"Pip told me you were looking into her suicide letters?"

"Yes, yes, I did that," confirmed Vida, kicking herself inwardly and hoping, against all the odds she knew, that the journalist would just skip over her obvious self-incrimination. She recounted Maggie's story to Stacey, being careful not to mention any names or point any particular fingers. Her focus was the science, her mantra a very tight keep-on-topic. For a few minutes, the journalist back-channelled appropriately, asked appropriate questions and appeased Vida's terror.

"So, Dr Henrikson, what are you working on currently? You mentioned a murder? Can you offer our readers any more information? It's such a fascinating subject. I'm sure everyone would like to find out more about what the science entails and how you're helping solve murders."

Damn her. Damn the journalist and her weasel ways. And damn herself for her naivety and stupidity. "I don't think it would be right for me to offer any comment on an ongoing investigation," she said, primly.

"An ongoing investigation," mused Stacey and again Vida kicked herself. This woman would be excellent in the field of Forensic Linguistics. She didn't miss a single language nuance. Silence was clearly the only way of evading this. "It won't be that difficult to work out which case you're working on, Dr Henrikson. Are you sure you wouldn't like to explain to the readers what your involvement is? It seems quite unusual for the police to get involved in this kind of science. Perhaps it might indicate a lack of confidence in themselves? If they're seeking external, academic," the word was laced with derision, "support then perhaps they're not able to solve the crime itself?"

Damn her again. Now she had no choice. If Vida stayed quiet, she risked making the police a laughing stock and that would do them, and her science no favours. "On the contrary," she started, "I believe that by involving this area of science," she emphasised the word, "the police are demonstrating a commitment to solving a case that is proving perhaps more challenging than the usual murder.

I've found them to be forward-thinking and open-minded in looking at ways to solve crime quickly and efficiently." Okay, so it was a little white lie. But delivered with confidence she felt sure that she'd rebutted the journalist's sneak attack.

"Well, thank you for that, Dr Henrikson."

Vida barely had time to reply before the journalist had rung off. She sat back in her chair, feeling simultaneously satisfied but also a little unnerved. She'd done her best, but she couldn't help thinking that a resounding no comment might have been the better option after all.

Chapter 29

There was still paperwork that needed attending to so Slater headed back to the station. He hated leaving things like that waiting until another day. A misfiled evidence sheet or overlooked witness statement could make the difference between a successful prosecution and one that made them look like incompetent idiots. Not that he didn't trust Louise to be accurate in her work. Everyone's work bore checking again though. Especially over nearly over 72 hours into a murder investigation. He liked being at the station after dark too, when the regular day teams had gone home, and the rooms felt shadowy yet somehow safe. The smell of sunlight on carpet and dust motes in the air was strangely reassuring to him. There was also the added bonus of him being safe from Sabryne in his police fortress.

Louise was still at her desk when he swung the door open. She threw a bright smile at him, making him feel bad about his reclusiveness. He quickly filled her in on his day's activities. It helped being able to say it out loud. Especially to someone who didn't look at him as though he was insane.

"Are you going home soon?" he asked, pointedly when he'd finished. He didn't have a life outside of his job, but he thought she probably had someone waiting at home for her.

She didn't seem to take any insult in his words. "Yep, just finishing off this file."

Slater nodded and wished her a good night before retreating to his own desk. There was a neat pile of papers in the corner waiting for his attention, but apart from that the space was immaculate. He read through the reports that waited for him, signing off appropriate requests, jotting down actions on his task list for tomorrow. He couldn't keep his mind from what Anna had told them though. It answered so many questions he'd had about Kitty and her behaviour. Had her family known? How could anyone be so callous towards another human being? Especially someone like Anna. She looked like a tiny woodland creature of a woman, nervous in the extreme, needing to be coaxed out. He couldn't imagine she'd been any different as a teenager. How could someone take advantage of such vulnerability? No wonder she'd felt like she needed to atone for her behaviour. But what had triggered the change? Was it just maturity that had made her realise how terribly she'd behaved? Or had something made her see sense before that?

"Boss? Gabe?" The voice broke urgently across his silence. Louise was standing white-faced in the doorway. "The cells. Raheeq." She didn't need to say anything else. He could hear the panic in her voice.

Lights on sensors followed him along the corridors and down the stairs that he took three at a time to get down to ground floor where the station's holding cells were, flashing on and then off again as he strode past them. The offices were dark as he past, heading towards the noise and hubbub of the main holding area. He felt unusually unnerved, anxious about what awaited him. The main door to the cells was open and a group of officers were crowded round Cell 5.

"Steven, what's gone on?" Slater asked the custody sergeant, desperately.

"Routine checks at 8pm. Found Khan on the floor. No pulse. Matt's in there now giving him CPR. Ambos are on their way. Not looking hopeful though."

"What the hell happened? Suicide?" Slater recalled the distress in the man's face yesterday when he'd been interviewed. He'd not considered him a suicide risk. Had he made a mistake?

"Not sure. No outward injury. Could just be an underlying condition. I'm presuming he didn't mention anything about a heart condition?"

"Not to me. I'd've said if I'd known anything relevant." The guilt made his tone harsh.

The custody sergeant took a step back and held his hands up. "I know, I know."

"Stand back!" The call came from the corridors as the paramedics pushed past with their equipment. Slater watched on helplessly as they took over the CPR, gauging and measuring, massaging and brusquely conversing with each other. He sent up a silent prayer to his mother's god. He wasn't sure he could stand another death on his conscience.

Dear you

I know what you did and I will make you pay, you faithless whore. I am your dark storm and I will have vengeance.

You probably think you're safe. You probably think that what you've done will stay in the past. I'm going to make sure it doesn't. I'm going to make you pay.

Maybe you don't think of it at all. I see you and I think that perhaps you've forgotten it. Is that the only way you could live with yourself? If you pretended that it had never happened. Pretended that she had never happened. I can't do that. I can't wipe her out of my memories. She's there every day, every minute in my brain, living with me, reminding me of everything she was and now will never be.

I wonder what she did to deserve what you did to her. Maybe nothing. Maybe she looked at you, or said something to you, or maybe she never even noticed you at all. She was like that. Her head in the clouds. A dreamer. You stole that from her. You stole everything from her. Why?

Chapter 30

The previous evening's phone-call with Simon had proceeded as predicted. He'd left it late before calling, perhaps reckoning on her being tucked up in bed so he could get away with just leaving a bright and breezy voicemail as though the argument had already been had and resolved. Unfortunately, the realisation that he genuinely didn't seem to have a clue what she was going through at the minute made the fight that much more vicious. She'd been drained and exhausted when he'd rung, tired of the words of hideous abuse dancing through her mind, emotionally over-wrought at the thought of everything Kitty had done and everything the girls she had betrayed had suffered. And once again with his impeccable timing and sense of understanding, her loving husband had managed to sideswipe all that to regale her with stories of the puppies and their lives in the olive groves of Italy. She wasn't entirely sure that this wasn't his way of trying to make her feel better: talking about irrelevant and superficial things. But she'd hoped for something more like understanding and sympathy. The fight had inevitably turned spiteful, stomping down familiar fault lines in their relationship, until she'd finally hung up on him mid-rant. What were they doing to each other?

In reality, the venom she'd spat at Simon, together with the bitterness she'd sobbed out afterwards had helped. Her anger for the perpetrators in these cases, for Kitty and Ash and Raheeq Khan and all the other unnamed people who had driven Maggie and maybe countless more to kill themselves was powerful, burning her stomach and oesophagus with rage. It had been cathartic to have a human to scream at, even if he'd no idea about what the real issues were. And after the rage had been assuaged, the gut-wrenching wails had disturbed the neighbours until she felt she could cry no more and she had immediately fallen into an untroubled sleep. She'd felt guilty about that when she awoke; how could she sleep peacefully when people were abusing girls all over her city?

Red-eyed and bleary, she sat at the kitchen table, nursing her coffee, with the piles of work she'd brought home from the office yesterday surrounding her. Working with the police was playing havoc with her marking plan and she now had a large pile of undergraduate essays that were going to be overdue for return if she didn't finish them today. She wasn't doing the undergraduates any favours by looking at them right now though. Her mind, let alone her heart, wasn't in it. How could she be expected to mark dry historical essays on cases that were long-dead when she had real victims to help? But was she actually helping the victims? She was helping the police find the person who had killed someone. But surely those people had deserved some sort of retribution for what they'd done. She knew teenage girls were often cruel; she'd experienced the truth of that herself at school when she was always a little bit nerdy, a little too round and far too solemn. But what Kitty had done to these girls, making them feel that they were special and then taking it all away in the worst way imaginable was barely thinkable. How could anyone be so cruel? Vida knew she was buying into all the social constructs of women's crime being worse because they were the caring gender, but she couldn't help it. Kitty was nothing that a female or a child should be; she was manipulative, and heartless and wicked. Did that sort of person really deserve justice?

But who was she to decide? She sighed and rubbed her forehead worriedly. She felt like she'd gotten herself in too deep this week. A world of murkiness and despair that she wasn't sure she was equipped to deal with. Wearily, she dragged herself to the present and checked her watch. Her first seminar was at 10am and she had barely an hour to sort herself out. Unless she wanted to give the administration yet another reason to side-line her and her science, she couldn't start missing lectures. She switched the radio on, hoping the facile music would shake the darkness out of her head. Maybe an ear worm would get in there instead and she could hum along to it. It worked for a while as she bopped around to Stevie Wonder's Superstitious as she finished applying her make-up. The news bulletin displaced her mirth though once more as she heard an ominous connection made between the police, Kitty Wakelin and her own name.

"Damn it." She was in for it now.

Chapter 31

Slater was exhausted by the time he dragged himself to work. He'd been unable to sleep properly. Every time he drifted off, he'd been yanked awake by thoughts of Kitty and Anna. Sabryne. Sometimes Vida. When he opened his eyes, the sight of Raheeq being worked on replayed itself in front of his face. He was in no mood for the small, bouncy woman waiting for him by his desk when he came in.

"DI Slater?" she asked, hopefully as he approached. He didn't answer, shrugging off his raincoat and hanging it up. The weather was still stuck in the same February gloom of drizzle and looming sky although the forecasters were promising snow later.

"Bloody snow," he muttered under his breath before turning to the woman. "Yes?"

"I'm Cathy in IT. I've been looking at the laptop of your victim, Kitty Wakelin?"

Female, and quite attractive, she was still wearing the IT uniform of jeans and a slogan T-Shirt together with the slightly unhealthy pallor of hours spent in a darkened and air-conditioned room.

"Sorry," he said. "I'm a bit tired. Yes. Have you found something?"

"May I?" she asked, logging herself onto his computer without waiting for a confirmation. She navigated her way through some files. "We've been combing the hard drive for anything relevant. Of course, you're never quite sure what's relevant until you find it so there's a lot of looking around. We're always particularly interested to see what people have deleted. You probably know that things that are deleted aren't always gone forever. Lots of people know that but then just don't bother doing anything about it. I suppose most people aren't doing anything criminal and just assume no-one's ever going to bother looking through their deleted files. It's not like the average person's family will trawl through their hard drive after they're dead, even if they could."

"Did you find something criminal?" Slater interjected, trying to get her on track. Maybe she'd saved up all the words she would have used in a normal work environment to unleash them as soon as she had an audience out of the box they were all trapped in.

"Oh no, not criminal. At least I don't think so. That's your job, isn't it? To decide if it's criminal or not. We found loads of deleted files. Lots of pictures, head shots, contract versions, emailed invoices from online shopping."

"Anything relevant?"

"Yes, of course, that's why I'm here."

Slater inhaled, praying for calm. Was she planning on getting to the point any time soon?

"Which was?" he prompted.

"This," she said, vacating the seat at the desk to enable him to sit at the computer. He took his place and scanned the document in front of him. "What you've got here is a series of letters or emails that Kitty has written.

We can't tell if she ever sent them to anyone. No way of telling if she'd printed them and we couldn't find any record of them in her email folder."

"Why would she write them and not send them?"

"I can tell you're not a woman," Cathy said. Slater looked at her sharply. Was that flirty compliment or sarcastic comment? Cathy blushed as though sensing his thoughts. "I mean, women have been known to write letters as a sort of journal sometimes. She might just have been writing them to get something off her mind."

"What?"

"Read them," she instructed. He turned his attention to the screen. Cathy had highlighted a collection of twenty or so document files.

"All of them?" he asked. He didn't particularly relish sitting and reading while she gazed at the back of his neck.

"I can print them off for you, but maybe just this one." She leaned over and double-clicked a file dated the end of January.

"If you could print them off, that would be great," he said, firmly, refusing to look back at the screen until she'd left him alone. She smiled, uncertainly but didn't move. "Today would be good?"

"Oh, yes, of course." She nodded and scurried off back to what he always thought as being the IT cave.

He turned his attention finally to the screen. It wasn't a particularly long document.

I am sorry. I know the words are never enough but I would do anything I could to make this right. That probably doesn't make you feel any better. I would give anything, and I mean anything to go back and do things differently. There are no reasons or excuses. I was young and so selfish and stupid and I never thought of anyone but myself. And I know I'm responsible for what happened to Aly. She was a sweet girl. I know she would have had a long and happy life and I stole that from her. Nothing I can ever do could make that right. But I'll be there.

"Slater?" He looked up as Louise approached. "I've just had info back from Kitty's bank. Her balance was certainly a lot healthier than mine. There's nothing particularly suspicious in any of her accounts; regular outgoings like rent and food. She doesn't seem to have splurged or anything. The only thing that stands out at all is this." She pointed to a line on the bank statements. "It's a regular payment to the Sheffield Women's Charity."

"So, she gives to charity? Even I manage the occasional charitable giving."

"It's not the charity, it's the amount. Over half of her income each month went to the charity. That's a massive amount some months, a few thousand."

Slater nodded. He wasn't overly surprised by it. It was just another piece in the Kitty jigsaw puzzle. They knew what she was like as a teenager, but something had happened to change that. Something so terrible that she'd spent her whole life trying to amend for it. He needed to talk this over with someone.

"Ma'am?" He knocked quietly at Hussain's door. She looked up and nodded him in.

"I think she went to her own death willingly," Slater started. "Suicide by murderer if you like." He outlined what he'd found out about Kitty, glossing over the not-strictly-following-protocol interview of Anna. The information she'd given them was valid, irrespective of how he'd got it.

Hussain snorted disbelievingly. "She doesn't look like the kind of girl who would feel repentance." She indicated through her internal windows to where the picture of Kitty was central on the murder board. It had been a publicity shot and Slater couldn't deny the truth that she looked like nothing more than a vacuous celebrity.

"She's just playing a role there."

Hussain still looked unconvinced. "If she was truly repentant then she'd have gone to the police, taken steps to stop what was going on. Silence and letting everything just carry on doesn't show shame. Just a pretence of guilt."

"She lived an almost hermitic life though."

"While raking in the dosh for being this role-model of female perfection?" The derision was clear.

Slater shrugged. Hussain wasn't wrong. It had been remorse on an individual scale. "It would explain the CCTV we saw," he said, determined to prove his point now. "She was very clearly walking alongside the killer. There was no coercion."

"Slater, you've not even proved that that was the killer. It could have been someone she was meeting for fun."

"No defensive wounds," he continued. "No sign of struggle at the entry to the alleyway. She went there willingly."

Hussain smiled at him. It wasn't a particularly comfortable smile. "Even if she did go willingly, does it find us her murderer? Does it get us anywhere closer to solving this crime? Does it help us solve this second murder you've decided to link in? I can't take this to the Super and tell him that no, we haven't solved the case yet, but it's okay because you think Kitty Wakelin went willingly to her death. We'll dismiss it as a suicide. Only... wait... remind me. Ashaz Khan, that was suicide too was it? He went willingly to his death? You're the one adamant that these two things are connected."

He bristled. What had been hoping to achieve when he'd approached her? A pat on the back and a resounding job-well-done?

"Did you happen to catch the local news this morning?" Hussain asked.

He was confused about the change in topic. "No, ma'am." He very rarely listened to the radio and didn't even own a television.

"Nice little news report about Kitty's murder. Together with a comment from a certain Forensic Linguist. Apparently, we're struggling."

Bloody hell. She wasn't wrong, but why had she told the world that?

"She needs to be taken care of." The tone was as sinister as the words she spoke.

"Ma'am?"

"Remove her from this case. If I see her in this office again, I will not be responsible for the consequences."

"Of course, ma'am. You're right. I apologise," he said, stiffly.

She contemplated his capitulation. "I don't know what's going on with you right now, Gabriel," she said. "You're normally my most reliable detective in terms of solving cases quickly and without any fuss. You've never been this bothered before about victimology. Is there something in your life that you need to tell me about? Should I be asking another DI to take over the cases?"

For a minute he thought about unburdening himself. Where would he start? His brother and the disastrous situation with Sabryne? His mum's pressure? He mentally slapped himself. None of these were reasons for not doing his job properly. And he couldn't explain why Kitty was bothering him so much. He didn't normally get this involved in a case.

"No ma'am," he said. "Nothing's going on. I'm sorry if I'm letting you down."

"Just stop trying to unpick every decision. Let the CPS work out why; we just need to find the who and the how." She looked at him. "We had a call from the hospital this morning. Raheeq was DOA. They're not certain what the cause is. Looks like some sort of heart failure."

"Bloody hell," he sighed.

Hussain shrugged. "No great loss to humankind. I daresay he'd've grown up to be just like his nasty little father and uncle. We got lucky catching him so early. Even luckier now he's shuffled off his mortal coil."

Slater thought back to the boy's face. He didn't think he was like his father and uncle. The trauma he portrayed at Maggie's death had seemed genuine. "I don't know, ma'am. Maybe he would've turned things around."

Hussain's smile oozed patronising sympathy. "All these years in the force, DI Slater, and you still see the positive in human nature. Trust me. The world's a better place without the likes of Raheeq Khan."

"Will there be any investigation?"

"Death in custody, bound to be. But if natural causes bears out then there'll be no questions to answer. Don't worry, Slater. None of this will come back to bite you."

"Yes ma'am. Thank you ma'am." But as he walked away, he couldn't shake off the sense of unease that still bore down on him, and the questions about the case that went far beyond the who and the how just wouldn't stop bothering him.

Chapter 32

"Have you seen this?"

Vida looked up as Myfanwy barged her way into her office. She'd made her 10am seminar by the skin of her teeth and had coasted through it, relying on lively students to bring their A-Game while she barely completed a pass. Myfanwy was brandishing a newspaper that she threw at Vida. Vida opened it out carefully, that feeling of sinking dread washing over her once more.

Police Have No Clues to Popstar Murder

She scanned the article quickly. Thankfully, there was no link made between Kitty's death and the murder of Ashaz Khan but that was about all there was to be thankful for. The takedown of Slater's operational prowess was brutal and harsh, and seemed to stem entirely from the fact he'd sought external help. Vida's own quote had been chopped down to nothing more than a statement that the police were finding the case unusually challenging. "Damn," she said out loud, rubbing her eyes wearily and holding out the paper for Myfanwy to take back. It didn't add anything to the news report she'd heard yesterday.

"What were you thinking?" Myfanwy asked, voice high, her face a picture of horror and disgust.

"It's been taken out of context," started Vida. Who was she kidding? Of course, it had been taken out of context; that was how the local paper got its news. "I'm sorry, Myfanwy. The reported called me directly at home.

She said Dr Lacewing had given her my name. I was just trying to do something good for the university."

"Well, you haven't. Since this whole thing began you've done nothing but harm. That's it, Vida, I am done with you and your ridiculous ideas. You can forget about running the course next year. You'll be asked to teach something else." She turned to march back out before throwing over her shoulder, "That is, if you're asked to teach at all."

Exhaustion threatened to break Vida's resolve to keep it together. She debated locking her door and trying to get some sleep in her office. If she was here, surrounded by people and noise, perhaps she would feel safe enough to drift off. She couldn't shake the thought though that one of those people might be a killer. How could she rest until she knew for sure that the killer had been caught?

She packed her things up, cancelled the tutorial she had later, and gathered her initial findings. She had to do something, even if that something was putting her career in jeopardy. This was more important. She hadn't wanted to go into the station again; she felt like she was infiltrating enemy territory in a not particularly convincing disguise as she slinked into the police station and asked for Slater. He had been annoyingly uncontactable though, not responding to her messages and there had been no other option but to come in and talk to him directly. Myfanwy's words rang loud in her ears though and she was fully cognisant of the fact she was potentially walking herself into a career suicide situation.

She couldn't turn away from Anna though and Maggie and all the others.

"Dr Henrikson?"

Damnit, her cover was blown straight away. She straightened her back and turned towards the formidable face of Hussain.

"I had an interesting conversation about you this morning." Hussain advanced towards her. There was a slight Birmingham twinge to her words. Normally the accent was reassuring; surveys carried out always picked it as being one of the friendliest accents. Together with the Yorkshire softness, it should make for an appealing combination. There was nothing remotely appealing about the woman marching up to her right now. "I made it very clear to your supervisors that your continued interference is no longer welcome in this investigation. And that was even before I heard your little star turn on the radio this morning."

Vida couldn't help the blush that rose to her cheeks. She rolled round the alternative responses in her head. Play dumb? Fight back? In the end, she ignored the pointed comment about the radio and fell back on her usual failsafe, appeasement. "I understand you had some concerns about the fact I was at the crime scene the other day. I can assure you that I've explained all that to DI Slater. In fact, it's him I'm here to see really. I've drawn some preliminary conclusions from the data he gave me, and I'd like to share what I've found with you." The very voice of reason. It was hard to argue with someone who was committed to being so reasonable she knew. It had wound Simon up enough times.

Hussain seemed about to snap out another response, when Slater rounded the corner and greeted her. "I was just explaining to DCI Hussain that I've got some preliminary findings," she said to him. Another arrow in her quiver. Hussain couldn't dismiss her now without seeming unreasonable.

Slater scowled at her. He'd obviously heard her comments in the press too. "Well, we are apparently struggling. Isn't it a good job that you're here to help," Slater said, with a sneer.

He was right to feel maligned, but she couldn't help the tears that bristled suddenly at her eyes. She blinked quickly, refusing to give in. "Well, the letters are not from a victim herself, are they? Look," she said digging the letter out of her file. "Look how she uses the personal pronouns, can't wipe her out, what did she deserve. She's talking about what someone's done to someone else."

"You said she?" Slater said.

"Yes, I think so. It's a weak result but the language analysed so far suggests a female author." She saw Hussain and Slater exchange glances. "Is that not what you expected?"

"Well, it's wrong," Hussain said, sharply.

Slater looked contemplative, his animosity forgotten. "It might be right," he admitted. "Witnesses have so far all suggested male, but it's a skinny figure and no-one's seen his face. Could be a woman."

Hussain rolled her eyes so hard that Vida was surprised they came back to the middle. "I don't think we'll send out the BOLOs just yet. As you've said, weak result. Thank you for your help," the inverted commas were clear, "but as I explained to your superior this morning, I think it would be best all round if you stayed out of the investigation."

Nothing like support in the sisterhood. Vida looked to Slater to see if he was going to speak up on her behalf. After all, it had been his idea to involve her in the first place. He was looking at his feet. Not the trousers in this relationship then.

Her annoyance grew. All the time she'd spent on this. Not just actual time but the enormous mental drain she'd felt, and she was being dismissed without even being given the opportunity to finish the job properly. How was she ever going to prove her science to the point where people accepted it if she were never allowed to see a case through? "You could look at it from the point of view that if I'm right, you're looking in completely the wrong place."

Hussain's face flashed anger. She scowled at Slater, clearly blaming him for the breach. "Of course," Hussain said tightly. Slater took a step back. Vida wondered whether he'd done it deliberately or subconsciously. "We do prefer our data to be taken from actual evidentiary conclusions however, rather than just a pseudo-science."

"Hardly a pseudo-science," Vida replied. She wished she could hit Hussain. Ravel up all the stress of the past few days and channel it into a harsh flat-handed slap that would sting her palm and leave a red mark on the supercilious woman. "Many years of research, theory and practice. And the fact is that you haven't solved the murders yet. Isn't that correct? DI Slater?" Vida looked to him and then took a step to stand next to him. Two could play at that game.

"She is right, ma'am," admitted Slater. "There can't be any harm in continuing to investigate the letters in this way. Like Dr Henrikson has pointed out, the first part of the analysis has thrown up something interesting. Why not continue the analysis? We can go back to the witnesses and see if they could be mistaken on the gender." He still had the air of a schoolboy asking his mother if he was allowed some sweets before tea.

"Apart from Raheeq," Hussain said. Slater winced. "Do you have an expected date of completion?" she asked Vida sharply.

"I've analysed the bulk of the letters now. From the three main contributors, I've given you some basic conclusions such as gender, age, approximate education level. I just need to compare syntax and lexis choice now to see if I can add any geographical specifics or something like that. I'm going to focus that analysis going forward on the writer of the typewritten notes as that is the one that links Kitty to Ashaz."

Hussain's eyes narrowed and she looked as though she was going to say something more, but she left it as a sharp sigh before spinning and leaving.

Slater let out a slow intake of breath before grinning, surprisingly, at her. "Thought you were going to come to blows then."

The tension dissipated; Vida returned the smile. She was inordinately proud of herself for standing up to Hussain. If only she could apply the same backbone to her encounters with Myfanwy. Maybe if she'd polished her shiny spine in the first place she wouldn't even be in this situation now. "Me too," admitted Vida.

"What about the letters being from different places?" Slater asked.

"You were right. As far as I can tell, the hate mail author and the author of the note found on the body the other day are the same person."

Slater looked relieved. He was obviously feeling the pressure as much as she was. That made her feel better, less like an over-thinking ninny. "Is there anything else you can give us at the minute?"

"Well, like I said, we're looking at a female. I think she's probably talking about a sister, but that's psychology, not really my area of expertise." She blushed.

"To be honest, that just increases our potential suspect pool at the minute," said Slater.

"I can guess. I can also conclude fairly certainly that you're looking at someone who's somewhere in their thirties."

"You can narrow it down that far?"

"Not on my own. That's on the back of a massive database that we've put together along with a few other universities we're in consort with across the globe. As a team we've analysed thousands, maybe even millions, of texts, picking out key words used more commonly by certain age groups. Problem is, it changes constantly of course. Today's thirty-year-old is tomorrow's forty-year-old and language changes and adapts all the time. Let's say it's an ongoing project."

"Impressive. Anything else?"

"Educated to degree level at least. Not an early school leaver." It didn't sound like much when she'd said it out loud now.

"And there's more to come?"

She wondered if he'd sensed her embarrassment. "Yes. I mean, I hope so. I mean, you know it's never going to find the killer. I can't be that specific. But maybe if you've got some different suspects, it might help narrow it down for you."

"Yes, I'm sure it will."

She looked at him, trying to work out whether he was being genuine or patronising. She didn't have enough energy to take patronising right now so took it as genuine. "I'll be in touch over the next couple of days with my finalised information. There are some things I've noticed about the letter writer that I think will help me pin it down further, but I just need to do some further research." It wasn't a lie, but as Vida made her way back to the university, the weight of the self-imposed deadline weighed heavily.

Chapter 33

The visit to the morgue seemed easier this time. Or harder maybe. Slater wasn't really sure which. The practicalities were easier, that was for sure. He didn't feel the same wave of lost life watching Ashaz being dissected as he had for Kitty. Maybe if he'd known what Kitty was before he'd attended her post-mortem, the difference wouldn't have been so stark. He was able to watch with more distance as the worker bees did their job, poking and prodding, slicing and saving. Dawson didn't seem to be aware of any difference however; his face was as green now as it had been the last time they visited.

But while Slater'd been full of optimism about getting Kitty's case closed quickly, achieving justice for this poor damsel, now he felt nothing but glum about their prospects. He was convinced that the two cases were linked but without proper scientific evidence, no-one else was willing to believe him. And no-one seemed willing to accept that Vida's work was proper scientific evidence, which he was finding more and more annoying. He wondered if this was how Newton had felt trying to get people to accept gravity, or Pythagoras with his spherical globe. He could only imagine how frustrating it was for her, to have her life's work knocked back at every opportunity by naysayers and suspicion.

"Anything you can tell me to close the case?" Slater asked Ellison as he emerged from the autopsy suite, rubbing lotion into enormous fleshy hands that looked barely capable of wielding cutlery, let alone a scalpel.

"Probably not much that can help you, Inspector. As initially premised, cause of death was a single slashing wound to the neck. No hesitation marks. Early blood tests indicate the presence of benzodiazepines in a concentration that would have been sufficient to knock him out."

"A clinical murder?" asked Slater.

Ellison viewed him with suspicion. "As you know, Inspector, I don't like to involve myself in vagaries and guesswork. The science is fact based, not supposition."

Slater stayed silent. Dawson shuffled beside him and Slater willed him not to open his mouth. He was sure the doctor would offer them a little more if they just waited.

Ellison sighed. "What I would say is that the passion does not seem to be the same as in the other murder. I understand you're trying to link them?" He made it sound like Slater was trying to bail out the Titanic with a mug and a wine glass.

"I believe they are linked, yes," Slater said, firmly.

"Obviously both victims were killed with a knife wound. There are some similarities between the two death-resulting wounds; both are clean cuts. The first murder however, obviously had several deep stabbing wounds. I believe we suggested at the time a great degree of anger. This second murder is, as you say, more calculating."

"Is there anything to exclude it being the same perpetrator?" Slater asked, desperate for anything now.

"No. Much depends of course on whether the second victim was in his chair before he was drugged. There are no bruise marks under his arms or any other signs of him being dragged so I would suggest that that was the case. He made his own way to the chair and was drugged whilst there. If that is true, then the same body type parameters as in the first murder also stand true."

"A woman could have committed these crimes?"

Ellison looked surprised for a minute. Slater hoped to god that it was just his natural sexism coming through, rather than anything really obvious which meant it could be a female killer. He didn't fancy going back to Hussain and telling her that Vida had already been proven wrong. Not to mention the conversation he would have to have with Vida. He felt a need to not let her down.

"Yes, Inspector. A perhaps slightly unusual female. Neither of these feel like female crimes I think. Much messier for one. But yes, the killer could have been female."

"And what about the knife wounds? Is there any chance we can match the weapon?" Dawson asked, hopefully.

"I doubt it," Ellison said. "The slashing nature of the wounds means it's nigh on impossible. Had the second victim been stabbed in the same way as the first, we would have stood more of a chance."

Bugger. No way of linking the two crimes forensically. "There's nothing else that could link the cases then?" Slater asked, a note of desperation weaving through his voice.

"Not from my end, Inspector, no." He gave a single nod and then turned, leaving Slater wanting to bash his own head against the wall in exasperation. He realised he'd been counting on the PM to throw up something useful. He was still no further forward.

He rubbed his temples instead of anything more violent. He'd had a constant feeling of nausea since this whole case began. Not even beating his opponents in the ice hockey ring had made him feel any better. He was drowning and could catch a single rope to hold on to. Apart from this bloody linguistic thing which was feeling more and more like some malevolent force was sawing at it from the other end to make sure it failed just as he needed it.

His phone rang. He checked the number. Sabryne. Did he want to talk to her right now? He was pretty sure her revelations were another cause of the nausea.

"I've got to take this," he said meaningfully to Dawson who shrugged and ambled off outside, probably to try and recover his colour.

"Hello?"

"Gabriel," she sing-songed. He felt his loins clench. She always caused that reaction, and he was never sure if it was pleasurable or tortuous. "I spoken to Anna some more and she give me a list to give to you."

"A list?"

"She wrote the names of some others."

"Other victims?"

"Other girls, yes. She say she knows they also were taken by these men."

"Will you text me a photo?"

"Yes."

"And tell her thank you."

"Of course, my baby."

This time, it was definitely not a pleasurable loin clench. "Don't call me that," he said, sternly.

"Why not?" she asked. He could hear the pout through the phone line.

"I'm not your baby. You shouldn't say that out loud either. What if someone overheard you?"

She scoffed. "They just think I talk to Caleb."

"Well, just don't."

"You not gonna thank me?" she asked.

"For what?"

"For helping in your investigation."

"Thank you, Sabryne, for helping in my investigation."

"Is nothing, my baby. We got to stick together. Especially nowadays."

"What do you mean? Are you talking about the baby?" he asked, rising panic infecting his voice. He checked over his shoulders to make sure he really was an unobserved as he thought he was. "You told me it was Caleb's, Sabryne."

"I not talking 'bout that," she laughed, gaily. He was glad that this was a telephone conversation. He didn't think he'd be able to resist the urge to slap her stupid, smug face if she were here. "I talking about this gang. Takin' girls off the street. I don't want to be next."

"We've found the people who were running the ring," Slater said. "I think you'll be safe." Like hard-as-nails Sabryne would ever have been a target for a gang of men who picked on weak and needy girls. She'd been supremely confident her whole life. Beautiful, intelligent, charismatic. Everything a mother would want in a daughter-in-law. Apart from the fact she was a Class A Bitch. "Send me that picture." He hung up before she could respond further. His phone buzzed a few seconds later with a picture of the names and a close up of what looked suspiciously like Sabryne's breasts. He stared for a minute, unable to help himself. "Bloody hell." He deleted the second message, scowling.

The first had five or six names on it. A couple of Eastern European sounding ones, a couple potentially Asian and two definitely Sheffield through and through. Maybe he could trade this little snippet of information with the team now investigating the sex crimes. He needed the names of the girls who had been abused. He wasn't sure how he was going to handle that though. Oh yes, we're sorry you were raped, but do you happen to be a murderer? He could imagine the complaints and uproar in the press if that was his approach. It was already shaping up to be another public disaster for the South Yorkshire police. He knew the national press were already on the case. And who could blame them? The force had sworn that it had cleaned up its act. Every time it got its foot out of one disaster, it stepped firmly into another one. At least the PR machine should be well adept at its unhelpful apologies and blatantly untrue vows that all wrong doing had been addressed. He needed to take interview strategy on advisement before he lit the touch paper to a doubtlessly incendiary explosion.

Dawson was stamping his feet outside, and rubbing his arms in a dramatic manner. "It's not that bloody cold, and you've only been out here for a couple of minutes," Slater said.

"It's very cold. Met Office reckon we could be in for an even colder snap. Promising snow for tonight."

"Great," Slater said. He hated the snow. It was one weather he couldn't really run in, hating the feeling of the surface that moved beneath his feet. "So, Mark. Next steps?"

Dawson looked surprised. Slater knew he didn't often ask his sergeant what they should do next. Maybe that was a fault. Right now though, he had to admit he didn't know where they should go. "Erm, dunno boss. Ashaz's brother, Hamid Khan will be landing at Manchester in a couple of hours. We'll need to interview him. Reckon we'll have to get in their sharpish before sex crimes whip him away."

"Right. He should be able to confirm Anna's version of Kitty's involvement. Hussain's not going to let us continue to treat these as one investigation unless we can confirm their connection." That data triangulation again. Hussain said it made investigations infallible in achieving convictions.

"Are you sure about this?" Dawson asked him.

Slater regarded him sharply. He wasn't used to his team questioning his judgement. But then he wasn't used to feeling like his judgement was questionable in the first place. "Yes," he said, with more conviction than he felt. "I am, Mark. I'm bloody certain they're connected. We just need to find out specifically what links Kitty and Ashaz beyond a general involvement in this sex ring and we're sorted."

And the clouds cleared. That was exactly what he needed, he realised. He'd been struggling to connect the dots because simple connection with a thing wasn't enough to cause the chain of events that had occurred. There had to be something deeper than that. Something that had caused Kitty to change her ways. Something worth killing for.

Slater contemplated the hangdog face he'd got in response to his statement. He wished suspects were as easy to read as the sergeant. "Go home, Mark, think about it. Maybe inspiration will strike over your tea. What is it tonight?"

"Depends on whether Sophie's had a good day with the baby. Either she's made something or I'm making myself a cheese sandwich." His morose expression had quickly been replaced by one that Slater could only describe as puppy dog excitement and Dawson bounded off eagerly.

Slater's own departure from the station was slower, a pace dictated by ensuring that his desk was empty, all paperwork had been filed in the appropriate places and that his to-do list had been updated in anticipation of tomorrow's continued investigation. Not that he was able to put anything more specific on it than "Find the mystery connection." He'd ruminate overnight on what exactly that might entail.

He'd barely taken three steps away from the station towards his car, hardly enough time to register that it was even colder now than it had been, before a wolf whistle caught his attention. He peered in the direction it had come from, eyes trying to make out who it was skulking in the shadows.

"Gabriel," the figure said, moving away from the corner of the building in front of him.

"Caleb," greeted Slater, jaw tight.

"You could look happier to see you little brother."

Slater remained silent, waiting for whatever it was his brother wanted this time.

"I know ma told you our good news. You're gonna be an uncle, man!" He made to punch Slater lightly on the arm, but Slater moved sharply out of the way.

"So Sabryne and me, we were thinking that we need some stuff to get things ready for the baby."

Slater made a show of looking at his watch. This blag for money was shaping up to be delivered in record time.

"I know, man, I know. You a busy man. Well, I a busy man too and I just came here and see if you want to make a contribution to the baby fund."

In times gone by, Slater would have asked questions. Why did they need the money? Where was the money going? Had they drawn up an appropriate budget to deal with potential income threats and bonuses? He'd learned after the first few times that it didn't matter what he asked, the money always ended up in some sort of Caleb blackhole. "Do you not think it's time you started looking after your own family?" he asked. "Now, you're going to have a family."

Caleb smiled, the dimple that had let him get away with a thousand childhood indiscretions appearing on his cheek. "You my family. You and ma. You know, she so excited about this baby. I sure that if you can't contribute to your new baby niece or nephew, ma will be more than happy to dig into her savings."

The dimple disappeared as the weight of Slater's arm and full body slam pushed Caleb back into the shadows against the wall of the building. "Don't even think about taking money from mum," he hissed as Caleb tried vainly to get out from his grip. "She doesn't have anything left to give you. You've drained her, Caleb. Just let her grow old in comfort."

"You such a little choirboy," Caleb spat. "You think you so good, but you know nothing about life. You just jealous I have it all. I have a woman who loves me and a baby on its way and you have nothing, Gabriel. Nothing."

The desire to blurt out the truth danced on his tongue, but he swallowed it hard. Fight gone, he stepped back from his brother. "How much do you want?"

"Two thousand should do it."

"I'll give Sabryne the cash."

"No," said Caleb, urgently. "I don't want Sabryne to know."

Slater laughed. "You think she won't know? She knows you. She knows you got no way of making £2000. She'll know you either borrowed it or robbed it. Trust me, she'd rather know you borrowed it. And it's that or nothing. I've told you before, Caleb. I don't want to see you. Not now, not ever. This is the last time. And it's only for the baby. It's going to need all the bloody help it can get with you for a father."

He turned and headed back towards his car. How true would his words be if the baby turned out to be his? Could he honestly say he'd be a better father than his brother? At least his brother loved and was loved. Could he say that about himself?

Chapter 34

Vida bolted upright, her heart thumping as she struggled to orientate herself. Whether she'd been forcibly evicted from the dream or yanked into the real world by something she'd heard she wasn't sure. She instinctively reached her hand out to Simon, hoping to feel his warm body to reassure herself that she wasn't alone. But she touched down on cold sheets and remembered that she was.

There was nothing concrete she could remember in her dream, so the sudden wakening must have been the result of something in the real world. She shuffled upright in her bed and listened keenly. Even in deepest winter she slept with a window open, disliking the claustrophobic headaches she got from sleeping in an airless room. There was no sound from the outside. The comforting city noises seemed quiet, far away. Pushing back the sheets and sliding her feet into slippers, she padded over to the window and pushed the curtain back.

Snow lay in a thick layer as far as she could see. Street, gardens, bins, cars and bushes were all indistinguishable bulges in a white landscape. The air was thick with cold, the sky an eerie amber as the ground reflected the streetlights back up. The alien landscape sent shivers running through her that went beyond the cold.

Vida was about to go back to the warmth of her bed when she noticed a series of indents in the snow. Footprints leading down the street and to her front door.

Was this what had awoken her? She opened the window further and craned her neck to look up the street but there was no sign of anyone beyond the trail of prints. Had they knocked? Why had they come and not stayed? A shiver went down her back, but she wasn't sure if it was the intense cold pushing into her bones or the thought of being alone in the house and what might happen. She wasn't a natural worrier, more likely to overlook potential dangers than see some where there were none, but she felt the sudden panic of her isolation. This was the first time since she'd moved to Sheffield that the snow had fallen this heavily. Perhaps if her errant husband had been at home the fear wouldn't have been so full. She just wanted a human voice to bring her out of the rising terror that was gripping her for no realistic reason. It was only 2am she noticed though, checking the clock. Not the hour that anyone wanted to be woken up by a grown woman in the middle of some ridiculous self-involved meltdown. She forced herself to laugh loudly, the sound jarring against the silence of the world around her.

"Don't be so daft," she told herself sternly. "You're being ridiculous. You've been home alone before. What do you think's going to happen to you?" Pulling on a sweater over her nightie, she went downstairs, pondering whether a hot milk or a whiskey neat would be the better option to put her nerves at rest. Probably the milk. If she was going to behave like a silly child, she may as well soothe herself like one.

The letter on her doormat stood bright white against the floor and immediately the dread came back. She contemplated ignoring it. Whatever it was could wait until morning. Who was she kidding? She knew what it was, and she knew that there would be no rest for her for remainder of the night. A strange part of her felt strangely satisfied. It was as though she'd known all along that this was going to happen. She couldn't have found out the things she'd found out, seen the things she'd seen, without it having an impact on her. She'd assumed, hoped that a feeling of disquiet and a promise to be more vigilant about the students in her care would be sufficient to be her side of the bargain. It felt almost inevitable that she wasn't to get away that easily.

She stooped and picked the white envelope up. It looked like the other one. She wondered whether the letters sent to Kitty and pinned onto a dead body had been on the same quality stationery. She'd only seen photocopies; it was another thing that she'd never ever contemplated before. Dr Vida Henrikson was printed neatly on the front of the envelope; clearly this was someone who was more proficient with mail merge than she was, and she found herself smiling slightly at the thought of a killer's mail merge database. Then she remembered she was on a killer's mail merge database and the smile fell from her face.

Ignoring the shaking of her hands, she slid a nail under the seal and pulled the envelope open.

Dear you

I know what you did and I will make you pay, you faithless whore. I am your dark storm and I will have vengeance.

You probably think you're safe. You probably think that what you've done doesn't matter. But you are working for the powers of darkness when you are standing against the righteous path. Justice will be ours and you cannot stand between them and the retribution He will mete out. You hide behind your science. You pretend that you are seeking out the truth. But the truth is made to serve my purpose. You will not stop me.

I will stop you first.

Nausea rose suddenly in her chest and Vida rushed to the kitchen to push her face under the cold tap, despite the frigidity of the night air. Her face felt aflame and she gulped down the icy water earnestly, choking gutturally as she battled the ongoing urge to throw up. Her neck soaking, she slid to the floor, connecting with the heat-sapping cold of the kitchen tiles. Her heart was beating violently, and she struggled to fight the tide of panic that tightened across her chest. Dropping the letter, she pushed her palms flat against the floor, watching the inexorable ticking of the clock and counting her breaths in and out carefully.

Her senses restored sufficiently to continue, she felt out the letter and brought it to her knees. There could be no doubt, even on the initial reading, that this was from the same person who had sent Kitty so much hatred in the mail.

"Shit," she murmured under her breath. "Shit, shit, shitty fucking shit." Why hadn't she minded her own business? Why had she insisted on sticking her oar into this case? What the hell had she been thinking?

A sudden noise outside startled her. She sat still, barely daring to breathe let alone having the courage to get up and investigate further. The certainty that the murderer had returned and was now outside grew. The trembling in her hands returned as she listened, ears piqued as much as possible to try and work out if someone was there. And if they were there, where exactly was there? The blood pounded in her veins, surging her heart into a unrhythmic drumbeat of fear.

An unnatural terror rose in her. The letter that had come through the door was an all too immediate reminder that she was vulnerable. A killer knew where lived. A killer had been to her house. A killer had stood outside while she was sleeping, wrapped in the innocence of her dreams, unaware of how close the threat was.

No further noises filled the silence. The dull glow of her mobile phone on charge on the kitchen counter caught her eye. Without daring to stand upright in case someone was waiting outside to catch a glimpse of her, she crawled across the floor and reached up to grab it. Redial.

"Slater?" she whispered, when he picked up.

"Dr Henrikson?" Despite it being the middle of the night, his voice held no signs of having been asleep. The relief of human contact was immediate, rushing through her. Even if the worst were to happen now then at least she wouldn't die alone. She would have someone with her, even if it was just over a mobile connection. But it also signified the fact that help was now on its way.

"I think the murderer is outside," she said. Despite her attempt at quiet, her voice sounded incredibly loud and the terror that someone might have heard her destroyed her nerves all over again.

"What?" His voice was disdainful.

Please, she silently begged, please do not make me explain everything. "I think the murderer is outside," she repeated, urgent and carefully enunciating every phoneme.

Whether it was the silent plea or the unmistakable terror in her voice, he got the message. "Sit tight, I'm coming over."

She tried to ask him to stay on the line, to keep that human contact with her but he'd hung up before she could say anything else.

She remained frozen in place, her bum now numb and uncomfortable on the hard floor, silent tears occasionally escaping and trickling down her face to drop on her dressing gown. The world seemed completely silent now, as though she had cotton wool stuffed in her ears and for an absent-minded moment, she wondered if it had started snowing again.

She screamed as the doorbell sounded. "Dr Henrikson?" the voice cried. It didn't sound like Slater. Panic rose again. What if it was her? The murderer? "Vida?" the voice came again, insistent.

She was being silly. The murderer wouldn't announce her arrival by waiting politely at the door. It wasn't the frontal assault she needed to worry about; it was the sneaking round the back when no-one else was looking.

"Coming," she called, her voice wavering, as she sought to prevent another onslaught of noise. She was conscious of the way they were disturbing the unnatural silence of the night. Maybe that was a good thing though. Maybe the murderer would be scared off if they were out there, like a hedgehog caught unawares in the background. Maybe she was like a fox though, wily and ready to front out any incursion. She struggled to her feet and still feeling the urge to move unnoticed, tiptoed to the front door.

She opened in a crack, then moved out of the way as the visitor forced the door open and pushed her way in. Vida nearly screamed again but it died in her throat as she recognised Hussain, her hair wet with fallen snow. Behind her, an officer stood, obviously waiting for instruction. Hussain nodded her head towards him, and he ambled off.

"Slater sent out an APB on the radio asking for attendance at your property. I was nearest so I came straight away. Met PC James on my way. He'll have a look around for you. Had to leave the car on the main road though. Looks like you're snowed in; the council won't want to waste budget clearing this little tinpot alley." Vida's lips tightened at the implicit criticism of her home. The woman clearly didn't like her; she didn't know why she'd bothered to come. "Let's go in, you can put the kettle on and tell me all about it." She practically pushed Vida towards the kitchen. Vida had noticed that she was in charge of tea-making. It obviously wasn't a skill that the higher ups in the police force thought was for them. The relief at having another person in the house though vastly outweighed the annoyance at being relegated to teas-maid.

Hussain obviously knew what she was about though. The familiarity of the actions of boiling the kettle and filling the cups soothed her. Her heart rate began to normalise, and she felt less like she might burst into tears at any given minute. She'd been scrupulously avoiding the white paper on the floor but now she scooped it up and gave it to Hussain.

"Something woke me up about twenty minutes ago. I thought it was just a cat or something maybe." She wished it had been a cat. She wished it had been anything apart from what it was.

"It's just a letter," Hussain said.

Vida glared at her, unable to tell if she really was dismissing her fears so easily. "From a murderer," she said.

"No," said Hussain. "From someone who we wish to interview in connection to a murder investigation."

She was making Vida feel like an irrational woman, clearly over-reacting to this invasion of her life. "From someone who knows where I live."

"That's hardly top-secret information. A quick google will bring up the addresses of most people these days. Perhaps if you hadn't been so quick to stick your nose in, you might not have even hit his radar."

"Her radar," Vida said. Hussain acknowledged her correction with a tight grimace. Vida wondered why Hussain had bothered coming. Seeing Vida stabbed to death would probably be a positive outcome for her. "You don't need to be here," Vida said. "Slater said he'd be here soon."

"Your personal Knight in Shining Armour," mocked Hussain. "Speaking of which, I thought you had a husband? Shouldn't he be here, protecting his wife's virtue and anything else he wants to protect."

"He's out of the country at the minute," Vida said. "I'm expecting him back in the next couple of days."

"I wonder if he knows about your relationship with Slater."

"There is no relationship. I've just been trying to help him, help you, solve a murder. That's all."

Hussain raised her eyebrows in a way that suggested that Vida's denial had done nothing but convince her more strongly that something was going on.

"Vida? Vida?" Slater's voice preceded him bursting through the front door and down into the kitchen.

"Well, if our prowler wasn't scared off before, he certainly would be now," Hussain said.

Vida scowled at her. "I got a letter from the killer. She knows where I live." She snatched it back from Hussain and gave it to Slater. He studied it, folded it up and put it in his pocket. "It's not the first one," she admitted.

Slater looked up crossly. "Not the first letter?"

"I got one at work. Not like this. Just a transcript with some highlighting."

"You didn't say anything," he said, shortly.

"I..." She didn't what? Want to acknowledge the reality of the threat?

He seemed to hear her words, despite the fact they were in her head. "Any sign of anyone around now?" he asked, carefully directly his question to Hussain.

She shook her head. "No. I've not heard anything since I arrived. Whoever it was, if there was someone, is long gone now."

Vida bristled at the implicit suggestion of delusion. "I didn't imagine it. I certainly didn't imagine that, did I?" she said, gesturing towards the pocket to which Slater had confined the letter.

"Whoever it was probably just wanted to scare you. Maybe it's not even from the same person."

"This is exactly why I didn't tell you about it. I knew you'd be dismissive. This is from the same person who wrote that hate mail to Kitty and who left that other letter on a dead body. It is. I can tell." She fought the instinct to fold her arms and stamp her foot. The anger was doing a good job of edging away the fear though.

"I suspect that if it is the same person, they've just done it as a warning. I don't think you're in any direct danger," Slater said.

Vida glowered at him. "I'd consider having a killer know where I live, having a killer personally sending me little messages, as direct danger."

"Well, perhaps we can leave a police car outside of the rest of the night?" The question was directed at

Hussain who gave a sharp shake of the head. "Well, I can ask the night shift to drive by a couple of times anyway."

"Is that it?"

"Budget constraints," Hussain said. "Perhaps if you just did as the killer says, it will all blow over anyway. Stop meddling in things that don't concern you and let us solve this case." She stood up, the chair grating against the floor with a loud noise that made Vida wince. "I'll hand over to you now, Slater. Secure the premises and then leave Dr Henrikson. No need to waste even more time on this." She marched out.

"Is that what you want?" Vida asked Slater. "For me to stop working on the profile?"

Slater looked awkward. "I know I asked for your help originally, but perhaps it would be best all round if you just left it there. Especially if the killer is threatening you. She might be harsh but Hussain's right. We don't have the budget to guard you indefinitely."

"But my profile might make the difference between you catching the murderer and not," Vida appealed. Slater's look though was one that you might give a child who'd just realised that their art wasn't quite as good as they'd always thought. "You don't think it has any value."

"I'm sure it does," Slater started but Vida could hear the falsehood and platitudes.

"Don't bother," she dismissed him. "If that's what you want then I'll stop. No point flogging a dead horse." There went her chance of getting Myfanwy back on side, but she'd end up in deep water if she kept venturing over this ice. "Check the perimeter," she said, mockingly formal.

He sighed and then got to his feet. She could hear him wandering into every room, crossing to windows, trying doors. "You should close your bedroom window," he said, as he came back downstairs.

"I'll take that under advisement. Now if you wouldn't mind, we've all got to get some sleep."

For a moment, he looked as though he was going to offer something, offer more. But then he shook his head. "Make sure you lock up behind me," he said.

She did. And she contemplated going back to bed but instead she sat on her sofa and watched the black of midnight turn slowly into the grey of another February day.

Dear you

I know what you did and I will make you pay, you faithless whore. I am your dark storm and I will have vengeance.

You probably think you're safe. You probably think that what you've done will stay in the past. I'm going to make sure it doesn't. I'm going to make you pay.

Maybe you don't think of it at all. I see you and I think that perhaps you've forgotten it. Is that the only way you could live with yourself? If you pretended that it had never happened. Pretended that she had never happened. I can't do that. I can't wipe her out of my memories. She's there every day, every minute in my brain, living with me, reminding me of everything she was and now will never be.

I wonder what she did to deserve what you did to her. Maybe nothing. Maybe she looked at you, or said something to you, or maybe she never even noticed you at all. She was like that. Her head in the clouds. A dreamer. You stole that from her. You stole everything from her. Why?

I wish you had known her as a child, had seen what she was like as a toddler and an infant. I'm sure you would have loved her. We all did. Maybe if you'd known her then, if you'd seen her, dancing around the living room with her teddy bear, or tucked up tight at night with her thumb in her mouth and her forehead warm, maybe then you wouldn't have done what you did.

Chapter 35

Slater looked at the team around him. He wouldn't necessarily describe them as defeated, but battle-worn for sure. The week of futile searches and dead-end interviews had taken its toll on all of them. He needed to keep them focused.

"So, what have we got? Let's take the positives first and then we can think about all those black holes we've still got to find. Two victims. Two very different approach MOs if I can call them that; neither of these murders was set up in the same way. We have Kitty who seems to have communicated with the murderer." He flicked his eyes towards Hussain's ever-disdainful look. "I think that she went to her murder quite... well not happily but resignedly shall we say. George, you've reviewed the CCTV footage and still we've got nothing to indicate that Kitty put up a fight on her way to the alley." George shook his head.

"I've finally got witness confirmation as well," Louise said. Out of all of them, she seemed still the most alert. Maybe it was because she felt like she was actually getting somewhere, unlike the rest of them. "I finished trawling the tweets and social media posts and located Kitty in the tapas bar. She features in the background of a number of other shots. There was some sort of works leaving do and lots of shots captured her."

"Anything to help us pin down her companion?" Slater asked, knowing as soon as he did what the answer would be. Louise wasn't a glory hunter; she wouldn't be sitting on a vital lead waiting for her moment to shine.

"No, sir. Nothing more really than we've already got. A slight figure, between five eight and five eleven. Dressed in black, no distinguishing features. Only thing of note is that they do look like they're socialising rather than Kitty being under duress."

"So the theory stands. Looking at those messages on Kitty's laptop that IT recovered, she went to her death willingly. That's nothing like Ashaz's murder though. No signs of defensive wounds true but the PM found he was heavily drugged, a benzodiazepine that wiped him out sufficiently for the killer to slash his throat. Very different locations of course. Kitty in the alleyway."

"Could the killer be saying something about her being a waste product?" asked Louise, thoughtfully.

"Possibly. And Ashaz was definitely left on display. Maybe a statement about the domestic setting. Monster in the living room?"

Hussain frowned at his words and he felt the rebuke. Her words yesterday still echoed in his ears. He'd lost his grip on the case. Created more questions instead of answering anything. Offered an unusual amount of psychobabble that he wouldn't normally even contemplate.

"Anyway..." he said, looking back at the team who were looking expectantly at him. "We've got two entirely different MOs in terms of location and staging, but they've both used a knife. Any news on that, Mark?"

Dawson shook his head. "Nope. Casts were taken of the wounds, but forensic services are backed up. We're looking at a two-week turnaround at the quickest. They also don't think they'll find anything useful, given the nature of the wounds." Slater felt sure he could hear a note of embarrassment in Dawson's words. Slater had pushed through the knife mapping despite Ellison's comments yesterday that it would be unhelpful.

"Damnit. We need a concrete link between the two murders. We have got the letters, and Dr Henrikson is certain that the author of the letter left at the Ashaz scene is that same as the author of the ones sent to Kitty. We also have a link between the victims." Was that the right word to use he wondered? When he first started the investigation, he thought Kitty had seemed like some sort of paragon. It turned out that she was the worst kind of betrayer and abuser. "Kitty worked as a groomer for the gang in the 2000s when she was around fourteen, fifteen. We don't know what caused her to leave the gang. Whatever it was, it was something that affected her ever since then."

"So, we're looking at victims of the sex ring then? As potential perps?" asked George.

Slater shrugged. "Maybe. Dr Henrikson suspects that it's not an actual victim, but a relative. Maybe a sister or a mother."

"Bloody brilliant," said Dawson. "We're not just looking at victims as potential suspects but all their bloody female family members?"

"Mark is right," said Hussain coolly from the doorway. Slater didn't bother looking at her this time to see the disapproval. "What you've got is a potentially massive group of suspects, with very little information to help narrow them down. Are you planning on alibiing them all DI Slater? Do we even have a complete list yet? How are you planning on carrying out the interviews?"

"We're starting to get some names through from the Harpocrates team," he said, mentioned the team tasked with sorting through the horrors of the Khans' recording suite.

"So no," Hussain said. "No complete list, no real idea of when it will come in, no idea of how exactly you're going to make this list more useful." She nodded as though agreeing with his incompetence. "You don't seem to realise the pressure of this case, DI Slater." He sat upright in his seat, staring just behind her shoulder to avoid meeting her gaze. He wasn't used to being called out on his failures. He wasn't bloody used to being a failure. It wasn't a pleasant feeling. He wasn't sure which was worse though; that he'd let Hussain down or that he'd let the victims down.

"No, ma'am," he said, firmly.

"What exactly am I supposed to tell the super? Or the press? They know nothing about this real life of Kitty Wakelin. As far as they're concerned, the city's golden girl is dead and the city's police force is bungling the case. Thankfully, no-one seems to have linked the second murder yet. I personally am still not convinced that they are even linked. A few words on a scrap of paper is hardly irrefutable proof. If they are linked and the press gets wind of that, the Sheffield Serial headlines will be front page before we've had chance to deny anything."

Anger was replacing the feelings of failure. He was doing everything he could bloody think of to do. They'd exhausted as many traditional lines of enquiry as they possibly could. Ninety-nine times out of 100, the case would have been closed by now. It was bloody ridiculous.

"Do you have suggestions, ma'am?" he asked, tightly.

"Stop communicating with your pet scientist, for a start," she snorted.

"She might give us the information we need to tighten this list down though," Slater objected. He knew it was unreasonable, but he felt attached to the blonde doctor and her science. "She gave us the details yesterday about education, gender, early thirties. That does help us tie it down. And she's confident that she can get something more specific still. It might give us the break we need."

"Mights don't solve the case, Slater." Her words sounded like they'd been lifted from a self-help guide. Dreams don't build houses, wishes won't repair friendships. All hippy new-age bollocks. Trouble was, that seemed to sum up the current investigation perfectly.

"We have some names from the witness I interviewed on Thursday," Slater offered, seeking her approval. "She provided the names of girls she knew who were connected to the ring. Louise, have you got the list of names?"

Louise handed him a sheet. He studied it. Paled.

"Slater?" Hussain prompted.

"Louise has run the names through the system, ma'am. There's the witness I interviewed off the record. Anna Szabo. Her middle name. It's Natalya."

"And?" The impatience in her voice came through clearly and Slater felt it grab at his throat. There was a sense of impending disaster. And he wasn't sure he'd survive this.

"The IT team found evidence of letters written by Kitty to one of her correspondents, apologising for what she did to 'Aly'."

A smile dawned on Hussain's face. It was not a pleasant look. "You interviewed her? Unofficially? And now she links directly into this hate mail business?"

Slater could do nothing but nod. He couldn't even bring his eyes to look up at her. He was sure the others were looking at him. Pity from Louise maybe, amusement from some of the others.

"Get out to her address now, Slater. Bring her in. I need to talk to Professional Standards to take advice on whether you even see this case through to the end." She glared at him. "Now."

Chapter 36

Vida smiled as she said goodbye to her seminar group. Despite her exhaustion, the normality of the session, exploring some of the intricacies of child language acquisition had distracted her pleasantly. It didn't take long though for the brooding to start again. She was out of her depth and didn't know where to go.

An incoming text brought her back to the present. An unknown number. For a terrible moment, that seemed to pull out and extend in front of her, she became certain that it was the killer. Trembling, she pushed her thumb to the home button, the iPhone unlocking in front of her and revealing a few short words. *It's Anna. Please can I talk to you.*

The relief washed over her entire body, seemingly catching up the residual tension from last night and this morning's confrontation with Myfanwy and taking that away too. Here was someone she could help. Someone she could talk to. Perhaps this would help her escape that feeling of futility. She messaged a hasty reply, asking for an address and hoping that it wouldn't be the same salon as Thursday. She didn't think she could cope with the evidently perfect Sabryne again. Anna named a cafe just off the Halifax road and the relief twinged again. It was a short walk away from the Infirmary Road tram stop; she could be there within twenty minutes.

It made a welcome change to ride the tram. She still used it rarely enough for it to be a bit of a novelty. Most of her transportation was on foot, walking the short distance from their house to the university, maybe into the city centre occasionally. There was something relaxing, almost hypnotic about the rhythmic sway and clickety-click of the pantograph as it slid over the cables. From the moment she sat on one of the roughly furnished seats, she had to fight the desire to just close her eyes and drift off. The fear that perhaps the killer was watching her right now was enough to keep her awake. She stood and moved further down and positioned herself standing by an open window this time, relying on the harsh February temperature to maintain alertness. The city trundled past her in shades of grey, moving from a bustling centre to near deserted streets the further out she got.

The heavy snow of the previous night having turned rapidly to slush, the walk from the tram to the cafe was unpleasantly wet and treacherously slippy. Thankfully, it was also short, and with heaters blowing full blast, the cafe made a welcome respite from the invasive dampness of the streets. Vida spotted Anna straight away, huddled in a corner, nursing a cup of steaming liquid. Ordering herself a cup of tea to match, Vida picked her way through the students' laundry bags and mothers' pushchairs. The room was hot and steamy with bodies and chat, condensation on the windows blurring the view to the outside and giving the illusion of being in a bubble.

Anna looked even younger than she had when Vida had seen her in the salon. A large, moth-eaten sweater enveloped her, tiny stick hands emerging from the sleeve, skinny jean-clad legs descending from the body. She looked up at Vida when she approached, smiled a weak smile and then gestured to the seat opposite.

"Thank you," she said. Vida sat down and for a while, they stayed silent, both nursing their hot drinks. Vida wasn't entirely sure what she'd come for. Or why Anna had asked her here instead of relying existing friends. Maybe Anna sensed a lost soul in her.

"I think perhaps you wonder why I ask you here?" Anna started, her rising tone giving the sense of a question.

"A little I suppose," Vida admitted. "I'm not sure I can give you any more help, Anna. And if you've got any more information, I think you need to take it to the police. They're the ones who can investigate this."

"I do not want to talk to the police," Anna said. "I do not have any more information. I just wanted to talk to someone, and I think maybe you feel as I do?"

Vida looked confused. She didn't think she had much in common with Anna, perhaps beyond her hair colour.

"I think perhaps you can understand what it is like to be that teenage girl and to want people to like you. Sabryne has been so good to me and she has given me so much. But she does not understand. She has been beautiful and popular all her life. Not like me. Not like you, I think?"

It was phrased as a question, but Vida recognised the statement in the words. Anna wasn't wrong either, even though it hurt to admit it. Vida was not and had never been beautiful and popular. She could see all too easily the road to being abused by these men and in another time and another place, it could have been her.

Chapter 37

Slater and Dawson stomped their way to the front entrance of the block to Anna Szabo's home. Her address was in one of the brutalist tower-blocks that still dominated the Sheffield skyline, hard grey against the dull mercury of the gathering clouds. Despite the thaw that had melted last night's heavy snow underfoot, the evening held the promise of more of the white stuff. A security system dangled uselessly from the wall, while the door hung ajar. To Slater's surprise though, the entrance hall was bright and clean. He'd expected to find a dark, urine-soaked entry way. There was the slight smell of bleach lingering in the air, but it was clear that the renters and homeowners in this block at least took pride in their surroundings. The stairs were a little more inauspicious, the darkness clearly hiding a multitude of sins and the aromas here were a little more human and a little less fragrant. The seventh floor was a long climb away and even Slater was slightly out of breath as they reached the top. Dawson, cricket-fit not necessarily football-fit struggled after him, dropping further and further behind.

"Bloody hell," Slater said as they emerged from the dark stairwell out onto the balcony that the flats came off.

"What?" Dawson asked and then "Bloody hell," as he saw what had made Slater exclaim.

A couple of uniformed officers were assembled outside of the door. It wasn't entirely clear what they were waiting for, but Slater had a sinking feeling anyway. His gut hit bottom when one of the officers stepped aside to reveal Hussain in the middle.

"She didn't hang about. She must have called up the uniforms before we'd even left the station. Shouldn't have stopped for that coffee you insisted on getting."

"Baby was up all night. Anyway, what is she even doing here?" asked Dawson. "Anybody'd think she doesn't trust us."

"Me," Slater said. "She doesn't bloody trust me." A feeling of dread crept up his back. It couldn't be a good sign if your superior officer didn't even trust you to carry out a search and retrieve. "Ma'am," he said, approaching her as she finished giving orders to the uniforms.

"Slater. About time. I've had a quick look through the windows. No sign of Anna here."

"I didn't realise it was so urgent," Slater said. He wished he could have hidden the slight reproof in his voice better.

Her eyes narrowed. "At this stage, DI Slater, given that lack of forward progress in other areas, I feel that all lines of inquiry are potentially urgent. Professional Standards suggested a senior officer might be helpful. To ensure that procedure is followed properly." She didn't need to add the unlike last time. "I need something to report back to the ACC later." She nodded to the officer who was standing waiting with the ram. A sharp blow and the flimsy front door swung open. Hussain didn't wait for any further indications, simply stepped through the door and started her own search.

"Do we follow?" Dawson asked in Slater's ear. "Or is it like the Queen and we have to wait for her to clear the premises first?"

Slater rolled his eyes at his sergeant. He wasn't so forthcoming when Hussain was within earshot. "Come on."

As they stepped in, Hussain had virtually finished her royal tour. "Looks clean," she said, sharply. "Make sure you have a good search though. If there is something, we need to find it."

"What if there isn't though?"

"Then there isn't anything," she conceded. "But at least I can explain what exactly we've been doing. Proper police work instead of pandering to our little science hobby. This morning's papers just reminded me of what a liability she is. If I see her at the station again, you'll be up on disciplinary. Do I make myself clear?"

Slater nodded, the only response remotely acceptable if he hoped to keep his job.

"And I expect you to be with Julia this afternoon. Thanks to your doctor's big mouth we need to put together a rebuttal. Make it clear that she's a complete fantasist who thinks she's working with the police whereas in fact we're having nothing to do with her."

Another nod. Hussain scrutinised him as though looking to see if there were any fractures in him. "Last chance, Slater. Either you get the results today or I get a fresh set of eyes on it."

"Yes, ma'am," he said quietly. She turned and left, shedding her latex gloves like a snakeskin and leaving a uniformed officer to scoop them up behind her.

"Come on. Let's get this done." Inside, Anna's flat was tiny but clean. Sparsely furnished, Anna had clearly tried to make it more homely with a few blankets and cushions. Slater couldn't help but make comparisons between this and Kitty's flat, victim and aggressor. There was something quite pitiful about how Anna had obviously tried to make it nicer, with cheap IKEA prints adorning the walls and a range of pastel colours on the wall. There were no family pictures though, no sign of any inhabitation beyond Anna's and that made him feel inexplicably sad. He didn't know why. It was the way he chose to live himself and he'd never viewed his own life as being pitiful.

A quick scan of the flat showed him a living room, kitchen, small bathroom and a bedroom, all decorated in the same humble manner, all spotlessly neat and well-cared for. Uniforms were busy in each room, rummaging through and Slater felt suddenly guilty about the mess that Anna would return to. Whether or not they found anything, they were turning her life upside down, rooting through her most intimate spaces in the same way the abusers had done a few years ago. It made him sick.

"Found anything yet?" Slater asked the officer in the living room. He was torn between wanting them to say no and wanting them to find something instrumental. What was the better outcome here? Disrupting a victim's life and finding nothing or realising that he was on the verge of letting a killer walk free?

"Nothing yet. Place is pretty well looked after. All clean."

Slater went into the bedroom, leaving Dawson furtling in kitchen cupboards. He debated reminding him to check the knives out but decided his sergeant would get affronted if he was prompted about such an obvious thing, irrespective of whether or not he had actually remembered it. An old-fashioned looking patchwork blanket was draped across a double bed, the only sign of personality in the bedroom. The rest was renter's anonymous. He opened the wardrobe and half-heartedly thumbed his way through the clothes, a few thin dresses, a couple of coats and jackets. A pair of sandals, some trainers and a single pair of heels were stacked neatly in the base. Even he owned more pairs of shoes than that. The chest of drawers was similarly lacking in contents; the top drawer revealed her underwear, plain white cotton. He handled this even more gingerly, but was thorough, knowing that it was a favourite hiding place. Nothing revealed itself. There was nothing amongst her t-shirts and jumpers in the second drawer either and finally the bottom drawer lay empty. The bedside drawers revealed little more than a typical hotel room. A jar of half-used moisturiser and a library copy of a Marion Keyes novel sat on top.

There was nothing here. Nothing to indicate Anna had anything to do with this. The relief he felt was immediate and immense. He wouldn't have been able to live with himself if the alternative was true; letting a murder suspect get away without even a formal interview was the kind of thing that dead-ended careers.

He got down on his knees to check under the bed. Not even a dust bunny; Anna's standards of cleanliness were impressive. Avoiding the temptation to groan slightly, from the disturbed night's sleep and the previous gruelling hockey practice, he got back to his feet. Finally, the washing basket, an old-fashioned Ali Baba type affair in the corner of the room.

On first glance it looked empty, but a second look told him there was some black fabric at the bottom.

"Gabe?" Dawson called him from the kitchen. Not wanting to confront what he'd found in the basket quite yet, he stood up and turned towards Dawson in the kitchen. He was flicking through a book open on the tiny kitchen table.

"What is it?"

Dawson pushed the book towards him. It looked to be full of newspaper cuttings, an old-fashioned scrapbook. "They're all stories about Kitty."

"Well, she's already told us that they had a connection."

"Not a friendly one," Dawson said, pointing out the pictures. Kitty's face stared out at them; or rather it would have done had the eyes not been gouged out. "Every picture's the same."

Slater shut the book. "It doesn't give us anything we don't already know," he said, but he was already turning back to the basket. He scooped out the garment and spread it out on the table as Dawson moved the scrapbook out of the way.

"Shit." The bundle turned into a black hoody. On the front, something darker than the black fabric gathered in a thick patch. Slater moved closer.

"Is that blood?" Dawson asked, his voice almost reverential.

"Looks like it."

Dawson grinned at him. "That's it, Gabe. About bloody time. Thought I was going to have to follow you onto the burning boat."

"Could still be nothing," he said, but the bubble of excitement was there. Immediately behind was the feeling of panic about missing something so big earlier. Served him right for breaking the rules. Bloody Sabryne and her bloody restrictions. He should have demanded that they made the interview official. He wasn't going to make that mistake again. Everything right down the line from now on in. "Okay, get that back to the lab," he ordered, gesturing for an evidence bag. "I want it cross-matched against Kitty Wakelin and Ashaz Khan."

Slater looked around again. Did this look like the flat of a murderer? Someone who had viciously stabbed two people to death? Someone who had planned and plotted? He thought back to what he'd said to Vida about there not being a type of person who would kill. It was true he knew. But surely there was the kind of person who wouldn't kill.

"Has anyone found a laptop? Or a printer? Or any supplies of similar paper to the letters that were sent?" The question was open but all he got were a few surprised looks and a couple of head shakes.

"Maybe the letters are just a coincidence," Dawson said. "Maybe she used the local library or something."

"I think you're probably right," Slater agreed. "The whole thing was a bit bloody Miss Marple, wasn't it? Did you find anything else in the kitchen? Any knives that could match?"

"Not unless she did it with a butter knife."

Slater's inner bully sat firmly on the questions that were still churning in his stomach. "Right, put a rush on the forensics. They can match blood type quickly and that will give us some broad info. But we've got to arrest her now. This is our triangulation point. Any ideas where we might find her?"

"Yes," said Dawson. "But I don't think you're going to like it." He'd wandered out on to the balcony and pointed now down to the square in the centre of the blocks. Slater pushed out of the hall and looked down.

"You've got to be kidding me," he scowled. "What the hell does she think she's playing at?"

Chapter 38

The walk back to Anna's flat had numbed Vida's feet again. It had been a nice invitation for her to make and Vida felt strangely protective of the girl. Anna was evidently proud of her home and it touched Vida to be invited into her private space. It must have been hard for her to trust people, especially when her trust had been so spectacularly betrayed by Kitty Wakelin. They chattered irrelevantly about television and music and world travel and food and for a few short metres, Vida felt the weight of the last few days lift.

"Oh," Anna said, suddenly as they crossed the quadrant between the tower blocks.

Vida looked up to see Slater and a stockier man striding towards them. Her face automatically broke into a smile which faltered as she saw the emotions on Slater's face. Anger, confusion, distress. It was not the face of someone who was happy to see her there. She stopped abruptly, her heart beating to get out of her chest. What if someone else lay dead here? Another victim slaughtered by this mad killer that Vida just couldn't get a handle on. Then came the guilt. While she'd been having a nice cup of tea and talking nonsense, she'd not been looking at the letters. She'd been distracted and worse than that, she'd welcomed it.

Her first emotion was quasi-relief then as Slater approached Anna. It wasn't her; he didn't want to add to her burden.

"Anna Szabo, I'm arresting you on suspicion of murder."

The relief turned to horror which turned very quickly to righteous indignation. Her gaze moved quickly from Slater to Anna and back again. He delivered the caution flatly, as though the words held no meaning for him. Anna looked wild almost, panicked. Slater took her by the arm, gently, and fed her carefully into the grip of the man next to him who started to steer her towards the car park. Slater's body language spoke of regret and defeat. His gaze was on the floor as he turned to follow the others.

"What are you doing?" hissed Vida, urgently. She grabbed Slater's arm and pulled him back towards her.

Slater looked at her balefully until she dropped his arm. "Arresting the prime suspect in this murder investigation."

"But it's not her! It can't be her! You heard her when she spoke; she's not a native English speaker. She doesn't sound anything like the person who wrote those letters. I've given you the profile. The only bit she fits is female."

"Well, maybe she didn't send the letters," he said, tightly.

"But you said that the person who sent the letters was definitely the person who killed them. Kitty wrote back, for heaven's sake."

"Well, maybe your profile is wrong."

Vida felt the anger rise. "It is not wrong," she said, through gritted teeth. "You know what, all along, you've been so negative about everything I do. Every time I've offered some piece of information, you've looked at me with that smug, condescending face. And yet, every time, every single time, I've been proven right. You wouldn't have found out about Maggie's death without me. Maybe none of this at all would have come to the surface if it hadn't been for the work that I was doing. And now, it's just too inconvenient for you to admit that perhaps the science is right. Perhaps you've got the wrong girl."

"We found a document on Kitty's computer referencing a previous victim we think, an Aly."

"Her name is Anna," she pointed out, trying to keep the obviously out of her tone.

"Her middle name is Natalya. Aly?"

"You only know about her because she approached you. She offered you help," said Vida, furiously. "Why would she tell you about the link if she was the murderer? She may as well have put it on a sign outside her front door."

"Sometimes people like to play games. And you said yourself that it seemed like the killer was more interested in making sure people knew what Ashaz and the rest of them had been up to. Getting away with it wasn't part of her plan."

"What sort of a killer doesn't want to get away with it?"

"The sort who thinks they're seeking justice. Justice needs to be public; it can't be done in secret."

"Is that it though? Because her middle name might have a diminutive shared by loads of other people? What about the fact the rape happened to her? We agreed that the letters sounded like they came from someone talking about some else. They use the personal pronoun."

"Psychologist reckons that that could indicate some sort of dissociative disorder."

Vida felt unreasonably jealous. She was the independent expert here and yet her judgement was being usurped by someone who hadn't even introduced himself to her.

"Listen," he said, urgently. His tone held the air of someone who knew he was about to break someone's heart. "There was other, more compelling forensic evidence."

"Well, it must have been planted."

Slater's face darkened. "I do not plant evidence."

Vida took a step back. He looked like he might be on the verge of losing his temper with her.

"Slater... Gabe... please listen to me," she started. "I'm convinced. One hundred percent. Anna is not the girl who wrote those letters. And if she didn't write those letters then someone else did. And that someone is far more likely to be your killer than that poor broken girl we met in the salon."

"All I can do is go where the evidence leads me," he said. "I know you reckon we need help. What was the headline in the paper this morning?" His voice was gruff.

Vida had the grace to blush. "I didn't say what they made it sound like I said," she said. "In fact, I was very complimentary about the police force and the way they are approaching this case using modern scientific methods. Don't turn your back on it now, Gabe. Not when it's so important. Anna's a victim in all this. You know she can't be the killer."

"Evidence tells me she fits the physical bill, she's got motive, we'll talk about opportunity at the station. I can't go beyond the evidence," he repeated.

"Well, I can," she replied, sharply.

"Vida, you shouldn't. Don't put yourself at risk. Remember the letter."

And she did. It came back to her, bringing with it sudden nausea, panic and a feeling of helplessness. Damn him for reminding her. Damn him for putting her in this impossible situation. "But if I'm right, Gabe, then I'm at risk anyway. Because you've not caught the killer yet. And until you do, I'm always going to be looking over my shoulder and wondering. I can't live like that. I don't believe anyone can."

He appeared to contemplate her words. "My hands are tied," he said, finally. "Hussain's made it clear that she believes the case is closed. We've got a case that will please the CPS. I can't continue to investigate a solved case."

Vida turned to leave.

"Just be careful," he said. "And if you do find anything, you know where I am."

The righteous anger she'd felt when she'd confronted him had vanished, leaving an uneasy mix of uncertainty and fear.

***

"What do I do?" she wailed, pacing up and down Caroline's much more ordered office. It wasn't just the view of the landscaped city park that created an air of calm and nature; Caroline had somehow managed to decorate her office with plants that thrived, a fish-tank that sustained actual life and neatly ordered bookshelves that looked pretty instead of overloaded.

"Calm down, for a start." Caroline gestured to the chair opposite her desk. She got up and quickly boiled the kettle, pouring hot water onto a tea bag and setting the mug in front of Vida.

"What is this?" Vida asked, suspiciously.

"Camomile and honey. Should help you remember to breathe. That kind of thing."

Vida sniffed at it. "But what do I do, Caro? They arrested her."

"Well, maybe she did it. It does annoy me when everyone is so willing to believe that the police are completely fallible. Why shouldn't they get it right occasionally? It's like all those petty parents who complain about us being too hard on their little Diddums. Like any of us became lecturers for any other reason that we love our subjects, and we want to teach."

"They're not right, though. He's not right."

"Who? That DI Slater? I can believe that. He was far too pompous to be right. He probably did join the police to bully other people."

"No," Vida said, absentmindedly. "His dad was a policeman too. But he isn't right on this I mean. There's no way Anna could have killed those people. I'd be able to tell."

"You're not always an excellent judge of character, Vida."

Vida's brow darkened. "It's not even that. I might not be able to judge character, but I do know words. She did not write those words, Caroline."

"Then prove it."

"But he won't listen to me."

"That's his decision then. You'll have done everything you can. And you can take it to her defence if she needs it."

"What if I can't narrow it down anymore?"

"Bollocks, Vida. You know sometimes you're so annoying. Of course, you can narrow it down. You're great at what you do. Just because Myfanwy Davies has spent the past few months telling you you're useless, there's no good reason to believe her. But you can do it, Vida. And for your own peace of mind, you need to see this through to the end. Prove she didn't write those letters. Find who did."

Chapter 39

"It's fine," said Hussain. "A good solicitor will be able to offer mitigation and reduce her sentence. She did the world a favour really. These people needed to be taken off the streets. And unfortunately, our justice system doesn't give space to deliver the real punishment these people deserve." He'd heard her thoughts on crime and punishment before, but never in such strident terms.

Anna had been booked in and was now sitting downstairs in the cells. He'd met her when the squad car brought her in and had tried to reassure her, tried to build on the fragile relationship they'd established at Sabryne's, but she'd been withdrawn and the look she'd given him had been pure hatred. He couldn't blame her. The hoody had been submitted to the Forensic service and he was just waiting for them to ring and confirm blood-type. He could start the interview now, but he wanted to make sure the blood was a type-match before he started the interview. It couldn't be necessary. It had to be relevant.

He'd taken his concerns to Hussain. She didn't seem as concerned. She'd praised him as soon as he walked through the door. He couldn't deny that the praise had felt good, especially when she mentioned that the ACC himself had passed on his congratulations. A job well done. But he couldn't get Vida's words out of his head.

"She doesn't match the profile put together by Dr Henrikson though," he said, stubbornly.

"Slater, I cannot begin to explain to you how much of a shit storm you are going to find yourself in if you do not stop mentioning that woman in my presence. She is a bloody liability. And you will be considered the same if you do not move on."

Slater shrugged, miserably. He couldn't remember ever feeling this dissatisfied after a successful case completion. "The profile is compelling though," he said, unwilling to let go completely. "Dr Henrikson says she's going to continue working on the case to exonerate Anna. I think she's formed some sort of bond with her."

Hussain snorted, derisively. "Well, I don't think we've got anything to fear from that quarter. As far as I can tell, the science is relatively untested in court. A judge probably won't even let her testify as an expert. The forensics on the hoody will come in, we've got motive, opportunity and now the means. CPS will be on board with this." She paused and seemed to be readying herself. "Despite the ACC's congratulations, Slater, he did also impress on me that there are going to be some questions for you to answer." She looked disappointed, but Slater couldn't tell if it was at him or for him. "You had met the killer previously and had not even sought to formalise that statement. I'm afraid the IPCC will want to look into that. I'm sure it will be straightforward enough, but they will want to ensure that there's no whiff of corruption that can come back and bite us when this gets to court."

Slater nodded. Perhaps that was where the unease came from. It wasn't with the case itself; it was with his own inadequacies. He'd interviewed a killer and hadn't even considered her as a possible suspect, despite the fact she'd effectively sign-posted herself as that.

Dawson knocked on the door. "Sorry to interrupt boss, ma'am, but Forensic Services just rang. They carried out the blood group test immediately. Found two different blood sources. First is O+, which matches to Kitty Wakelin but also 36% of the population. Second is B+ which is a match to Ashaz Khan's blood-type but is also common amongst Eastern Europeans and Asians from the Central Asian region."

"It's enough," Hussain said, smiling. "I presume you urged them on to DNA match with our victims?"

"Yes, ma'am," Dawson said before backing out of the door.

"It's enough," Hussain repeated.

It was enough. "I'll get the interview started now," Slater said. "With any luck, she'll confess before we have to go too far. If she is interested in justice then I can argue that a confession will make it better for her; it will put the focus on Kitty and Ashaz and what they did wrong rather than on her own crimes."

"Clear strategy."

With Hussain's approval singing in his ears, he shrugged off the last of his uncertainties and headed back out to his team. This case had given him a sick feeling from the very start but at last, it was looking like things were finally going to be sorted. He needed to embrace that and start looking forward to the spoils of a successful prosecution. Dawson had said right at the start of the week that this was going to be career make or break. He was going to make damn sure it made him.

Chapter 40

Vida stared at the table that she'd made of the letter writer's common features. She'd already pinned down gender, age and education bracket. She needed something much more specific now that she could show excluded Anna as the possible writer of the letters. It still seemed patently obvious to her that the writer of the letters was the killer. Why else would they have left a letter on Ashaz's body? How else could they have left a letter on his body for that matter? She needed something.

The more she needed it though, the more it eluded her. All she could see was what she'd already seen.

"Right, fresh eyes," she told herself, standing, stretching and shaking her head. "You can do this." She felt like a prize fighter before the biggest fight of the year and danced a little between her feet to try and inspire the same kind of passion in the words as they showed for their fists. "Limber up, Vida, limber up." She stretched her shoulders and then wiggled her fingers before sitting back down.

It was no good. The words were still incomprehensible to her. It felt like she'd almost lost the ability to read, let alone define anything linguistically. "Damn."

She wandered into the kitchen and made herself some white toast and butter. The one advantage to Simon not being there was that she could indulge herself in childhood treats like white bread. He refused to buy it when he was at home, preferring instead to use the sourdough starter he kept on the windowsill and addressed as though it was their first-born. Taken together with a hot cup of tea, the hot butter-laden toast was just the prescription she needed to refresh herself.

Returning to the study, she saw that Jamie had emailed her the first of his analysis. His email was friendly, perhaps overly friendly, and Vida couldn't help but cringe at the platitudes he'd included. He wrote like a woman she noticed, his emails full of indirectness, hedging and super-intensive politeness markers. It didn't make her feel more inclined to help him.

She looked at the analysis. It was a write up of the research he'd done in Birmingham, interviewing a range of Urdu speakers, from first generation immigrants through to seventh or eighth generation immigrant families. Interesting and wide-ranging, Vida knew that it was going to have real impact on the database she was trying to establish of different locations' speech patterns.

Her mind was so far away though, in a cell with Anna, on Slater's shoulder, even in Simon's olive grove with a dog, that she nearly missed it. A single line, a throwaway comment that she would make him strike out of the analysis because it brought nothing to an understanding of how and why the language patterns evolved. "Several respondents used the word 'gully' where non-Birmingham speakers might use passage or road or drive." She flicked back to her table, then scrabbled through the photocopied letters on her desk. There it was "We played in the gully at the back of our house, splashing in suds that were left from the car washing." She'd read it and assumed that it meant there was some sort of drop at the back of the house, a traditional gully in the sense of a ravine made by water at some point. It had struck her as slightly unusual, but nothing so out of place that it stood out. But perhaps it was an indication of the writer having spent time in Birmingham, probably as a child given the word was connected to her childhood. She scanned through the rest of the table, looking for anything else that could support the conclusion. Cop was used as a transitive verb in the past tense. To suggest that someone was apprehended for something. It was enough. Two geo-linguistic points that located to the same origins. Flicking back to her profile, she dotted down 'spent time in Birmingham, possibly as child.' Whoever it was, wherever they'd come from, it was clear that they were based in Sheffield now and seemed to know the city well enough to navigate successfully through the streets without being too obviously spotted. That took street skill. Vida added 'Living in Sheffield now.' So it was obvious. Sometimes the obvious overlooked became as important as anything else.

She returned to the letters, rejuvenated by the discovery. It was always the smallest things that unlocked everything. She pored over it, determined to notice every small anomaly. There, 'I you will make pay.' A non-standard sentence, written in Subject-Object-Verb syntax when Subject-Verb-Object would have been standard in English. Another thing that she'd missed earlier as her brain had read what she thought was there, rather than what was actually there. It was a common problem when reading in bulk. Languages that commonly used the SVO structure included a wide range of Asian languages. Even though Ancient Greek and Latin had started this way, the Romance and Germanic language trees had evolved from the base of the Indo-European tree, the European languages going from one side, the Indo-Iranian from the other. Could this writer have been bilingual? Possibly English wasn't her first language after all. Or if it was, she'd been raised in an immigrant family where they spoke another language too. It excluded Anna though, as Hungarian was firmly on the European side of the tree. She jotted it down on her list. Definitely not Hungarian. Possibly Asian.

That made her wonder. She'd noted some of the language as being religious. 'Faithless whore' clearly indicated some religious leanings. The venom in the adjective spoke of an organised spirituality. But what about the Messengers? She googled the term quickly and found herself wading through a host of responses about various TV shows and films. Whatever the word connoted, it was obviously connected to fear and horror. She added 'religion' to her search terms. This time it brought up things connected to Islam. She drilled down. Messengers seemed to be a subset of prophets, bringers of divine revelation from Allah. She read more. There was a reference to Allah sending Messengers to investigate potential crimes before meting out justice. Was that it? She added it to the profile and then sat back and looked at what she'd got. Female. Early 30s. Well-educated. Childhood spent in Birmingham, currently living in Sheffield. Could she narrow the second language down any further? Not conclusively, she didn't think, but perhaps suggestively. The most recent census of Birmingham demographic put the Asian group at nearly 300,000, with Pakistani Asian making up over half of that. Urdu was the national language for Pakistan and also used the SVO syntax. So did Punjabi though which was another common Pakistani language. She noted them both down, adding a hesitant question mark after each. A Pakistani origin would also connect with the possible Islamic influence; Indian which was the second largest demographic after Pakistani would be more like to have a Hindi influence.

That was it. She sat back in her chair. Was there anything else? She scanned through the letters one last time. Nothing else jumped out at her. Feeling a combination of nerves, satisfaction and downright paranoia, she clicked send.

She'd done what she could. The profile was flying through the ether to Slater. It was as precise as she could be. Perhaps as precise as she'd ever been thanks to Jamie's Urdu research and the focus she'd put on it. It felt more important than anything she'd done before. Even being part of a team to find the missing Jenny a few years ago. It certainly felt more real. That case had been distant and in the past tense; this one was here and now.

She looked restlessly around her study, fighting the urge to ring Slater and give the report orally as well as in writing but she knew that wouldn't do any good. Maybe she should go down to the station now and demand that he looked at it. She didn't think he'd appreciate that though and if Hussain caught her, she'd probably make Slater delete the file before he'd even opened it. Maybe she should ring Caroline and meet her for a drink. Maybe email Jamie and tell him how instrumental he'd been in putting the profile together. It might spur him on to finish the project. Maybe she should forward the profile to Anna's solicitor. It could provide ammunition for him to get Anna out of there.

Her stomach still churned with an unhealthy mixture of nerves and fear. It wasn't over, she knew. She just needed to make Slater see that too.

The doorbell rang.

Chapter 41

Slater slumped at his desk. Anna had refused to confess, remaining wide-eyed and traumatised through the whole thing. He'd thought he'd seen her crack a little when he pointed out that the hoody had the blood-types of both victims on it, but she'd just shaken her head and refused to comment. Even when he'd patiently explained to her that if she confessed now then the judge would look favourably on her during sentencing. 'Anyone would be able to understand why you did what you did,' he'd said, gently. No comment was all he got back. That and the accusation he read in her eyes every time he asked her a question, no matter how gently he tried to frame it.

The incident room was an abandoned ship as the rest of the team had headed to the pub, their mood jubilant, feeling more energised than they had for the previous week. There was no doubt in their minds that they'd solved it. He envied them their certainty. He kept telling himself that all he needed was one more thing. If the DNA came back positive. If they found the weapon in the area around Anna's flat. If she talked and gave them something. There were still a lot of ifs in his mind for saying the case had been solved satisfactorily for everyone else. He didn't begrudge the others their peace of mind though. He'd sent his credit card along with Dawson to put behind the bar with a promise that he'd join them later. Maybe he would.

He opened his email, scanning the inbox in the hope that the Forensic Service had beaten all known human records and had produced the DNA results in record time. No such luck. His heart sank a little when he saw an email from Vida. For a moment, he debated just deleting it. They had their killer. Forensics would be on their side. Motive and opportunity as far as he could tell, given that Anna had refused to give them an alibi.

He opened it. Read the profile. It didn't match anything about Anna. In fact, Vida had made it clear in very strident terms that there was no way that Anna was the writer of those letters. Where did that leave him? It was easy enough to convince the team that the letter writing actually had nothing to do with the killing. Not so easy to convince himself. Groaning, he pressed print, collected the profile and set off to the Harpocrates Op room.

Both the victim and assailant walls were considerably more populous than they had been when he visited yesterday. Around ten men had been added, their faces bleak and unsmiling but apart from that no different to any man you would pass on the street. It made him sick. But not as much as the victim wall which now had around 50 headshots pinned up, varying ages and races but all with the same fear and horror etched on their faces.

"You've made progress," he commented to a young male officer who had looked up as he'd entered the room. Like his own incident room, it was deserted apart from this paperwork warrior who looked as though he'd got a backlog of three years' worth of filing to complete.

"Some," the man said, modestly.

"Do you have dates for these?"

"Some," he repeated.

"I'm working on the Kitty Wakelin and Ashaz Khan murders," Slater offered.

"Oh yeah? I hear congratulations are in order for that. Got your killer today, didn't you?"

Slater gave a small smile. "I'm just following up a loose end really. Looking for someone, a woman, who was abused around 2010 to 2012 maybe? I'm not sure when."

"The wall's in chronological order." The officer got to his feet. 'This end is our most recent victims. Towards the left we go back as far as maybe 2005. We've probably got another fifteen years on that but thankfully, they're more sporadic. So, these ones here," he said, indicating a group of women on the left side of centre, "are the ones around your timeline."

Slater studied the women. You couldn't judge a book by its cover, he knew that, but some of these women could be superficially excluded. "Have you got names for them?"

"Most of them." He returned to his desk, made a few mouse clicks, typed something and then got up as the printer whirred into action. "Here you go. These are all the ones we've put names to. The unnamed women are at the bottom with their pictures."

"Thanks."

"No problem. Hope you get your loose ends knitted in," he said, cheerfully, before returning to his paperwork mountain once more.

Slater laid the sheets of paper out on his own desk. Around twenty women. Ran through what he knew. Not much about the victim herself apart from the fact that she must have had a sister or a close female relative who would now be in her thirties. That wouldn't exclude that many of them, he thought bitterly. What else? Well, if the sister grew up in Birmingham, there was a good chance that the victim did too. Similarly, the Islamic and Pakistani connection. He drew a line through the thirteen obviously white women. Including Anna's face. She was almost unrecognisable as the same woman he had downstairs in the cells, waiting for the axe to fall. He'd thought she looked young now, but in 2011 she looked barely twelve. The terror in her eyes was entirely adult though, holding the sort of knowledge that no child should ever have to know.

He was left with seven women. Five known names and two unknowns. He ran each of the names through the computer, excluding two more women as being recorded as Hindi, one as being Italian and one as being a single child orphan. Three left, one known, two unknown. The final name inputted into a google search produced a vignette of a happy and successful woman. Unscientific perhaps, but Slater didn't see that this level of success would cause the level of hatred seen in the murders. He was still looking for his complicating factor.

He stared at the two unknown women, trying to make out something that would give him the answer to their identities. Both Asian, both beautiful, one younger than the other, looking like she was around fourteen whereas the other looked like she could be in her twenties. There were no distinguishing marks on either of their faces.

His phone rang. "Slater?"

"DI Slater. Ellison here. Just wanted to let you know, we've determined COD for Raheeq Khan."

Please let it be natural causes, Slater prayed. "And?"

"Overdose of insulin."

"Insulin? How? I mean... how did that happen?"

"I'm afraid it looks like murder. No sign of it being self-induced. Found a small puncture wound on his thigh. Correlates to a mark in his trousers. Your officers reported no needles or anything at the scene, so someone else must have delivered it and walked away afterwards."

"But he was in the cells?" Ellison was silent. "You mean, it was someone in the station?"

"That's for you to find out, Slater. But unfortunately, that would be the first place I looked."

Slater thanked Ellison and hung up. Murdered? But why? As punishment for Maggie? But who? Brain whirring, he picked up the phone again and rang down to the custody suite. "It's Slater. I need the names off the sign in sheet for visitors to Raheeq Khan."

Somewhere in his brain, a synapse suddenly fired, crashing into a name that the Custody Sergeant gave him. He hung up without saying anything more. Hands shaking as he clutched the printout tightly, he crossed to Hussain's office. Her door was shut tightly, but not locked. The lone family picture still stood on her desk. "Shit," he swore, his voice low as though he was afraid that if someone heard him, caught him, he'd have to explain what he was doing in her office and at the minute, any way he couched this was going to sound completely insane. He picked up the picture, holding the unknown women next to it, feeling his heart pound and his stomach plummet as the commonalities between the younger unknown victim and the girl he presumed was Hussain's sister swam into focus.

"Shit," he said again. It wasn't conclusive. Lots of girls looked like each other. Especially in old photographs; they didn't have the digital accuracies of modern photography. Returning to his desk, he plugged Hussain's name into the search box. Millions of results appeared. Breathing slowly to try and keep his tremors in check, he added policewoman. The results narrowed, stories now full of praise for his superior officer. Highlighting her quick rise, her promising future and her fighting gender and racial barriers. Still, nothing helpful. He added family and found himself drowning in more results. The name was too common for him to distinguish anything helpful. "Think, Gabriel," he urged himself.

He navigated to a genealogy website and plugged in Hussain's name and year of birth. If he could locate her parents, then perhaps he could locate her sister that way. Cursing, he filled in the information to give him immediate access to the website and then sent the search out. Over 83,000 results came back. He narrowed it down by month and date. Still hundreds of results. If Vida was right though, he could potentially narrow it down further. Birmingham. He tried to remember anything that Hussain had ever told him about her family. Barely anything as she was so secretive. Maybe this was why. He was sure though that she'd told him once that her father was a pharmacist and that he'd been disappointed when she chose a career in the police over a career in pharmaceuticals. He scanned down the list, adding parental names as he went. The list reduced finally to around thirty sets of parents.

This whole process felt so slow and the waiting for search results to run was agonising. At the same time, this finally felt like he was back on form, like a blockage had been cleared. The excitement was electric. Each parental name went into the search box, lined out as they had multiple children, or just one child, or had children who were now dead. Seventeen pairs in and he found his first parents to two girls, one Zahra Hussain, born 1985, one Aaliyah Hussain, born 1997. "A," he breathed. "Aaliyah."

He switched tabs and plugged Aaliyah's name into google. The first result was a Sheffield Star headline: Tragic Teen in Terror Plunge to Death.

Chapter 42

Hussain stood on her doorstep. "Dr Henrikson, may I come in?"

"Why?" asked Vida, suspiciously. "If it's about the profile then what I said stands. I don't care what your so-called forensics say. Anna did not write those letters and if she didn't write the letters, then she didn't kill those people either."

"I'm concerned for you," Hussain replied, angling her head onto one side and affecting something that looked like worry on her forehead, although Vida noticed that it didn't reach her eyes.

"Why?"

"DI Slater has informed me that you're planning on continuing your search for the so-called murderer. I'm very worried that you're putting yourself in the sights of a potential killer."

"I don't really care," said Vida, forcing the declarative certainty into her voice while feeling the interrogative wavering inside. "I can't let an innocent woman go to jail for something she didn't do. Especially because that means that the someone who did do it will still be free. I can't live with that on my conscience and I'd be surprised if you could."

"Dr Henrikson... Vida, may I come in? I'm concerned about the impact this case has had on you and I'm sure you wouldn't want to have this conversation about your personal mental health in view of everyone on your street.

I understand you've been under a lot of pressure at work recently. If news of anything like this reached the university, I'm sure it would not look good for you."

"My mental health is fine," replied Vida, defiantly, but she stepped aside to let Hussain in.

Chapter 43

Slater rubbed his head, following the story link. Aaliyah Hussain, fourteen years old with immense promise and life in front of her had thrown herself off a high-rise building in Birmingham. The death was clearly suicide as they had several witnesses who'd seen her going up there, but the causes were unknown. According to her family and friends, there was no reason at all why she would have killed herself. The girl, known as Aly, had simply everything to look forward to in life.

He looked back to the printout he'd taken from the Harpocrates Op room. He could still be mistaken. The similarities could all be in his head. But he knew it wasn't. This girl, captured in her moment of agony, was Aaliyah Hussain.

And he'd told her sister that Vida was still looking into the case.

Chapter 44

Vida had prepared tea for two in silence, with no desire to make polite conversation with the woman in front of her. For her part, Hussain looked serene, almost beatific in her posture and gestures. Vida placed the tea down, excused herself to go to the bathroom and returned to find Hussain still sat in the same position.

"You can stop pretending to be interested in my mental well-being," Vida said, sitting opposite Hussain. She was a beautiful woman. Could be stunning if she broke a smile occasionally maybe.

"On the contrary, it's not a pretence. After I had that very illuminating conversation with your Myfanwy at the university, I came to understand that unfortunately your position is looking precarious and I'd hate for you to fall off the edge of anything."

"It's no good anyway. I finished the profile and it one hundred percent excludes Anna from being the letter writer. I'm going to make sure that her solicitor gets it, and I will volunteer my services to be an expert witness if they need. She didn't do it and I'm going to make sure everyone knows that."

Hussain smiled. "You're very passionate about this. I suspect that's your weakness. You're getting too involved. Trust me, when you work with criminals every day, you have to stay dispassionate. They will horrify you with the depths of their depravity. Just look at these so-called men.

Years of torture and horror. Finally though, the Messengers will come for them."

Vida looked up, sharply. "Pardon?"

"It's a common idea in Islam, Vida, that Allah will mete justice out with the help of the Messengers. I'm sure these men will get what they deserve. Maybe not as much as Kitty and Ashaz did, but as much justice as our little criminal justice system can give them before they face the Day of Judgement."

Vida shook off her suspicions and took a slurp of tea.

"I'm sure you don't think that these men deserve to get away with what they did?"

"No, of course not," said Vida, fiercely. "But nor do I believe that Anna should take the blame for something she didn't do."

"Perhaps it was someone else then after all."

"Perhaps," Vida said, slowly. She didn't know where Hussain was going with this and her head was beginning to feel a bit groggy. Doubtlessly, it was a result of last night's lack of sleep and this morning's focus on getting the profile finished.

"What did your little profile conclude?" Hussain asked, her voice strangely sing-song.

"Female, early 30s, well-educated, probably raised in Birmingham, probably a Muslim, maybe a Pakistani Urdu speaker." Vida's tongue felt thick in her mouth.

"Maybe," Hussain said, as though conceding a point. "Or maybe," she leaned forward, "that's all a fiction created by a little Forensic Linguist who's in danger of losing her job and thinks what she needs is a shiny little case to make herself indispensable."

Vida felt confused, even more exhausted. She didn't understand what Hussain was saying.

The knife that Hussain withdrew from her bag and slid across the table, on the other hand, was all too clear.

Chapter 45

"Shit," Slater said as he rushed to his car. Any other suspect and he'd be asking for backup, maybe even SWAT to help get the suspect out. How on earth was he supposed to tell them that he thought his superior officer was the killer? Everything he'd found out about the police in the past few days, all those official eyes turned away from Maggie and all the girls before her, made him pretty damn certain that even if he had a smoking gun, the powers that be would still be reluctant to make anything approaching a public scene. He'd be laughed out of the building. His own career would be over, even if it was subsequently proven that he was right. Nobody would want to work with him again. He'd got no choice but to go on his own.

Chapter 46

The pain in her neck brought her back to consciousness, a sharp twinge on the right where her head had lolled too far over. She was still sat in her own kitchen, but now she'd been firmly tied to the chair. Her head felt like it was full of cottonwool and she wondered how much time had passed.

A sharp noise behind her, the clatter of metal on metal, made her yank her head round, causing the dull throbbing to be viciously painful. Hussain was there, hitting each of Simon's beautiful copper saucepans with the blade of a large knife. Vida was no expert, but it looked suspiciously like blood smeared on the surface of the steel. She struggled against the bindings but soon realised that she was fastened tight. Her armpits ached slightly. Hussain must have pulled her hard to get her into the chair. Vida was gratified to notice a sheen of sweat on the woman's forehead. Maybe this was one advantage to being slightly on the bulky side.

"You're awake," Hussain said, spotting Vida's scrutiny.

"I don't understand," said Vida.

"Well, of course not. You're not really that bright, are you? Just like playing with word searches and the like. Of course, the barbiturates probably don't help your mental clarity but I'm afraid they were necessary. I can't have you interfering in the case."

Vida was horrified. "You're mad!" she said.

Hussain smiled, tightly. "Not at all." The smile fell from her lips and left nothing but direst fury. "I'm completely sane and I will have justice."

"You're a murderer," Vida said, weakly.

"No," Hussain corrected. She seemed to be enjoying this. "You are."

Chapter 47

The snow had started falling again as Slater approached Vida's house. He'd left his car at the next street as he'd driven up and noticed Hussain's own vehicle parked opposite the address. That couldn't be a coincidence. He abandoned his car and carried on on foot, pulling his coat up around his ears and hurrying along. His mind was racing with all the possibilities of what he was going to find. Of all of them, Vida lying dead somewhere was the one that terrified him most. What if she was right and he was wrong and he was just too late to save her.

Chapter 48

Vida tried to laugh. It came out as a painful-sounding croak. "Me, a murderer? Nobody will believe that."

"Oh, but they will," Hussain said. "All the evidence is here. There's been a well-documented over-stepping of the mark. You were seen at the murder scene. I raised my concerns with your superior and she confided in me that your department is under threat, there have been complaints about your professionalism and oh yes, your husband seems to have left you. Poor Dr Henrikson. You just couldn't take the pressure." This was all delivered in a deadpan tone, Hussain walking up and down in front of her, waggling the knife.

"Nobody will believe that," Vida repeated, but even she could hear the doubt in her voice.

Hussain bared her teeth in an approximation of a smile. Her humanity seemed to have vanished, leaving a hollow and vicious banshee in front of Vida. "They won't have a choice. Especially when I, a fine officer of the law have to fight off a brutal knife attack and you are killed by your own weapon. A weapon, by the way, that will have traces of Kitty and Ash's blood."

She placed the knife in front of Vida. "It's so tragic," she continued. "Driven insane by pressure, you obviously thought there was no way out. Desperate to find your feet again, you created this whole thing to try and make your science famous and secure your position."

362

"But it's all linked with the abuse. How am I supposed to have known about that?" asked Vida, hoping that perhaps some sort of rationality might inject some sense into proceedings.

"It's obvious," Hussain trilled. "Maggie had obviously written about it and you found out all about it. You decided this suited your purposes and lined it all up."

"But I didn't get involved with Maggie's case until after Kitty had been murdered," Vida pointed out.

Hussain's face flushed and she hissed angrily. "It doesn't matter. Who's going to argue with me? Who's not going to believe a police officer?"

Chapter 49

Slater cursed Vida for living in a terraced house as he approached. The back yard backed straight onto someone else's and so he had no choice but to enter in the front. Whether the door was locked and whether he could do it without being noticed was not anything he really wanted to contemplate.

The snow crunched lightly underfoot. In the houses around him, through glowing front windows, he could see families huddled together, old couples watching television, a young mother nursing a tiny baby. All the while, Vida could be lying dead. All because of him.

He slid up her garden path, saying a silent prayer of thanks for the fact the gate was already open. He didn't want anything to alert anyone to his presence. The front window of Vida's house was dark, only the faintest glow coming from the door to the hallway. He presumed that meant that any inhabitants were in the kitchen.

He stopped at the door. Was this madness? Was he being completely stupid here? Hussain was a police officer, and a bloody good one. He admired her and the quick, efficient way she dealt with the cases that came through their team. Surely, he was wrong about this. He had to be wrong about this. She couldn't be a killer. Could she?

He couldn't risk it though. Pushing down on the door handle, he tried to open the door as silently possible. The rubber smack of the insulating seal letting go seemed impossible loud to him and he paused, the door half-open, waiting to see if anyone else had heard it. There was no sign though of anyone else.

Nudging the door open further, he slipped inside the hallway. Now inside he could hear voices. Vida's first and then Hussain's. He wasn't wrong. He was so horribly right.

But at least Vida was still alive. It was up to him to keep her that way.

Chapter 50

"Even if they do believe you," Vida said, "is that what you want?"

"What do you mean?" snapped Hussain. She'd picked the knife up again and was gently running the flat of the blade against her palm.

"Well, it means that the case becomes about me. One mad little lady trying to make herself look better. Instead of being about Kitty and Ashaz and what they did. Is that what you want? You must be doing this for a reason. For someone. Who's the she in the letters? Your sister? Don't you want her to get justice?"

"Aaliyah," Hussain said, softly. "It means exalted. And she was. She was perfect. She would have had a life of love and happiness and joy. My sister and my hope. Pure and honest and everything that was good in the world. But they took that from her. That bitch said Aaliyah had bullied her. That she needed punishing. But Aaliyah would not. Could not. It was nothing but a lie. To try and make herself feel better."

"Don't you want that to be known? Don't you want her name to be known? You don't want Kitty and Ashaz to be seen as the victims, do you? They need punishing."

Hussain looked at her. "What do you know of punishment? I have punished them. I have punished them in ways you cannot imagine, and Allah will also punish them beyond. I need no more. Aaliyah needs no more."

She stopped, suddenly, listening. Vida struggled to hear what had caught her attention but could make no sounds out beyond the familiar buzz of the fridge and ticking of the kitchen clock.

"DI Slater," Hussain said eventually, without turning her head. "I don't suppose I'm surprised you're here. You just couldn't let it go, could you?"

Chapter 51

As soon as she said his name, his feet became rooted to the spot. Perhaps if he didn't move any more, she'd think she was mistaken. Who was he trying to kid? The house was tiny. All she had to do was take a few steps into the hall and he'd be there. There was nowhere to hide.

Reluctantly, he propelled his wobbly legs into the kitchen. "How did you know I was here?"

"Your aftershave," Hussain said, simply. She was stalking up and down the kitchen, her posture as upright as it ever was, her bearing the same as at all the crime scenes they'd attended together over the years. There was an unnatural gleam in her eyes though, a sheen of sweat across her forehead despite the chill of winter in the kitchen, and a panic in her gait. A caged animal, waiting to escape. Almost against his own will, he dragged his eyes away from her to check on Vida. She was huddled in a chair, arms bound behind her back, and feet tied to the legs of the chair. Her hair was dishevelled, and she had a long scratch down one cheek. Apart from that and the intense fear in her eyes, she looked in good shape.

But for how long?

Chapter 52

"I'm glad you're here, anyway, Slater. You can help me arrest the killer," Hussain said, gesturing towards Vida with the knife. Slater looked confused.

"You mean Vida?"

"Yes, of course. This is all part of her plan to get herself noticed. She's criminally deranged." Hussain said it all so monotonously, so calmy that Vida had no difficulty in believing this version of events. "Of course, it's tragic really. But we had no choice, you understand that, don't you?" Hussain pleaded with Slater, who still looked like he hadn't caught up with what was happening. "When she came at us with the knife, we had no choice. You had no choice." Her voice was deliberate now, emphasising each word to Slater.

Chapter 53

"I can't do that," Slater said. "Why would I use the knife?"

Hussain looked at him, a weight of disappointment in her eyes. It was a look he'd become familiar with recently, but it had never been delivered with such pathos. "Because she attacked me with it, Gabe. And you fought valiantly to protect your senior officer."

She slowly and deliberately drew the blade of the knife across the lifeline on her palm. "Oh, look," she said, as though noticing some small creature at the side of the road, "a defensive wound." For a moment they all watched as the blood welled up, bright against her dusky palm. She clenched her fist and let some drops fall to the floor.

"You're mad," Slater said. And for the first time, he saw just how mad she was. All this time he'd assumed that yes she might be a killer, but she obviously had a reason for it. But this, right now, this was insane. "I'm a police officer. I can't do that."

"Your dad was a police officer," Hussain said.

"What do you mean?"

She snorted. "Bloody hell, Slater. You can't seriously imagine your father wasn't as corrupt as the rest as the bloody force. You think a black man could progress in the 1980s any more than an Asian woman in the 2010s can? He was as dirty as every single member of that team. Every one of them turned a blind eye." She shook her head and gave a derisive laugh. "I knew you were naive, but I had no fucking idea that you're as blind as you seem to be. Did you never ask anyone about him? Try Scotty," she said, naming one of the oldest Duty Sergeants in the station. "He'll tell you about the time they had to get five men to pull your dad off a little bastard who'd said something he didn't like."

Slater felt sick. She couldn't be telling the truth. Surely, he would have known. Someone would have said something to him. He looked across to Vida and tried not to react to the unbridled sympathy in her eyes.

"That's not true," he said, finally. "My dad was a good copper. Everyone says so."

"Oh, everyone does, do they?" Hussain mocked. "Haven't you realised by now that everyone's as bad as each other? You've been reading those files. You've seen the way woman after woman reported the abuse and all those little obedient coppers swept it all under the carpet. Who cares if a junkie got raped? Probably begged for it in exchange for a few crumbs. Stupid little Eastern European bitch? Probably did it for a tenner. And what about those Muslim slags? Probably gagging for some real cock. Woman after fucking woman... hell, that's being kind to those bastards... kid after kid reported what had happened to them and what did all those good coppers do? Absolutely fucking nothing."

She approached Slater, the knife low in her hand. He wanted to keep his eye on the weapon but there was a burning intensity in her eyes that drew him constantly. He had no problem seeing her as an avenging angel right now. There was something ethereal about her. "And what about your brother," she whispered. "How long, Gabe, before Caleb oversteps the line and you have to choose between your professional honour and protecting him?"

Chapter 54

Vida watched as Slater closed his eyes. The accusation had hit him hard.

"We could be a great team, Slater. We could rebuild the force. Take it where it needs to go. Just look at the work you've done on this case. You've solved it."

"She solved it," Slater said, nodding to Vida.

"I think you'll find that she's the murderer." Hussain smiled. A wolf's smile if ever there was one.

"You think we'll be able to sell that story?"

"Why not?" Hussain shrugged. "It's obvious she's in trouble. She's going to lose her job at the university, inappropriate relationships with students and an inability to keep her fucking nose out of things that don't concern her. Clearly, she wanted something to raise her profile. Classic arsonist who sets the fires to be the hero. She was seen at the scene of Ash's murder. We've found the knife here." She twisted the knife in the air, more carelessly now, stabbing and slicing as though fighting an invisible target. "You and me, we came to arrest her. She was showing an unhealthy interest in the case. She knew something that only the killer could have known. There was a fight and she got stabbed. End of case. We get accolades and promotions. Just imagine how proud your mother would be then. Of you, this time."

Vida could see that it was swaying Slater. She tried to communicate desperately with him, eyes urging him to do the right thing.

Chapter 55

The scary thing was that it was a fairly convincing narrative. Of course, questions would be asked, but they'd be easily deflected by two senior police officers. And who was there to counteract their version of events? "What about her husband?"

"He can't even be arsed to stay in the country. I don't think there's anyone who would kick up a fuss really. We'd certainly be doing the university a service; they think she's a massive liability right now."

Slater could see the hurt in Vida's eyes. It hit him more than her fear had. She was holding herself together amazingly well, but barbs about her professional life obviously hit hard. He felt an unexpected bond with her. It wasn't easy being a professional outcast. Hussain was offering him a way out. Perhaps he'd belong in a way that he never had belonged before. It would be a powerful thing to have her support, professionally and perhaps personally. All the stress about being connected to Caleb and his disastrous life would be gone. With her on his side, he needn't fear exposure.

"And Raheeq? He was just a boy."

Hussain blazed. "He was no boy," she spat. "He was a man. Like his father and his father before him. Rapist monsters who used girls and threw them away like they were nothing."

"But he didn't do anything to your sister."

"But he would have done. And that man.. That other man... he escaped easy. A death at home in his bed surrounded by loved ones. That's no punishment. Allah demands vengeance in his place. Aaliyah demands vengeance."

"But Ellison told me it was murder. They'll never believe that she did that." He gestured towards Vida.

"In the police station. I think we'll find the evidence we need to prove that it was suicide. Perhaps we just overlooked the syringe in his cell. Who's going to question it? Who's going to demand anything else? His family are rapists and murderers. They have no voice against us."

He looked again at Vida. The look in her gaze was stark, brutal in its earnestness and need. But did she outweigh all the good he could do? How simple his life would be with Hussain behind him? Slater felt sick. There was no way out of this. Whatever action he chose, his career was destroyed, he knew that. If he took Hussain out, he'd be a police pariah. No-one would want to work with him. He could pretty much call his career quits right there. All those years of hard graft. And what would his mother say? He could almost see the sadness on her face, not to mention the probable glee on Caleb's. But the alternative? Was that worth even contemplating? The life he wanted to lead. But could he lead it knowing that he'd got it though foul means. The foulest.

Chapter 56

The more Vida fought to keep calm, the more her panic seemed to rise in her throat. Pushed awkwardly into the corner, her back against the wall, waves of exhaustion were threatening to topple her to the floor. She was sure that the first time she moved, Hussain would slice her open.

She forced her thoughts away from despair and into the room, watching Slater and Hussain. It was obvious that Hussain was offering Slater something that appealed. What did she matter to him? All she'd done was be a thorn in his side. He'd made it obvious he found her annoying. Why wouldn't he trade her for a lifetime of protection? Her brains made a mental inventory of all the people who would miss her. Her parents definitely, probably Caroline. Maybe Simon but she knew he wasn't the sort to perform any long-term mourning period. It surprised her a little to find out that she didn't actually care about that. What struck her more was the short list. Too short.

Chapter 57

In his years of policing, Slater had never been involved in a knife fight. Occasionally, a drunken idiot might have pulled a knife on him when he was in uniform, but a swift baton blow to the arm disarmed him. Here there was no drunken idiot and no baton. All there was was a deadly woman who'd already killed three other human beings and showed no signs of being remotely repentant. Vida must have sensed his wavering though and before he could decide one way or another, she'd planted her feet on the floor, gone onto tiptoe and thrown her whole body, chair attached at Hussain.

Hussain stepped back and screamed, her face puce with fury. She rushed at Vida, knife out, and Slater knew, finally that he had no alternative. Thought was gone as he shot forward, trying desperately to insert himself between the two women, trying to ignore the large knife but also being far too aware of its danger.

The three of them wrestled desperately on the floor, Vida writhing furiously to try and get her arms and legs free of the chair. There was the sickening sound of bones cracking and he knew that something had broken somewhere. Vida's scream of pain told him everything and her body went immediately limp, providing the perfect target for Hussain's frenzied attack. The floor was soon slick with blood and sweat and Slater couldn't see well enough to work out where it was coming from.

His last few moments were a blur of hands and arms, the knife being thrust, hitting the wood of the chair then sinking unmistakably into flesh. The air filled with his own guttural scream as the air punched out of his belly.

Then the silence of the street, with its flowing, flocking flakes seeped into the house, bringing with it the thick air of a snow-laden night. Everything stopped.

Dear you

I know what you did and I will make you pay, you faithless whore. I am your dark storm and I will have vengeance.

You probably think you're safe. You probably think that what you've done will stay in the past. I'm going to make sure it doesn't. I'm going to make you pay.

Maybe you don't think of it at all. I see you and I think that perhaps you've forgotten it. Is that the only way you could live with yourself? If you pretended that it had never happened. Pretended that she had never happened. I can't do that. I can't wipe her out of my memories. She's there every day, every minute in my brain, living with me, reminding me of everything she was and now will never be.

I wonder what she did to deserve what you did to her. Maybe nothing. Maybe she looked at you, or said something to you, or maybe she never even noticed you at all. She was like that. Her head in the clouds. A dreamer. You stole that from her. You stole everything from her. Why?

I wish you had known her as a child, had seen what she was like as a toddler and an infant. I'm sure you would have loved her. We all did. Maybe if you'd known her then, if you'd seen her, dancing around the living room with her teddy bear, or tucked up tight at night with her thumb in her mouth and her forehead warm, maybe then you wouldn't have done what you did. We played in the gully at the back of our house, splashing in suds that were left from the car washing. She was so beautiful and so full of life.

I saw you on the television the other day. You are a rising star it seems. Your future is all ahead of you. That must be so exciting. How do you think your family would feel if I took that away from you now? If I took your future, the way you took hers. Everyone shall taste death; it could be soon for you. The Messengers are waiting to take you beyond to taste the penalty of burning.

I promise.

Epilogue

The Lagotto Romagnolo was bred originally to retrieve game from the water but had lately turned its skills to truffle hunting in the Italian mountains. Somewhat smaller than a labradoodle, they had a thick curly coat and a short snout, looking almost bovine in appearance. Having been raised by monks in an olive grove outside Bologna, Billy the Italian truffle hound was also poorly socialised and liable to get himself involved in situations that he should have known better than to be involved in. He did have an innate sense of direction however, and as soon as he'd bolted from the taxi he'd arrived in, he'd found his way to what would be his home. Maybe he'd followed the footsteps that crept their way towards the front door. More like it was because an open door and warm looking glow offered shelter from the bitter snow. His luckless owner, thankful that he didn't have to explain to his wife just where his 1500 Euros had gone if the dog had been hit by a car, barely registered the open door as he chased after the dog, desperately calling his name. The smell was slightly unusual to the human perhaps, reminiscent of when he butchered his own pig, but the dog didn't seem to notice.

"Oh shit," the man muttered. "What the hell has gone on here? Vida?" he said, his voice breaking as he recognised the blonde head of his wife in amongst the human debris on the floor. He started to move forward but found himself locked in place. The dog didn't show similar reticence and was merrily snuffling amongst the pile. Simon finally found his phone and with quivering fingers dialled the police. "Police, ambulance I mean. I don't know… my wife... something terrible has happened." He gave his address, communicated as best he was able the scene in front of him.

"How many wounded would you say, sir?"

"I don't know. Three maybe. Please come quickly, please. My wife... Vida?"

As his plaintive voice finally called the dog to attention, a blood-slicked hand opened and closed.

"Simon?" her voice said.

Dedication

They say it takes a village to raise a child... and the same is true of writing a book. My word-heavy baby. There's lots of people I want to thank, who have helped me and continue to help me in my writing.

For all those friends and family who have performed the role of first reader for me, especially Bec, Heather, Jane, Fay and Caroline. And all those other friends and family who have been my cheerleader every step of the way, especially Lisa.

For my fellow Crimies on the University of East Anglia Crime Writing Masters course, who helped shape Vida and Slater and gave them breath when it looked like they wouldn't make it past the first 10,000 words.

For my creative writing club, Emma, Niamh and Sophie, who have been helping me get my ideas down for over ten years now.

For my mum and dad, who have been cheering me on since Day One.

For my husband and children, who have put up with me when they probably would have preferred to murder me.

And lastly, for my own Zahra Hussain. Who isn't a murderous psychopath but is a strong and wonderful woman, without whom this book would never have been plotted and written.

And to the future, for all my readers and everyone who spends time with Vida and Slater. I hope you've enjoyed them! Please leave a review on Amazon or Goodreads if you've got the time.

Printed in Great Britain
by Amazon